Sweet Venom

BETTY ROWLANDS

Sweet Venom

Hodder & Stoughton

First published in Great Britain in 2004 by Hodder and Stoughton
A division of Hodder Headline

1 3 5 7 9 10 8 6 4 2

A CIP catalogue record for this title is available from the British Library

ISBN 0 340 82681 9

Typeset in Plantin Light by Phoenix Typesetting,
Auldgirth, Dumfriesshire

Printed and bound in Great Britain by
Clays Ltd, St Ives PLC

Hodder and Stoughton
A division of Hodder Headline
338 Euston Road
London NW1 3BH

To Phil Pride, marking over a
decade of friendship and co-operation.

Sweet Venom

I

'Isn't this is a beautiful spot, Lissie?' said Sylvia. 'And what a wonderful view!' Her eyes shone and she paused to lean on a gate leading into a field. Her daughter, quietly observant, felt a rush of gratitude at the animation in her expression and the healthy glow in cheeks that a few months ago had been pale and wan and full of care.

'Yes, it is lovely,' Melissa agreed. 'I never get tired of it. Look, you can just see the church.' She pointed across the sloping pasture, dotted with sleek black and white cattle, to the square Norman tower of Cotswold stone nestling among a clump of trees.

'So you can. It's a dear little church, so welcoming, and your rector is such a kind man, and his wife is so friendly. In fact, there seem to be any number of friendly people in the village.'

'Yes, the folk in Upper Benbury are on the whole a pretty sociable lot. I hope you'll be able to settle into village life and not find it too quiet after the town.'

'Oh, I'm sure I shall. He looks pleased with himself,' Sylvia added, switching her attention to a cock pheasant. Disturbed at their approach, he had scuttled across the lane ahead of them and fluttered up to perch on the dry stone wall that enclosed the field. He was now strutting along the top of it like a chanticleer lording it over hens in a barnyard, his colourful plumage glistening in the sunshine.

Melissa chuckled. 'He won't be so pleased with himself in a month or two when the shooting season begins.'

Sylvia's face fell. 'Oh dear, is there much of that round here?'

'Local landowners breed them for the guns. Organised shoots are a thriving industry these days. Country life isn't all gambolling lambs and picture postcard cottages, you know.'

'No, of course it isn't, but it does seem a little unfair to breed things just for people to shoot at, don't you think?'

'To be honest, yes,' Melissa agreed, 'but I have to admit I do enjoy a bit of roast pheasant.'

'Ah, now you're talking!' Sylvia stepped back on to the road. 'Shall we walk on a bit?'

'Of course, if you're not too tired.'

'Lissie, it's only ten o'clock in the morning! Of course I'm not tired.'

'You're still convalescent. The doctor said you should take things easily for the next few weeks.'

'Now stop fussing, there's a dear. I'm feeling stronger every day, so let's walk on. I want to see that house you were telling me about – what did you say it's called?'

'Cold Wells Manor. It's quite old – late eighteenth-century, in fact.'

'That's a strange name.'

'There are some springs down in the valley that the locals know as Cold Wells.'

'And who lives there?'

'A family called Cresney. I pointed them out to you in church last Sunday. Two brothers, Aidan and Quentin, and their wives Caroline and Sarah.'

'I remember. I noticed they hardly spoke to anyone after the service.'

'They're one of the less sociable families, although Aidan – he's a retired barrister, by the way – is on the parish council. He's not particularly popular because now and again he takes a controversial stand on certain local matters, especially about planning applications. Because of his professional background he often manages to talk people into dropping their objections, sometimes against their better judgment, because they can't put up strong enough arguments against him.'

'A bit like your father,' Sylvia remarked, half to herself. Melissa made no comment. Having just embarked on a new life as the wife of her agent of long standing, the last thing she wanted was to be reminded of the bitter years of separation and misunderstanding and the dreadful act of violence that had, eventually, brought about her reunion with her mother.

They walked on for a few minutes in silence. Then Sylvia said, 'So the two couples share the house? Is it divided into separate dwellings like ours?'

'You can hardly compare it with Hawthorn Cottage and your granny annexe, Mum. It's a large, rambling place – or so I'm told. I've never been inside it and very few people in the village have either since the Cresneys bought it and carried out extensive alterations. They're an odd family.'

'In what way?'

'According to Henry Calloway, who was rector at the time, there were just the three of them when they first moved in – Aidan, Caroline and Sarah, Quentin's wife. It was almost a year before Quentin appeared on the scene and it had been assumed that Sarah was either a widow or divorced. Until then, Henry said, he was welcomed at the house when he delivered the parish magazine, but after the younger brother mysteriously turned up they sort of cooled off.'

'Where had Quentin been?'

'No one knows. The gossips had a field day; some thought he might have been in hospital, or some kind of care home, or possibly in a detox unit after getting hooked on drugs. You've probably noticed he doesn't look anything like so robust as his brother, and he was even more frail-looking in the early days. It was even whispered that he might have been in jail.'

'With a barrister brother to defend him!' Sylvia gave a sudden mischievous giggle.

'It would be ironic, wouldn't it?' Melissa agreed. 'Not that I go along with that explanation for a moment; I don't see Quentin involved in mayhem. He doesn't seem the type.'

'Ah, but doesn't the least likely one turn out to be the criminal?' said Sylvia.

Her daughter gave an indulgent smile. 'Mum, you've been reading too many of my books.' Under the pen name of Mel Craig, Melissa was the author of a string of successful crime novels.

'Perhaps Aidan put him up to it and Quentin bungled it.' Sylvia's eyes gleamed with enthusiasm for her theory. 'You hinted just now that Aidan was a bit of a bully.'

'He's a very strong character, yes, but I'm not sure I'd go as far as calling him a bully. He's unlikely to be a criminal, though, not with his reputation to think of. Anyway, we're nearly there.'

'I can hear running water.'

'That's one of the springs.' The lane had been sloping

gently downhill for the past couple of hundred metres and Melissa pointed to a sparkling ribbon of water that trickled down the steep bank on their right. 'There's a bend in the lane a little way ahead and the house is just beyond. You see the back of it first, but at this time of year it's partly hidden by the orchard.'

'It's like something out of a picture book!' Sylvia exclaimed as the property came into view. 'Look at all those lovely red apples . . . and there are beehives as well, lots of them.'

'I understand Aidan took up beekeeping after he retired. Mrs Foster sells his honey in the village shop.'

'I must buy some.' Sylvia stepped forward to take a closer look. 'I've never seen so many beehives before, except from a distance. Or so many bees,' she added, backing away again. 'There are thousands of them buzzing around.'

'So there are.' Melissa peered through the trees at the nearest hives, round which dense clouds of the insects were dancing. 'That's unusual.'

'Do you think they're swarming?' Sylvia retreated still further.

'I don't know much about bees, but I'm pretty sure they don't swarm in August. Something might have upset them so I think we'd better keep our distance.' Melissa glanced at her watch. 'It's half past ten; if we turn back now we'll be just in time for coffee. Joe always brews up at around eleven when he's home.'

Sylvia gave her daughter's arm a squeeze. 'You have such a nice husband, Lissie dear. It's good to see you so happy, and so kind of you both to welcome me into your home.'

'It's nice to have you, Mum.'

Mother and daughter wended their way contentedly

homewards. Neither of them had noticed the patch of white on the ground beside a small wooden shed, barely visible in the long grass under the fruit trees. Even had they done so, it was unlikely that they would have recognised it as one of the sleeves of a beekeeper's protective outfit. Still less would they have realised that it contained a man's outstretched arm, or that the owner of the arm was dead.

2

'Aidan's been gone a long time, hasn't he?' Sarah Cresney checked her watch against the longcase clock in the corner of the sitting room where she and her husband were taking their morning coffee. 'He said he'd be only a few minutes.'

Quentin, immersed in the *Guardian*, looked up and said absently, 'Been gone where?'

'Don't you remember, he popped his head round the door half an hour ago to say Caroline had a headache and was staying in bed, so he'd be having coffee here with us this morning, after he'd seen to the bees.'

'Very magnanimous of him.'

'What's that supposed to mean?'

'It means he might wait to be invited instead of announcing he'll come to us for coffee. He just takes it for granted that we'll be honoured by his presence.' With an irritable gesture Quentin threw the newspaper aside, took a mouthful from his cup and pulled a face. 'This coffee's nearly cold. No doubt he'll have something to say about that.'

'It was hot when I poured it out. It's cooled down because you've been sitting with your nose in the newspaper instead of drinking it. Aidan's right, you should be doing something more positive with your time than mooching around the place reading and doing crossword puzzles.'

'Such as what? It's not easy for a man over fifty to find employment.'

'I'm sure there's some part-time work you could do, or perhaps some useful voluntary service. It's not as if we need the money after what you and Aidan screwed out of Poppy.'

'I object to the word "screwed",' said Quentin with a frown. 'It was only what was my due according to the law – Aidan made sure of that.'

'That's true,' Sarah conceded. 'Still,' she went on, returning to her original theme, 'it would be good for you to have an interest. You could help him with the bees, for example. That would be a complete change for you. Now he's chairman of the local Beekeepers' Association it means a lot of extra work for him. You could take some of that off his shoulders.'

'You know very well I'm not the least bit interested in bees. To tell the truth, I'm scared to death of the beastly things. I never go near the hives if I can help it.'

'Neither do I, for obvious reasons, but I was thinking more of the paperwork, organising the committee meetings and so on. You wouldn't actually have to handle the bees. Anyway, there's no risk if you know what you're doing, Aidan says. They never sting him.'

'They wouldn't dare!' Quentin's scowl robbed the remark of any suggestion that it might be construed as a joke. 'Anyway, why can't Caroline give him a hand? She's his wife, but she doesn't take an interest in anything he does. All she cares about these days is playing bridge or going to the theatre or shopping with her friends.'

'Well, we know why that is, don't we? I suppose in a way

you can't blame her. After the way he carries on – I can't think why she puts up with it. I–' She broke off and peered into the coffee pot.

Seeing her colour rise, Quentin said, 'You were going to remind me that *you* didn't put up with it, weren't you?'

'Don't be stupid. It was different with us. You didn't get involved with a married woman, whereas your oh-so-respectable brother–'

'Sshh!' Quentin glanced round with a look of apprehension on his pale, rather dull features. 'For God's sake, Sarah, why do you have to bring all this up when we're expecting him at any minute? We're not supposed to know about . . . you know. What if he heard you?'

'Sorry, it just slipped out. Let me pour you some fresh coffee. This is still hot. I'll give you Aidan's cup and get another one for him when he arrives. You know,' she went on after a further glance at the time, 'it's very strange. It's a quarter past eleven and he's such a stickler for punctuality. What do you think I should do?'

'I don't see why you have to do anything.' Quentin picked up the paper, refolded it at the crossword page and settled back in his chair with the fresh cup Sarah handed him. 'If he wants us to know about his change of plan, no doubt he'll let us know in due course.'

'Perhaps Caroline's feeling worse. Do you think I should go round and find out?'

He shrugged. 'Please yourself.'

'I think I will. I'm sure there's something wrong.' Sarah left the room. Quentin, absorbed in checking the solution to the previous day's puzzle, was only vaguely aware of the sound of his wife's footsteps on the flagged path leading to the front door of the main part of the house where his brother and sister-in-law lived. There was a communicating door with the rooms that had been adapted to accommodate him and Sarah after their reconciliation, but his autocratic brother had made it clear that – except in severe weather or in case of an emergency – it was to be regarded first and foremost for his own convenience. Sarah accepted the condition as part of the price they had to pay for their comfortable existence, but for Quentin it was one of many sources of resentment.

It was barely a minute after she left that he heard her come running back and he sat up with a start as she shouted through the open window, 'Quentin! Come quickly! Aidan's lying on the ground in the orchard – he must have been taken ill.'

He started to his feet and hurried outside. Sarah pointed with a trembling hand. 'There, behind the shed,' she said, her voice hoarse and trembling with fear. 'You can just see his arm.' She broke into a run, then pulled up short and let out a thin scream. 'Oh, my God, it's horrible!' she gasped and turned away, covering her face with her hands.

Quentin, a few paces behind her, stopped and stared, aghast. A figure he assumed from the beekeeper's white protective clothing to be his brother was lying on its back under an apple tree a few feet from the nearest hive. The air around was alive with bees and the creatures were crawling all over the recumbent motionless form, but the ultimate horror was what had happened to the face. Inside the veil, it was virtually invisible beneath a dark, seething, angrily buzzing mass.

Without a moment's hesitation, Quentin turned and fled. 'Get back to the house!' he shouted at Sarah. 'They'll be after us next!'

Sarah, her face white as death, was doubled up at the side of the path, noisily throwing up into the grass. She lurched after him, coughing and retching, one hand clutching her stomach. The minute they were back indoors she rushed into the kitchen and collapsed over the sink.

'We have to do something!' she gasped when at last the spasms subsided. She filled a glass with water and rinsed her mouth. 'We can't leave him lying there – he'll be stung to death.' Tears spilled from her eyes and she began to sob. 'We must help him, get him to a doctor.'

'How?' said Quentin helplessly. 'They'll only attack us if we go near him.'

'You could turn the hose on him. That might drive them off.'

'I'm not going out there again.'

'You're going to leave your brother to die?'

'I'm not going to let them kill me too.'

'Then I'll try. You'd better go and tell Caroline what's happened.'

'No, it's too risky. I've got a better idea.' Quentin grabbed the phone and began stabbing buttons. 'Colin Palmer keeps bees – he'll know what to do.'

Sarah made for the door. 'I'm going to connect up the hose. One of us has to do something, even if–'

Quentin seized her arm and pulled her back. 'No, wait. Let's see what . . . Colin, is that you? Quentin Cresney here. Something terrible's happened . . . we need help . . . urgently.'

'He's only been dead for a short time – less than a couple of hours,' said Doctor Charman. He glanced at his watch and muttered, 'Certified dead at twelve thirty,' while writing on a form he took from his case.

'We could have told you that,' said Quentin. Catching a disapproving look from his wife, he added, 'I mean, he was still alive at about a quarter to eleven. He said he'd be with us in a few minutes – he was going to join us for coffee.' He gave a short sardonic laugh. 'It was his proud boast that no one who knew what they were doing with bees ran a serious risk of getting stung. Fat lot of good his expert knowledge did him, didn't it?'

'I had no idea being stung killed anyone so quickly,' Caroline whispered. It was the first time she had spoken since Colin Palmer and another beekeeper whose help he had managed to enlist had driven off the bees with powerful jets of water before carrying Aidan's body indoors and laying it on the kitchen floor. Meanwhile, Sarah had raced round the house to make sure that every door and window was firmly closed.

The doctor shook his head and put away the stethoscope with which he had been vainly trying to detect a spark of life. 'Frankly, neither did I,' he said. 'Since none of you heard any cries for help, I'm inclined to think he died almost instantly of anaphylactic shock, but only a post mortem can tell us for certain.'

'I have a friend who used to live in Africa,' said Colin. 'He got badly stung when he was attacked by some wild bees. Somehow they managed to get inside his veil and he suffered something like a hundred stings before one of his servants rescued him and managed to get him to hospital. They said it was a miracle he survived.'

'Yes, I remember hearing you tell Aidan about it.' Caroline's voice was so weak it was barely audible.

'Do you think we should cover him up?' Colin suggested.

'Good idea. He's not exactly a pretty sight, is he?' muttered Quentin. He was staring in fascinated disgust at the swollen discoloured features. 'That'll teach you to be so darned cocky,' he added in an undertone that only his wife, standing close beside him, was able to hear. She pressed her lips together and shook her head, frowning at him, but he ignored her.

'I'll get something,' she said and hurried out of the room as if glad of an excuse to get away. She returned a few minutes later with a sheet and handed it to the doctor, keeping her eyes averted. He unfolded it and spread it over the body, to an audible sigh of relief that drifted like smoke round the room. 'What happens now?' she asked.

'I'm afraid I have to inform the coroner,' said Doctor Charman. 'It's routine in the case of an unexpected death,' he added, as if anticipating a chorus of objections, although no one made any comment. 'Assuming he gives permission – and I see no reason why he shouldn't – you can make arrangements with a local undertaker to come and collect him.'

'Do we have to wait in here?' Caroline faltered.

Sarah appeared to become suddenly aware that as the only other woman present she should be making some effort to comfort her sister-in-law. She moved to her side and rather tentatively put an arm round her shoulders. Almost impatiently, Caroline moved away. 'I need a drink,' she said in a flat emotionless voice.

'I think we could all do with one,' said Quentin. 'Sarah, will you . . . ?'

'Yes, of course.' She glanced down at the figure on the floor, now discreetly hidden from view, and then at

Caroline. 'Not in here, though. Perhaps in your house?'

'I suppose so,' said Caroline vaguely. 'This way.'

Like figures in the dream sequence in a ballet, they all slowly followed her from the room. At the same moment, there was a ring at the Aidan Cresneys' front door.

3

In the subdued silence that had fallen over the group, the doorbell sounded unnaturally loud, almost threatening. Everyone jumped, came to a halt and exchanged uneasy glances.

'Whoever can that be?' whispered Caroline.

'Perhaps it's the press wanting a story,' Quentin suggested. 'Can you picture the headline in the *Gazette*? "Killer bees loose in the Cotswolds".' He gave a feeble giggle and glanced round for appreciation of his attempt at black humour.

There was a moment's embarrassed silence before Sarah said, 'I don't think that's very funny, Quentin.'

'Sorry, perhaps not in very good taste,' he mumbled. 'Well, aren't you going to answer it?' he added pettishly, turning to Caroline, who was staring at the door as if transfixed.

Sarah went to the window and peered out. 'It's Roger with the post. I'll go if you like.'

'Would you?' Caroline whispered.

'No, I will,' said Quentin. Before his wife could move, he headed out of the room and made for the communicating door leading to the main part of the house. He flung it open and marched across the hall to the front door with the others trailing behind him.

The postman was standing on the doorstep with a bundle of letters in his hand. 'Sorry I'm so late, Mr Cresney, I was held up by–' he began and then broke off as he realised his mistake. 'Beg pardon, Mr Quentin, I didn't expect to see you.' He cast an anxious glance round the group. 'I noticed Doctor Charman's car on the drive and I said to myself, I hope no one's been taken poorly.'

'I'm sorry to inform you that my brother collapsed and died this morning after being badly stung by some of his bees,' said Quentin. His voice was wooden, showing no trace of emotion.

Some of the colour drained from the postman's ruddy features. 'What a dreadful thing!' he exclaimed. 'However did that happen? Mr Cresney was so experienced with bees. He lent me some overalls and showed me the inside of one of his hives a few months ago and they were as quiet as anything.'

'Some of them must have got inside his veil, that's all we know at the moment,' said Quentin. He held out a hand for the bundle of letters. 'I'll look after those. And from now on you will kindly address me as Mr Cresney.'

Behind Quentin, eyebrows were lifted and glances exchanged. 'Oh, er, yes, of course, Mr Quen . . . Mr Cresney,' the postman stammered, after a momentary hesitation when it seemed as though he was unsure whether he was hearing aright, 'and please, Mrs Cresney . . . all of you' – his eyes swept round the group – 'accept my condolences at the tragedy. I'm sure everyone in the village will be very shocked.'

There was a general murmur of thanks as the postman backed away, almost missing his footing on the bottom step in his confusion. Quentin closed the front door and gave a cursory glance through the envelopes before putting them on the hall table. 'I'll sort this lot out later on,' he said. 'Let's have that drink. In your sitting room, Caroline?' He took a step towards a half-open door across the hall.

Like a waxwork suddenly coming to life, Caroline stepped in front of him in what seemed a deliberate move to cut him off. She went to the table and began sorting the letters and packets, retaining the majority of them in her hand. 'I'll speak to Roger tomorrow and tell him to deliver all the post separately from now on,' she said. It was the first time since receiving the news of her husband's death that she had spoken in anything like her normal voice. She pointed to the handful of remaining envelopes. 'Those are yours and Sarah's, Quentin. You can leave them there if you like until you go back. This way, everyone.' She led them past the carved oak staircase, opened a door and beckoned them in. 'This is Aidan's study; it's where he keeps the drinks.'

'I can't hardly believe it!' Mrs Foster, postmistress and proprietor of Upper Benbury's only shop, gaped at Roger the postman through the security screen, her eyes wide and her pale eyelashes fluttering in astonishment. 'Mr Cresney gone, stung to death by his own bees! Mind you,' she went on, 'I remember once saying to him when he brought in the honey I'd ordered, "Mr Cresney," I said, "I do hope you're careful with those creatures. I don't trust them, the nasty vicious things." "Oh, there's no danger if you know what you're doing, Mrs Foster," he said, in that highty-tighty way he had, but I told him how my sister got stung once and swelled up like a balloon. Had to go to hospital and it was touch and go whether she came out again,' she added with a certain relish. She shook her head in bewilderment. 'Mr Cresney dead! I can't hardly believe it!' she repeated.

'It seems the poor gentleman got stung more than once,' said the postman. He eyed the security door at the end of the counter. 'Aren't you going to let me in, then?'

'Oh, yes, sorry.' She pressed the buzzer to release the lock and he stepped through the door, carefully closing it behind him. 'All this cloak and dagger nonsense,' she grumbled. 'Anyone would think this was the Bank of England instead of a village post office.'

'Ay, things have changed since the old days,' he agreed.

The bell jangled, indicating the arrival of a customer. Mrs Foster pushed open the door leading to her living quarters. 'Go through to the kitchen, Roger. I've just made the tea.' She turned to greet the newcomer. 'Ah, good morning, Mrs Craig . . . that is, Mrs Martin. Do excuse me, I keep forgetting, and I'm that mammered this morning, after what Roger's just told me.' Mrs Foster hailed from a neighbouring county and was apt to resort to dialect words from her childhood at moments of crisis.

'Has something happened?' said Melissa. 'You look quite pale.'

'You'll never guess what's happened! Poor Mr Cresney's been stung to death by his own bees.' She repeated what Roger had told her, adding a few details of her own.

'How absolutely dreadful!' Melissa exclaimed. 'My mother and I went for a walk down the lane to Cold Wells this morning and we noticed the bees seemed agitated. We decided to turn back for fear of getting stung.'

'Something must have upset them, I suppose,' said Mrs Foster. She glanced across her little shop at the grocery shelves. 'That'll be the end of supplies of Cold Wells honey,

I suppose,' she said sadly. 'A pity, that – it's a good selling line. People come from all over the place to buy it. Some of them take two or three jars at a time.'

'Perhaps one of Mr Cresney's beekeeping friends will look after his hives and keep up your supplies,' suggested Melissa.

Mrs Foster brightened. 'I do hope so.' After the initial shock of the tragedy, her business instincts had resurfaced. 'One thing's for sure, Mr Quentin won't want anything to do with them. Gets all agitated if he sees a wasp round the fruit.'

'Yes, he does seem a nervous gentleman. He must be very upset about his brother – and poor Mr Cresney's wife must be terribly shocked.'

'No doubt.'

Something in Mrs Foster's tone caused Melissa to raise an eyebrow. She waited for a moment, half expecting a further comment, but as none came she said, 'Perhaps we should let Mr Hamley know. I think I'll call in at the rectory and leave a message on my way home.'

'I'm sure that would be a kindness. Now, what can I get you, Mrs Martin?' Surprisingly for someone who thoroughly enjoyed a good gossip, Mrs Foster seemed disinclined to pursue the subject.

Melissa consulted the list in her hand. 'Joe wants to make omelettes for lunch and we're short of eggs. A dozen, please, and while I'm here I'll take half a pound . . . I mean, two hundred and fifty grams of Cheddar cheese and a packet of muesli.'

Mrs Foster served her with unusual haste and disappeared into the room at the back of the shop before Melissa had time to put her purchases into her shopping bag. Plainly, she was anxious to rejoin the postman in the kitchen to discuss the tragedy in more detail.

The principal topic of conversation during the preparations for lunch at Hawthorn Cottage was, naturally, the death of Aidan Cresney and particularly the bizarre manner of his passing.

'What baffles me is how the bees got under his veil,' said Melissa. 'I suppose there must have been a hole or a split in the seam that he hadn't noticed, but from what I know of him it seems unlikely. He was normally so meticulous about everything, especially at parish meetings, always insisting on dotting i's and crossing t's . . . but I suppose even Aidan wasn't infallible.'

Joe, busy beating up eggs for the omelettes while Melissa grated cheese and prepared a salad, said over his shoulder, 'If he accidentally left something undone so one or two could get in, he might have started flailing around at them and made them angry.'

'But surely, with his experience, he'd be aware that would happen and keep calm.'

'Maybe he's been so careful in the past that he's never actually been stung before.'

'I doubt if he'd have left any of the fastenings undone,' Melissa continued, 'and from the way Mrs Foster described it, he was attacked by an entire swarm, not just one or two.'

'Well, we know how she exaggerates.'

'True, but when Mum and I walked down the lane near the house this morning we did notice the bees seemed unusually agitated. You expect to see a few of them coming and going from the hives, but there seemed to be thousands and they were making a terrific noise.'

'Have you told your mother, by the way?'

'I haven't spoken to her since I came back from the shop. I suggested she have lunch with us, but she said she was going to eat off a tray in front of the telly and then have forty winks. She's getting more and more independent, which I suppose is a good thing.'

'Independent and tactful.' Joe gave his wife a quick hug. 'We're only just back from our honeymoon after all.'

'True. She's really being very sweet, and she thinks she has the best son-in-law in the world.'

'Quite right, too!' Joe released her in order to tip the beaten eggs into a pan of hot butter. 'Ready for the grated cheese.'

'Coming up.'

While they were eating, Melissa remarked, 'You know, I was saying to Mum only this morning, I've always felt there was something a bit mysterious about the Cresneys.'

'How so?'

'Of course, you weren't here when Quentin appeared on the scene. Until then, they weren't exactly neighbourly, especially Aidan who's always given the impression that he's much too superior to hobnob with *hoi polloi*, but I often used to meet Caroline and Sarah in the shop and they always seemed quite amiable and willing to chat. It was only after Quentin moved in that their attitude seemed to change.'

'In what way?

'It's hard to explain. For a start, they hardly ever come into the shop or show their faces round the village any more, except in church when they just say polite good mornings and disappear. You must have noticed that. And Roger reported that letters addressed to Mr and Mrs Quentin Cresney started appearing. Up till then, it was just Sarah who got letters and he used to put them through her letterbox. Then, all of a sudden, Aidan told him to deliver all the letters to him – even the ones addressed to Sarah.'

'Did Sarah agree to this?'

'I doubt if she'd have dared raise an objection. Aidan would probably have wiped the floor with her if she'd tried. There's always been something about him that puts everyone at a disadvantage – he had this very authoritative manner and the way he used to put people down was quite breathtaking at times.'

'And now his breath has been taken,' Joe remarked as he helped himself to salad.

'And by his own bees,' said his wife. 'It does seem very odd to me.'

'You know your trouble' – Joe made a mock pass at her with the salad server – 'you can't forget you used to write crime fiction.'

Melissa laughed, a little sheepishly. 'I suppose I was subconsciously seeing it as what the police describe as a suspicious death, but I'm sure it's nothing of the kind.'

'Just the same, it'd be interesting to know exactly what happened.'

'I dare say Gloria will be able to enlighten us next time she comes.'

'Is she the Cresneys' cleaning lady as well?'

'No, but there's not much going on in the village that she doesn't know about.'

4

They had just finished their lunch when the doorbell rang.

Melissa pushed away her plate and stood up. 'I'll go while you make the coffee.'

'I'll bet that's Mrs Thorne,' Joe predicted, pulling a face. 'She's heard the news from Mrs Foster and it's given her a brilliant idea for a plot for a crime novel.' Cynthia Thorne, a comparative newcomer to the village, was an avid reader of crime fiction and had been ecstatic on learning that one of her favourite authors was actually a neighbour.

Much as she enjoyed praise from a fan, there were times when Melissa found Cynthia's effusiveness a little wearisome. 'Gosh, I hope not,' she sighed. 'No matter how hard I try, I can't persuade the woman that I'm not writing any more mysteries.'

'Whatever you do, don't invite her in,' Joe begged. 'She'll stay for ever. Tell her we're just going out or something.'

But it wasn't Mrs Thorne, it was John Hamley, the rector of Upper Benbury and the adjoining parishes. 'I hope I'm not interrupting your lunch,' he said when Melissa opened the door.

'Not at all, we've just finished. Joe's making coffee; would you like a cup?' She stood aside for him to enter. 'We're in the kitchen; do go through.'

'Thank you. You can probably guess why I'm here.'

'The tragedy at Cold Wells?'

'Exactly. Thank you for letting me know so promptly. I went to the house straight away to see if I could help and to offer what comfort I could. Thank you, Joe,' he added as he sat down and accepted a mug of coffee.

'I imagine they must all be in shock,' said Melissa.

'Caroline certainly is. Yes,' he went on in response to their look of surprise, 'almost the first thing she said when I addressed her as Mrs Cresney was to say, "Oh, please, rector, call me Caroline."'

'That wouldn't have met with his lordship's approval,' said Joe.

'No, far from it. He was always a stickler for formality, and of course his brother and sister-in-law followed suit.' John poured milk into his coffee, stirred it and took several mouthfuls; Melissa had the impression that he was making the actions deliberately slow to give himself time to think.

'Did you see the others – I mean, Quentin and Sarah Cresney,' she asked after a moment.

'I did, after leaving Caroline. They were back in their own part of the house.'

'You mean they'd left her on her own?'

'She made it quite clear that it was at her own request. As I said, she was obviously in shock, but she was quite calm, or perhaps controlled would be a better word.'

'Well, I suppose we all react to tragedy in our own way,' Joe commented.

'And from what little we know of the Cresneys, we somehow expect them to behave differently from most,' said Melissa. 'Except, of course, that Caroline and Sarah are only Cresneys by marriage. Now that the most powerful influence has been removed from their lives it makes you wonder what effect it will have on the family as a whole.'

'Quite,' said John. 'To be honest, I found the reaction of all three of them . . . disturbing. That's why I've come to you, Melissa. Alice says that at one time you were quite friendly with Caroline and her sister-in-law.'

'Not exactly friendly. That is, we never became particularly close and so far as I know they've never chummed up with anyone else in the village. I suggested several times they might like to come to a WI meeting with a view to joining, but they always made some excuse.'

'I imagine Aidan Cresney would have discouraged it,' Joe remarked. 'He wouldn't have had much time for the WI; he'd have considered them way beneath his, and by extension his wife's intellectual level.'

'Probably,' Melissa agreed. 'Now and again, when we organise a trip to the theatre or a concert that's open to non-members, we invite them along as guests. Once or twice the wives accepted and appeared to enjoy themselves, but needless to say Aidan didn't honour us with his presence.'

Joe gave a wry smile. 'I don't suppose for a moment anyone would have wanted him; he'd have spent the entire interval pointing out the flaws in everyone's performance.'

'Sure to have done. Anyway, since Quentin turned up they've kept their distance even more than before.'

'Not exactly a sociable family, I'm afraid,' the rector agreed with a regretful shake of the head. 'Still, they come to church regularly and the parish is very grateful for their support.'

'John, you described the family's reaction as disturbing,' said Joe. 'What did you mean?'

'I found a total absence of any outward signs of grief. As I said, Caroline was composed but perfectly courteous and thanked me for coming, but when I called on the others I had the distinct impression that my visit was unwelcome. Mr Quentin mumbled something about getting in touch with me shortly about arrangements for the funeral and then practically showed me the door. And just as I was leaving, he said, "I'd appreciate it if from now on you'd address me as Mr Cresney." I understand from Mrs Foster that he said the same thing to Roger.'

'On the rare occasions when they appeared as a family, Quentin always seemed to be almost subservient to his brother,' Melissa remarked. 'In fact, I always had the impression that both he and Sarah were well and truly under his thumb. Now I suppose Quentin sees himself as the head of the family and entitled to the same deference as his brother commanded.'

'What about Caroline? Was she subservient?'

'Detached is the word that springs to mind.' Melissa considered for a moment before continuing. 'I've always wondered if there might have been some kind of tragedy or trauma in her past and that she was somehow . . . I don't know, covering up. There's a kind of remoteness and dignity about her that reminds me of a picture in the Wallace Collection in London. It's of a lady called Eleanora de Toledo; it used to fascinate me and I went to look at it every time I spent a day in town. I felt sure she had some kind of secret sorrow and it turned out that I was right.'

'How do you know?' said Joe curiously.

'I looked her up in *Britannica* and found she'd had the misfortune to marry into the Medici family and suffered all kinds of ghastly tragedies – one of her sons was murdered by another and her husband subsequently killed the brother. She died in mysterious circumstances and it was thought the husband might have been responsible for her death as well.'

'You're not suggesting Caroline is covering up something similar?' said the rector with a smile.

'Hardly. It was just something about her general demeanour that struck a chord the first time I met her.'

'So long as you aren't thinking of using the story for some grim Gothic melodrama,' said Joe. 'I don't think Cynthia Thorne would approve.'

'Perish the thought!' Melissa smiled for a moment at the absurd suggestion and then grew serious again. 'We shouldn't be making jokes at a time like this. John, do you think I could help? It's true that any conversations I've had with Caroline in the past have been pretty general, and she's never revealed anything about herself or her family, but she's always been perfectly friendly. Perhaps I should pop round and see her. She might find it easier to talk to a woman.'

'She's got her sister-in-law,' Joe pointed out.

'I suppose so, but from what John said it doesn't sound as if they're particularly close.'

'It would be a kindness.' There was gratitude as well as approval in the rector's reaction. 'Alice said she'd try and find time but she's always rushed off her feet during the school holidays, and anyway she's hardly spoken to Caroline apart from the usual polite chat after the service on Sunday mornings.'

'I'll go this afternoon.'

After a few minutes' deliberation, Melissa decided not to chance walking through the orchard to the front door of the house. The bees seemed quiet enough now; the activity round the hives was, so far as she could judge, fairly normal and there was none of the angry buzzing that had made her and her mother turn back that morning. She shuddered at the thought of what the sound had indicated and tried to imagine what might have happened. Perhaps Aidan had become aware of some abnormal behaviour, gone to investigate and been attacked. Perhaps in his haste he had failed to check that his protective clothing was properly fastened, with appalling consequences.

Whatever the explanation, she could not bring herself to walk that way, so she followed the drive indicated by a painted fingerboard reading 'Cold Wells Manor'. She walked slowly, partly on account of the fierce heat of the late summer afternoon and partly to give herself a little more time to decide what her approach should be. She had written and brought with her a card offering sympathy; if Caroline made it clear that she did not welcome her call she would simply leave it with an assurance that if there was anything she could do etc etc. The usual trite phrases, she thought with a sigh. But what else could one say? Her mind went back thirty years to her own experience of bereavement, when her young lover had died never knowing that she was carrying his child. She had heard precious few words of comfort then.

Through the tall neatly clipped beech hedge concealing the lower part of the house she caught an occasional glimpse of bright colour that suggested a well-stocked flower garden, an impression reinforced by the masses of climbing roses surrounding the upper windows. She knew, from the regular sight of a Land Rover turning down the lane leading to the house, that the Cresneys employed a local firm of garden contractors. It fitted with her mental image of the family; somehow one did not associate either of the Cresney brothers with hands-on experience of lawnmowers, fertilisers or potting sheds.

Such alterations as were necessary to convert the house into two separate dwellings had been carried out internally, so that the only visible change was the construction of a separate entrance that faced north towards the church. A short distance further on, the gravelled drive had been widened to form hard standing, presumably for visitors' cars, although this afternoon it was empty. People were not exactly queuing up to offer their condolences.

Melissa did not slacken her pace, but carried on walking towards the main front door on the east side of the house. As she reached the corner of the building a man's voice called out, 'Mrs Martin!' and she turned to see Quentin Cresney standing in front of his half-open front door.

He was not an impressive figure. Aidan, a well-built man with a commanding presence, had been almost a head taller than his younger brother, who was thin and delicate-looking. Aidan had carried himself upright, his head thrown back so that he appeared to be surveying the world and all it contained from a position of authority; Quentin walked with a slight stoop. Melissa recalled hearing the chairman of the parish council saying in exasperation, 'Aidan Cresney doesn't so much express an opinion as present his view on anything as a fact and challenge anyone to refute it.' She could not imagine Quentin ever offering an opinion of his own, let alone disagreeing with anything Aidan said. Yet from what John Hamley had told her and Joe, he was making an effort, as head of the family, to assert himself. It struck her as rather pathetic and she instinctively felt a wave of compassion; Aidan was going to be a hard act to follow.

She walked back a couple of paces and said, 'Good afternoon, Mr Cresney. I was so sorry to hear of the tragedy – you must all be very shocked.'

'Thank you.' He did not sound particularly shocked, or appear to appreciate the sentiment; in fact, his tone was almost curt as he continued, 'If you were thinking of calling on my sister-in-law, I advise against it. She's probably resting.'

'In that case, I won't ring her bell, I'll just pop this through the door.' Melissa held up the card she was carrying.

To her astonishment, Quentin held out his hand and said brusquely, 'You can give it to me. I'll see she gets it.'

Melissa felt her sympathy draining away, then told herself not to be uncharitable. Quentin too had been bereaved. Had he spoken more gently, she would have handed him the card, but it had been less a request than a command. He was making it clear that he had taken on his brother's role. Coming from Aidan, the words would probably have brought instant compliance; from Quentin they induced a perverse desire to defy him.

'Thank you, but I'll deliver it myself to spare you the trouble,' she said and without waiting for his reaction continued on her way.

She was about to push her card through the letterbox when the door opened and Caroline stood there. 'I saw you go past the window with something in your hand,' she said. 'I guessed you just intended to deliver it and go away, and I do so need someone to talk to. Will you please come in?'

'Of course.' Melissa stepped inside and Caroline closed the door behind her. 'I'd have rung the bell only your brother-in-law waylaid me and told me you were resting.'

'The interfering toad!' Caroline muttered through her teeth.

Melissa saw that her hands were shaking and her blue eyes filmy with unshed tears. On impulse she held out both hands and said, 'Oh my dear, I'm so very sorry!'

Caroline stared at her dumbly for a few moments. Her mouth was working; plainly she was fighting for control. Then she lost the battle, covered her face and wept.

5

Instead of grasping the hands that Melissa held out to her, Caroline staggered backwards, collapsed on to the seat of an old-fashioned hallstand and sobbed her heart out. In an attempt to offer some comfort, Melissa sat down beside her and put an arm round her shoulders. Immediately, she became aware of a slight but unmistakable stiffening of the heaving body, so she withdrew her arm and sat quietly waiting for the storm of grief to subside. Presently the racking sobs became less violent; Caroline began blindly wiping her swollen eyes and tear-stained cheeks with her hands, sniffing and gulping but gradually regaining control.

'Where can I find some tissues?' Melissa asked.

Without raising her head, Caroline pointed towards a door on their left. Melissa pushed it open and found herself in a small cloakroom. The lower half was panelled in dark wood, with equally sombre wallpaper above. On a shelf over the washbasin was a box of peach-coloured tissues. She picked it up and offered it to Caroline, who pulled out a handful and began scrubbing at her eyes and face. Then she blew her nose, hiccuped and said in a hoarse whisper, 'Sorry to make such an exhibition of myself.'

'For goodness' sake, there's no need to apologise. You've had an appalling shock; letting go is probably the best thing you could have done.'

'Maybe.' Caroline's gaze slid past Melissa to some indefinable point in the distance. 'I'd forgotten what it was like to let go.'

Uncertain what response, if any, was expected of her, Melissa waited for a few moments and then said gently, 'Your throat must be pretty dry after all that crying. Can I get you something to drink? A cup of tea, perhaps?'

Caroline gave a start, as if her mind had been elsewhere. 'Sorry, what did you say?' Melissa repeated the question and was rewarded with a half-hearted attempt at a smile. 'Thank you, that would be very kind.'

'Right. If you'll point me in the direction of the kitchen–'

'I'll show you.' Still dabbing at her reddened eyes, Caroline led the way across the hall. On the way she caught a glimpse of herself in a gilt-framed mirror and gave a little gasp of dismay. 'Oh my goodness, I look awful!' she exclaimed. 'I must do something to my face – please excuse me.'

'No problem. I'll see to the tea while you freshen up. Which door is the kitchen?'

Caroline, already halfway up the curved staircase that dominated the galleried hall, stopped, leaned over the banister rail and pointed. 'That one. If you wouldn't mind putting the kettle on, I'll be down in a tick.'

'That's okay, just take your time.'

'It's so good of you. We could have our tea in the sitting room. It's got a lovely view of the garden.'

'That sounds a nice idea.'

'With you in a few minutes.' Caroline scuttled up the rest of the stairs and disappeared.

Melissa located the kettle and filled it from a large brass tap at a white porcelain butler's sink. While she was waiting for it to boil she glanced curiously at the old-fashioned fittings that reminded her of kitchens she had seen in old farmhouses or small National Trust properties. An Aga stood in an alcove that had doubtless once contained an ancient cooking range, but the wooden dresser, shelves and work surfaces appeared to date, if not from the year the house was built, at least from Victorian times. Apart from an electric kettle and a toaster there was no visible evidence of modern appliances, but a soft humming noise enabled her to locate the refrigerator, its door disguised by a panel of stripped pine to match the other fittings. As she opened it in search of milk, it occurred to her that a dishwasher and washing machine might be similarly camouflaged; she was tempted to investigate, but resisted. Such things, she reflected, even had they been available, would have been unnecessary in the days when servants were cheap and easy to find, but surely essential in the twenty-first century. It crossed her mind to wonder how much help Caroline had in the house, and whether it was her choice or that of her husband to preserve it in what she imagined to be the state in which they bought it.

She began opening cupboards at random in search of crockery. Then, on the pine dresser opposite the Aga, she spotted a tray already laid for afternoon tea and beside it an old-fashioned tea caddy. There were two bone china cups and saucers and a silver teapot with matching milk jug and sugar bowl, all neatly arranged on a lace tray-cloth. It came as no surprise to find loose tea and a silver caddy spoon rather than teabags.

She had just made the tea and was standing at the open door of the kitchen waiting for Caroline to reappear and direct her to the sitting room when a telephone began to ring. At the same moment, Caroline came running down the stairs and, without appearing to notice Melissa, hurried into one of the rooms on the opposite side of the hall. The sound of the ringing grew louder as she opened the door and then stopped as she picked up the phone. Melissa heard her say, 'Hullo,' and then, making no attempt to lower her voice, 'Why didn't you call earlier? Didn't you get my message? What? I said it was urgent. Listen, something absolutely dreadful's happened. Aidan's dead.' There was a longer pause during which she seemed to be listening to the person on the other end of the line. Then she said, 'It must have been very nearly instantaneous. The doctor said it was probably anaphylactic shock, but there might have to be a post mortem. That's all I can tell you for now. I've got someone here, I'll call you later.' There was the sound of the receiver being put back in its cradle and Melissa, aware that it would be embarrassing to be seen standing in the open doorway as if she had been eavesdropping, hastily withdrew into the kitchen. When Caroline entered a moment later she was fiddling with the tea-things in an attempt to give the impression that she had only just finished her preparations.

'That's good timing,' she said brightly, 'and you've done wonders with your face,' she added, noting the carefully applied make-up that went some way to conceal the effects of the prolonged weeping. 'I found this tray already laid, so–'

'Oh, yes, I'd forgotten; I prepared it a little while ago. Aidan always. . .' Once again, Caroline seemed to slip into a brown study.

'So if you like to lead the way?'

'Yes, of course.' The widow made a visible effort to pull

herself together, but Melissa sensed that she had been disturbed by the telephone call.

The sitting room overlooked the extensive back garden, which was enclosed by the beech hedge that Melissa had noticed on her approach to the house. It had high recessed windows with shutters, and French doors that opened on to a paved terrace. A flagged path led across a wide lawn to a circular pool in the centre, where a stone nymph held aloft a scallop shell from which water cascaded over a group of stone cherubs lying at her feet. Rosy pink water lilies floated on the surface, their green pads glistening in the sunlight; colourful borders surrounded the lawn on three sides. Birds sang, bees buzzed among the flowers. A tranquil scene, one that gave no hint of the horror that had occurred nearby only a few hours earlier.

'If you wouldn't mind putting the tray there.' Caroline pointed to a small circular gate-legged table set between two armchairs facing out on to the garden. 'Do sit down while I pour,' she went on, as if suddenly remembering the duty of a hostess. 'I didn't put out any biscuits or cake; Aidan never allows anything to eat between lunch and dinner. He says it's unhealthy to eat between meals . . . that is, he used to . . .'

Her voice trailed away and the blank expression came back into her eyes. The hand that reached for the silver teapot was trembling so violently that Melissa said hastily, 'No, let me; you sit down,' and gently pushed her into a chair.

By the time they had finished their second cup of tea, Caroline had stopped shaking and some of the colour had come back into her cheeks. She wiped her mouth with a fresh tissue, picked up Melissa's empty cup and saucer, stacked them carefully with her own and replaced them on the tray.

'Thank you, that was just what I needed,' she said politely. 'Now, what was I saying?'

As she had not spoken a word for the past ten minutes except for a murmured 'thank you' when handed her tea, Melissa had to think quickly. 'You were saying your husband disapproved of eating between meals,' she said after a moment.

'Oh, yes, so I was,' said Caroline. 'He was absolutely right, don't you agree?'

'Oh, I'm sure he was.'

'He was right about so many things,' Caroline went on. She had an earnest, but slightly absent expression; Melissa sensed that she was not so much trying to make conversation as thinking aloud. There was silence for a moment or two, broken by a somewhat peremptory knock at the door. It opened before Caroline had time to say, 'Come in,' and Quentin Cresney appeared.

'I heard voices so I guessed I'd find you in here,' he said.

Although Melissa knew the man by sight, their only contact before today had been a polite exchange of greetings after morning service on a Sunday. On those occasions he had been in the company of his brother and their respective wives and had seemed an insignificant figure, his slightly hangdog appearance in sharp contrast to Aidan's commanding presence. Now, as he stood facing his sister-in-law, she was aware of a subtle change in his manner. He was holding himself more erect than when he had intercepted her a short while ago and there was a slight lift to his chin; it was as if he had stepped out of the shadows into the limelight, like an understudy suddenly having to play the lead.

Caroline said, 'Melissa, I believe you've met my brother-in-law.' The two exchanged polite nods. 'Mrs Martin very kindly called round to offer her condolences.' Her voice was even, but from her unsmiling demeanour it was clear that she did not welcome the unceremonious interruption.

'Oh, er, yes, of course.' For a moment, the new air of confidence wavered. 'Sorry to barge in.'

'What do you want, Quentin?'

'Sarah says, would you like to come and have a meal with us this evening? We don't think you ought to be on your own, and anyway you probably don't feel much like cooking.'

'That's very kind. What time shall I come?'

'Say six o'clock.'

'That's a bit early, isn't it?'

'There's a lot we have to discuss.'

'Indeed there is. All right, tell Sarah I'll come at six. Is that all?'

'Er, yes, I'll tell her. See you later, then.' He withdrew and closed the door behind him.

Melissa glanced at the ormolu clock on the mantelpiece above the massive stone fireplace and stood up. 'It's nearly half past four,' she said. 'I'll be getting along now.'

'It was so good of you to come,' said Caroline, and there was a warmth in her tone that Melissa felt was genuine.

'Not at all.' As she was leaving, Caroline repeated her thanks and Melissa said, 'If there's anything I can do, don't hesitate to ask.'

'So how did you find things at Cold Wells?' asked Joe when Melissa returned to Hawthorn Cottage. 'Did you get the same impression as John Hamley?'

'In a way. Quentin tried to get rid of me, but Caroline seemed really pleased to see me, said she needed someone to talk to, and then sat down and cried her eyes out.'

'That sounds as if she doesn't feel like talking to her brother-in-law and his wife.'

'I don't know about the wife, but she hasn't got much time for Quentin. She referred to him as an interfering toad and she put him down quite smartly when he came barging into her sitting room without waiting for her to respond to his knock.' Melissa gave a brief account of the exchange between the two. 'There seems no doubt that he's trying to establish himself as the new head of the family and I don't think Caroline cares much for the idea.'

'That ties in with what Roger told Mrs Foster.'

'Yes.'

'So what did Caroline want to talk about?'

'She didn't really talk at all, apart from one or two odd remarks when it seemed as if she was talking to herself and didn't really expect an answer.'

'What sort of remarks?'

'Something about not having been able to let herself go for ages – that was after all that crying. And she apologised for not offering cake or biscuits with our tea because Aidan wouldn't allow eating between meals.'

'There doesn't seem to be much doubt about who was boss.'

'No, and now Aidan's gone I sense there's a power struggle in the making. You know,' Melissa went on thoughtfully, 'there's quite a creepy atmosphere in that house. Everything has a retro look about it.'

'How d'you mean?'

'Acres of dark panelling and William Morris wallpaper,

the sitting room's a clutter of overstuffed furniture and knick-knacks, the kitchen's a museum piece and the downstairs loo has an overhead cistern and chain that look as if they came out of the Ark.'

'Lots of people go for that sort of thing. Isn't Victoriana the new cool or something?'

Melissa pulled a face. 'Maybe, but it wouldn't suit me; I'm not sure that it suits Caroline either, but if that's what Aidan liked she wouldn't have had much option.'

'He does seem to have been pretty difficult to live with,' Joe agreed. 'Just the same,' he went on with a shudder, 'I can't believe the poor chap deserved such a gruesome death. It's like something out of a horror movie.'

'That's true, but mercifully it was over very quickly.'

'How do you know?'

'Caroline had a phone call while I was there from someone responding to a message she'd left earlier. She said something about Aidan being dead and it was dreadful, but the doctor had said it was probably anaphylactic shock so it must have been very nearly instantaneous.'

'Well, I guess that must be some comfort to them all.'

6

Caroline's first action after saying goodbye to Melissa was to turn the key in the communicating door between the main part of the house and that occupied by her brother-in-law and his wife. 'If you think Aidan's death has given you the right to come barging in whenever you feel like it without so much as a by-your-leave, Quentin Cresney, you can think again!' she muttered. She withdrew the key and hung it on the hook that Aidan had put at the side of the door for that purpose.

Next, she returned to the sitting room to fetch the tea-things. For several minutes she stood with the tray in her hands, staring around her and hating everything she saw. Her gaze travelled from the dark panelling, topped by a shelf bearing a row of dingy ironstone plates, that covered the walls to within a couple of feet of the beamed ceiling; it rested briefly on the Victorian chiffonier with its fussy detail and its display of hideous ornaments before moving on to the cumbersome armchairs and the faded oriental rugs scattered on the wooden floor. Her mind went back to the day Aidan brought her to the house for the first time. There had been much about it that appealed to her: the setting was idyllic, the rooms were light and well proportioned and it was evident that the place had been kept in good order throughout. She remembered sitting on one of the deep, cushioned window-seats, looking out at the beautifully kept gardens and saying, 'This would be a lovely room if it had decent furniture instead of all that grisly Victorian tat. The whole house needs redecorating, of course, and a modern central heating system and a new kitchen, but I do like it. It's got lots of potential . . . if you think we can afford it.'

That had been the point at which she met her husband's eyes and saw in them an expression that had become all too familiar: the look of almost malevolent satisfaction at having yet again deceived her into supposing that she had any say in the matter. He had replied simply, 'It's just as well you like it, because I've bought it, lock, stock and barrel.'

'Oh.' She had been nonplussed for the moment, although not altogether surprised. It had been naïve of her to suppose that he would have consulted her in advance. Then she had rallied and said cannily, knowing that it would please him to have his decision endorsed, 'That was a shrewd move, Aidan.' She had gone on to say something about the contents being worth a small fortune because Victoriana fetched ridiculous prices at auction, intending to add that this lot would probably raise enough to engage an interior designer to advise on renovating the place. But at the sight of the sardonic smile that flickered round his thin lips the words died in her throat. She knew instinctively that he had no intention of changing anything.

Looking back, she asked herself how it was that she had failed to read the signs in the early days of their acquaintance. They had been plain enough; the relationship between Aidan and his younger brother alone should have made her stop and think, but she had been so dazzled by his charm and the strength of his personality – to say nothing of his brilliant brain, his professional reputation and all the material and social advantages that went with them – that she had shut her mind to any evidence of the darker side of his nature.

She went out of the room and closed the door behind her, resolving that things were going to be very different from now on. She rinsed out the cups and saucers and inverted them on the scrubbed wooden draining board. She glanced round the kitchen and shuddered; once things were settled and she had control of the money, she would start here. Then she recalled Quentin's words: 'there's a lot we have to discuss,' and put thoughts of future plans on hold for the time being.

She decided to relax in a hot bath before changing for supper. She went upstairs to her bedroom, *her* bedroom from now on, she reminded herself, hers alone. She sat down in front of the dressing table and studied her face in the mirror. The outward effects of prolonged weeping were beginning to fade, but it had left her physically exhausted and emotionally drained. At the same time she felt a profound feeling of relief. Melissa had been right when she said that giving way had done her good. In the early days of her marriage, there had been many occasions when Aidan reduced her to tears. The biting sarcasm such a display of weakness would invariably provoke had forced her to develop a degree of self-control she could hardly believe she possessed.

Well, she thought as she went into the en suite bathroom and turned on the taps, if the outpouring of emotion had fulfilled an immediate need, that self-control, together with the stress-relieving drugs prescribed by her doctor, would stand her in good stead in the difficult days to come. She could expect to be showered with messages of condolence from well-meaning people, who in their turn would expect her to show conventional signs of grief. She would have to be on her guard and not give the slightest indication of the sense of release that, after the initial shock of Aidan's death, had all but overwhelmed her. She tried to recall how much, if anything, she had betrayed to her recent visitor about her feelings for her late husband. She could not recall volunteering anything significant; certainly Melissa had asked no questions nor shown the slightest inclination to pry, merely offering sympathy and help if it should be needed. She seemed a person one could trust to be discreet. It might be good to have another confidante, someone she could open her heart to if she felt the need. Feeling comforted, she slipped out of her clothes, stepped into the bath and enjoyed a long leisurely soak.

'Why on earth have you come to the front door?' Quentin demanded in response to Caroline's ring.

'Because I've locked the communicating door and it's going to stay that way,' she said calmly. 'I've decided it's best if we respect one another's territorial boundaries from now on.'

'But I thought–'

'I know what you thought,' Caroline interrupted. 'You thought that without Aidan here to lay down the ground rules you could come and go into my part of the house as and when you felt like it, the way he used to go into yours.' Quentin's mouth opened and his eyes saucered as if he could hardly believe his ears.

For a second or two they stood facing one another. Inwardly, Caroline too found it difficult to believe that she had spoken in such a confrontational manner, but in the event it was Quentin who yielded. His eyes slid away from hers and he moved to one side, inviting her to enter with a vague movement of one hand.

'We're having drinks on the patio,' he announced over his shoulder as he closed the door behind her. 'We'll eat in the dining room, of course, but as it's such a lovely evening–'

'What a good idea,' she said politely.

'I'm glad you approve.' She thought she detected a slight acidic edge to the remark, but merely smiled and nodded. 'What will you have?' he went on. 'We're on gin and tonic, but if you fancy anything else–?'

'Gin and tonic will be fine.'

'Well, you know the way. I'll fix your drink,' he said and headed for the kitchen.

She forbore to mention that she had already had a fairly stiff one to give her Dutch courage for the interview. She knew exactly the line she wanted to take, but it was not going to be easy to be assertive after having played a subservient role for so many years. She had stood at her sitting room window while sipping her drink, gazing out over the garden and trying to nerve herself for what she sensed would be a clash of wills. She experienced for a moment the eerie sensation that Aidan's ghost was hovering beside her, infusing her with some of the disdain he had always shown for his younger brother's weakness of character.

Sarah came forward to meet her sister-in-law as she stepped out through the French doors on to the patio, took her by both hands and kissed her gently on the cheek. For an instant, Caroline felt herself stiffening, but forced herself to relax and return the greeting.

'Come along and sit down, dear.' Sarah indicated the semi-circle of cane chairs with green and yellow cushions, arranged round a circular glass-topped table on which stood two half-finished drinks and a bowl of crisps. 'We thought it would be nice to sit here for a little while. It's really pleasant now the sun's not so hot. I can lower the awning if you find it too bright,' she added.

'No, it's fine thank you. I thought we'd probably be out here so I've brought my sun-glasses.' Caroline took them from her handbag and put them on.

Sarah adjusted hers as if to reassure herself that they were still in place. There was a short silence while they settled in their seats. Then she said, 'I hope you managed to get a little rest this afternoon. I understand Melissa Martin called to see you. That was kind of her.'

'Yes, wasn't it?'

'Here we go – one G and T.' Quentin emerged, bearing a tray on which stood a tall glass containing gin, ice and lemon, and a small can of tonic water. He placed them on the table in front of Caroline with a flourish. 'I've left you to put in your own tonic. I hope that's okay?'

'Thank you, that's fine.'

'Do help yourself to crisps.'

'Thank you.'

Quentin sat down, picked up his own glass and said, 'I suppose in the circumstances it wouldn't be quite the thing to say, "Cheers", would it?'

'Hardly,' said Sarah. Caroline said nothing.

They drank in silence for a few minutes, gazing across the garden, each busy with private thoughts. Quentin was the first to speak.

'It's early days, of course,' he began, and it seemed to Caroline that his voice was pitched slightly higher than normal. Nerves, she thought to herself. He's going to say something that he's afraid I might disagree with. 'We do realise that you're still suffering from shock – we all are – and you probably don't feel like making any major decisions just yet, but there are certain things that have to be attended to like registering Aidan's death and arranging the funeral and so on.'

'Yes, of course.'

'So what I . . . that is, what we thought, Sarah and I . . . I mean, we want to make things as easy as possible for you . . .'

His voice tailed off, rather lamely, Caroline thought. She looked at him over the rim of her glass and felt a mingled sense of triumph and pity as for the second time his eyes avoided hers.

'If you're offering to attend to the formalities, I'd be very grateful,' she said politely.

'Yes, well, we don't know yet if there's going to be a post mortem, but even if there is, it shouldn't take long. The doctor seemed pretty sure about the cause of death, so if that's confirmed he can issue a death certificate and it should all be quite straightforward. We should know by tomorrow. I understand the rector has already called to offer his condolences.'

'Yes, wasn't it good of him? He said something about another visit to discuss funeral arrangements. We can discuss what hymns we'll have once we've fixed a date.'

'There'll be notices to the press,' Quentin went on. 'I understand the undertakers will see to that for us if we let them know what wording we want. I've drafted something.' He took a sheet of paper from his pocket and offered it to Caroline.

She took it from him, folded it without reading it and slipped it into her handbag. 'Thank you, Quentin, I'll read it later,' she said.

'Of course,' Quentin said, and once again his voice rose to a slightly higher pitch, 'there will be all sorts of business matters to deal with.'

'Naturally.'

'It occurred to me . . . us' – here he shot a brief sidelong glance at his wife, who responded with what appeared to be a nod of encouragement – 'that Aidan probably wasn't in the habit of discussing his business affairs with you.'

It was a correct assumption, but Caroline had no intention of revealing the fact. 'What gave you that impression?' she asked.

'Oh, er, it was just, knowing Aidan, it seemed likely.'

Caroline helped herself to a crisp, ate it, took a mouthful from her glass and said, 'Quentin, what is this leading up to?'

He cast another glance at his wife, who covered Caroline's free hand with her own and said gently, 'Don't think we're trying to interfere, Carrie, but we thought it would be a good idea to let Quentin look after the business side of things for you.'

'By way of a power of attorney,' he added.

Caroline drew her hand away. 'Excuse me, but I've always been under the impression that Aidan took care of your business affairs as well as his own,' she said.

'It's true we normally acted on his advice,' Sarah agreed, 'but he always explained things very clearly to Quentin, which obviously means that he has a much better grasp of such matters than you.'

'Possibly.'

'Almost certainly, if you don't mind my saying so.' Quentin finished his drink and stood up. 'How about a refill while you're thinking about it?' he said.

As he held out a hand for her glass, Caroline noticed that it was shaking slightly. 'Thank you,' she said, 'it's very kind of you to suggest it and I don't need time to think.'

'So that's settled, then,' Quentin beamed. 'I'll arrange for our solicitor to prepare the necessary document for you to sign.'

'That won't be necessary,' said Caroline.

'Oh, my dear, I'm afraid it will. It all has to be done legally, you see.' His manner became faintly patronising as he added, 'Don't worry, we'll make it as easy for you as possible.'

'That's very kind of you,' she repeated, giving him the warmest, friendliest, most grateful smile that she could manage, 'but I wouldn't dream of putting you to so much trouble. I shall be consulting my own solicitor as soon as possible and seeking his advice.'

'But surely . . . ' Quentin blurted out. 'I mean . . . Aidan and I used the same firm and I sort of assumed . . . '

Caroline, who was by now beginning to feel a little tipsy, had difficulty in restraining a giggle on seeing the look of dismayed astonishment that passed between her brother-in-law and his wife. 'Yes, I know you and he have been hand in glove ever since you returned to the fold, Quentin,' she said. 'That's why I think it might be better if I had some independent advice. In any case,' she went on as he appeared on the point of raising a further objection, 'don't you think it's a bit early to start this kind of discussion? After all, Aidan's only been dead for a matter of hours.'

'Oh . . . well, perhaps you're right,' he said, with obvious reluctance. His pasty features drooped in a sullen scowl and he went off to replenish their drinks without another word.

7

The atmosphere at the dinner table was, not unnaturally after such an overt clash of wills, noticeably strained. Nevertheless, all three participants did their best to maintain the pretence that it was a natural reaction to the devastating event that had shattered their lives. At nine o'clock, Caroline pleaded a return of the headache that had been her excuse to remain in bed that morning. She declined coffee on the pretext that it would keep her awake and took her leave.

Sarah saw her out; at the door, having glanced over her shoulder to make sure that her husband was not within earshot, she said in a low voice, 'I told Quentin he should wait a few days before mentioning the power of attorney business. It's too soon for you to be bothered with such things, but I do hope you'll reconsider when you've had time to think it over.'

'I shall do whatever my solicitor advises,' said Caroline. 'Goodnight, Sarah, and thank you for a lovely meal.'

'You're sure you'll be all right? I could stay with you tonight if you don't want to be alone. I'm sure Quentin wouldn't mind.'

'Thank you for the offer, but I'm sure Quentin will want you with him and I assure you I'll be quite all right.' *And you don't know just what a relief being on my own is going to be,* was the unspoken thought that followed the final words.

Back in her own house, Caroline slipped out of her clothes, put on her nightdress, a negligee and slippers and sat down at her dressing table. She took off her make-up and brushed her straight dark hair, noting with satisfaction that there were still only a few flecks of grey and that her fine skin was in good shape for a woman on the wrong side of thirty. She smiled and gave herself a little salute before going into the bathroom to clean her teeth. Then she went downstairs to the sitting room to fetch a book. Reading in bed was a luxury she had almost forgotten.

She had barely settled down when the telephone rang. 'I thought you were going to call me back,' said a reproachful voice on the end of the line.

'Oh dear, I quite forgot. I'm so sorry. Quentin and Sarah invited me to dinner and I've not long been back.'

'That was kind of them. How are you now?'

'All right, I suppose. At least, I thought I was.' A sob rose without warning into Caroline's throat; for a moment she was unable to speak. 'Oh God,' she whispered, 'you should have seen his face. It was horrible, all swollen, almost unrecognisable. I'll have nightmares about it for weeks. I had no idea bees could do that.'

'Don't think about it.'

'I'm trying not to. I keep asking myself if it really happened. It's like a bad dream. I never–' Her voice failed again.

'Take it easy. At least, it was over quickly. Hang on to that thought.'

'I keep seeing him–'

'You've had a severe shock. You must expect a few after-effects.'

'Yes, I suppose so.'

'At least you have Sarah and Quentin to look after you.'

Caroline's distress gave way to scorn. 'Look after themselves is more like it. You'll never guess what they want me
to do.'

'What?'

'Give Quentin a power of attorney so he can handle all
Aidan's affairs on my behalf. He didn't actually have the
document ready for me to sign, but no doubt he would have
done if there'd been time.'

'What did you say?'

'I told him to get stuffed – not in so many words, of
course, but I think he got the message. Sarah apologised
later for the way he came out with it. Said he should have
waited until I'd had time to adjust.'

'I'm sure he was only trying to be helpful.'

'Well, he's going about it the wrong way.'

'He's going to need time to adjust as well, don't forget.
He's been under Aidan's malign influence far longer than
you have.'

'Yes, I suppose so. Another thing annoyed me; when
Roger, our postman, arrived Quentin started taking charge,
telling him to address him as Mr Cresney instead of Mr
Quentin from now on.'

There was a chuckle at the other end of the line. 'You're
kidding!'

'No, it's true. Then he grabbed all today's letters and said
he'd sort them out later. And we were in our . . . in *my* house
at the time.'

'I suppose that was a bit much.'

'It was a bloody cheek. You remember I told you that
Aidan used to have all the post delivered here so that he
could get the first look at it?'

'I remember. The old tyrant liked to keep a check on everything that came into the house, even if it wasn't addressed to him, didn't he?'

'Right. He never showed me any of his unless they were personal to the two of us, but if there were any for me he always demanded to read them. When Quentin started chucking his weight around, it gave me a real jolt. I was determined to make sure he didn't get the same idea so I picked up the letters, took out the ones addressed to Aidan and me and gave him his and Sarah's. And I told Roger to make separate deliveries from now on.'

'That makes sense. Caroline, you are going to be okay on your own, aren't you?'

'I suppose so.'

'Good. Give me a call if you feel in need of a chat.'

'That's what Melissa said.'

'Melissa who?'

'Melissa Martin. She lives in the village. She's actually Mel Craig, the crime writer. She came to see me this afternoon; she's been so kind.'

'I see.' There was a short silence before the caller said, 'Well, goodnight, sleep well.'

There was a click followed by the dull hum of dialling tone. It made Caroline think of bees and she gave a little moan and put her hands over her eyes in a futile effort to blot out the hideous memory of her dead husband's distorted features. She put the book aside, went back to the bathroom and swallowed a couple of tranquillisers. Even with their help, it was a long time before she fell into an uneasy sleep.

At a little before eleven the following morning there was a knock on the door of Hawthorn Cottage. Melissa and Joe, busy at their respective desks in the upstairs room they shared as a study, exchanged glances.

'Not expecting anyone, are we?' he said.

Melissa shook her head. 'It's probably someone selling something.'

'Ignore them and they'll go away.'

'I'd better see who it is.' She pushed aside the script she was working on and stood up. 'It's almost coffee time anyway.'

To her surprise, Caroline Cresney was at the door. She appeared composed, but her face was pale; although there were no traces of the previous day's tears there were dark smudges under her eyes that had not been there before. 'I hope I'm not disturbing you,' she began.

'Not at all. Come in.' Melissa held the door open and Caroline, after a moment's hesitation, stepped inside. 'Perhaps you'll join us for coffee – I was just about to make some. If you don't mind coming into the kitchen, we can talk while the kettle's boiling.'

'I was going to phone, but I don't have your number,' said Caroline as she followed Melissa along the passage. 'I couldn't find it in the book and the operator wouldn't give it to me.'

'We're ex-directory,' Melissa explained. 'The number's on here with my website and email address.' She took one of her business cards from a drawer, gave it to Caroline and pointed to a chair. 'Why don't you sit down and tell me what I can do for you?'

'Thank you.' Caroline put the card in her handbag and sat fiddling with the strap while Melissa bustled about preparing the coffee. Then she said, 'I wonder if you could recommend a good solicitor?' The words came out with a rush, as if she had rehearsed them but needed to pluck up her courage to speak.

Melissa was surprised at the question, but was careful not to betray it as she said, 'Well, Digby Morrison looks after my affairs and has done for years. He's a partner in Barnes and Morrison in Cheltenham. I've got his number here.' She checked in her personal directory and wrote it on a scrap of paper.

'Thank you.' Caroline tucked it away with the business card. 'It's just that I need some really sound legal advice,' she explained.

'I'm sure he'll give you that. I've always found him very reliable.' Melissa filled the cafetière, put it on the table and moved towards the door. 'I'll just tell Joe the coffee's ready–'

'No, wait a minute.' The note of pleading in Caroline's voice and the earnest, almost frightened look in her eyes, stopped Melissa in her tracks.

'Is there something else?' she asked.

'It's just that . . . I hardly know how to put this, but . . . Aidan never spoke to me about his business affairs, so I've no idea–'

'A lot of husbands are like that, I believe. They think women haven't the brains to understand high finance!' Melissa deliberately made her tone jocular, but the remark brought no answering smile.

'In Aidan's case I'm pretty sure it was because there were things he didn't want me to know.'

'What sort of things?'

Caroline continued fidgeting with her handbag, avoiding Melissa's eyes. 'I don't know,' she mumbled.

'I take it you have access to his papers?'

'There's a filing cabinet in his study, but I've no idea what's in it. He always kept it locked.'

'Do you know where he kept the key?'

'No.'

'Was it in his pocket when he died?'

'It might have been. I never thought to look.'

'That's natural. You were too upset. Where is Aidan's body now?'

'At the mortuary, I suppose. The doctor wanted to carry out further tests before he'd issue a certificate.'

'Then he's the one to ask.'

'Yes, I suppose so. Thank you for your help, and . . . ' She hesitated once again. 'I'd be grateful if you didn't mention this to anyone in the village. I mean, I don't want–' She broke off in evident confusion.

'I wouldn't dream of it,' Melissa assured her, 'and if there's anything else I can do, just give me a bell.'

'You're very kind.'

'It's not a problem. Now, what about that coffee?'

Caroline shook her head and stood up. 'If you don't mind, I'd rather not stay now. I have a lot to see to.'

'I quite understand. Another time, perhaps.'

'That would be nice.'

'Well, what do you make of that?' said Melissa, as she explained the reason for Caroline's visit while she and Joe were drinking their coffee. 'I'd have thought Aidan's affairs were already handled by a solicitor.'

'Maybe they were, but it's obvious he didn't tell Caroline.'

Melissa helped herself to a second cup of coffee and stirred milk into it. 'No doubt all will be revealed when she gets into the mysterious locked filing cabinet,' she said thoughtfully. 'I wonder–'

He assumed an expression of mock dismay and raised a hand in protest. 'Please, stop wondering! I get worried when you use the word "mysterious".'

'I wonder if he made a will,' she continued, as if he hadn't spoken.

'Almost certainly, from what you've told me about him.'

'With his legal background, he could have drawn it up for himself, but he must have appointed an executor.'

'Quentin, perhaps?'

Melissa shook her head. 'I doubt it, but you never know. In any case, I can understand Caroline wanting independent advice. That brush I had with Quentin yesterday was quite revealing. If I were in her shoes, I wouldn't trust him with the money to buy me a lottery ticket.'

The following day was Wednesday, the day when Gloria Parkin came to do her weekly stint of cleaning at Hawthorn Cottage and at the same time bring the Martins up to date with the latest news and gossip. Joe escaped to the study before she arrived, in a state of great excitement and bursting to share the blend of information and highly coloured speculation that she had gleaned during the forty-eight hours since Aidan Cresneys' death.

'Mrs Wilson, the Cresneys' cleaning lady, said you could've knocked her down with a feather when she heard about it,' she confided as she put on her apron and pulled her cleaning materials from the kitchen cupboard. 'She said she couldn't hardly believe it of Mr Cresney, he were that careful over his bees and he knew exactly what he were doing. She reckons there must've been a hole in his overalls what let they bees in to do their dreadful work.' The final words were uttered with a dramatic roll of Gloria's toffee-brown eyes.

'Yes, we think that must have been what happened,' Melissa agreed. 'It must've been a terrible shock for the family, especially for his wife.'

'Ah, that weren't what I heard,' said Gloria mysteriously.

'What do you mean?'

'Mrs Wilson said Mrs Cresney – Mrs Caroline Cresney that is – were cool as a cucumber when she went there yesterday morning. She reckons she won't be doing much grieving.' Gloria gave a meaningful nod that set her blond curls bouncing.

'What makes her say that?'

'She reckons Mrs Caroline weren't a happy lady and that Mr Aidan were a real tyrant. She said she often noticed an atmosphere when she were there, and once she overheard them having a row over a game of bridge.'

'I didn't know they played bridge.'

'He didn't, but she do. She got some friends what plays regular, but he'd go out of his way to find something important she had to do on her bridge days to stop her going.'

'That was a bit mean.'

'Seems he were like that. She had to keep her arrangements quiet till the last minute. And that weren't all.' Gloria dropped her voice dramatically. 'Billy Wilson were in the Woolpack talking to my Stanley a while back and he said his wife were tidying up in the Aidan Cresneys' bedroom at Cold Wells one day and she found a shirt with make-up on it in the laundry basket.'

'It was probably his wife's,' said Melissa.

'She said it were a sort of pinky shade, not the colour Mrs Cresney wears.'

'Are you suggesting Mr Aidan was having an affair?'

'Shouldn't be surprised.'

'Well, I'm sure they had their problems, but I can tell you Mrs Cresney was very upset when I called on her the afternoon of her husband's death.'

Gloria looked faintly disappointed, then perked up as a further thought struck her. 'Being upset didn't stop her doing the washing, did it?'

Melissa looked blank. 'I don't follow you.'

'Mrs Wilson, she do the washing on a Tuesday, but she said when she looked in the basket it were empty.'

'Maybe Mrs Cresney felt she had to do something practical rather than just sit about. People do odd things sometimes when they're in shock.'

'S'pose so,' Gloria agreed reluctantly. 'Well, the place won't clean itself, so I'd better get on.' At the foot of the stairs she turned and said, 'When's the funeral going to be?'

'I've no idea.'

'Oh.' Gloria's face clouded again. 'I thought Mrs Cresney might've told you when she came to see you yesterday. She were on the phone asking for your number and when she couldn't get it she went out and Mrs Wilson thought–'

'Mrs Wilson seems to be good at putting two and two together and making five,' said Melissa, in what she hoped was a tone of disapproval. She had no intention of giving Mrs Wilson the satisfaction of knowing that at least one of her assumptions was correct.

8

After Gloria's departure, Melissa said to Joe, 'You won't believe what Gloria and Mrs Wilson have been saying about Caroline Cresney.'

Joe paused in the act of laying the table while Melissa prepared soup for their lunch. 'Nothing Gloria says would surprise me,' he said. 'Who's Mrs Wilson anyway?'

'Caroline's cleaning lady. They've been comparing notes and Gloria passed on all sorts of titbits.' Melissa related the scraps of gossip, causing Joe to raise his eyebrows. 'And on top of all that they got very exercised over the fact that Caroline did a load of washing herself instead of leaving it to Mrs Wilson.'

'Perhaps she found another shirt with make-up on it and didn't want Mrs Wilson to see it.'

'That occurred to me, but I didn't say so to Gloria. I wonder,' Melissa went on as she ground black pepper into the soup, 'whether Caroline knew about the other shirt – the one Mrs Wilson found.'

'Probably not, or she'd have washed it herself.'

'Yes, I suppose so. Joe, do you suppose Aidan was having an affair?'

'If he was, you'd have thought he'd have been a bit smarter at covering his tracks.'

'I'm surprised he didn't notice the make-up on his shirt, but everyone makes mistakes at times.'

'Aidan certainly did – a fatal one,' said Joe. The conversation, which up to that point had been fairly light-hearted, assumed a more serious note. 'I wonder,' he went on, 'whether we shall ever know exactly how the accident happened.'

'We'll have to wait and see. I'm sure if any details emerge, Gloria will let us know.'

Joe went to the sink, filled a jug with water and put it on the table. 'You shouldn't encourage her,' he said.

'You should know by now that Gloria doesn't need any encouragement. By the way, before she left she asked if Mum needed any help – said she could probably squeeze in an hour a week as a favour.'

'That was thoughtful of her.'

'Yes, wasn't it? I told her Mum's quite happy doing her own housework at present, but I'd pass the message on.'

'She's settling in really well, isn't she?'

'Yes, it's such a relief. She's made several friends already; as a matter of fact, she's off on a jolly into town today with Cynthia Thorne.'

'Good Lord, whatever does she have in common with that old chatterbox?'

'She organises the church flower-arranging rota and she recruited Mum the first Sunday she was here. The next thing, she's roped her into her flower club; they have a meeting every Wednesday followed by lunch.'

'Well, good luck to her – so long as she doesn't start inviting her loquacious friend back for tea. You might find yourself joining the party as well.'

Melissa shook her head. 'I don't think there's any fear of that. Mum's being very meticulous about our "respecting one another's boundaries" as she puts it. There'll be no prizes for guessing what the ladies will be discussing over their lumps of Oasis today,' she added.

'You mean the death of Aidan Cresney?'

'What else? They'll go to town on it, what with all the gossip about the dodgy state of the marriage and hints that Caroline won't be eating her heart out with grief–'

'To say nothing of doing her own laundry a few hours after the event,' Joe interposed with a grin. 'What's the betting old Mother Thorne will be on your back before long, trying to persuade you there's material for a plot?'

'I'll tell her one body isn't enough to make a murder mystery – you need at least two and preferably three,' said Melissa cheerfully.

'That's my girl.' Joe put an arm round her and peered into the pan of soup she was stirring. 'My, that smells good. Is it ready yet? I'm starving.'

'Coming up. Bring the bowls over here, will you?'

'How about a walk after lunch?' suggested Joe as they sat down to eat.

'Good idea. We've done enough desk work for one day.'

Later, as they were returning from their stroll along the valley path linking the two villages of Upper and Lower Benbury, they saw a car pull up outside Hawthorn Cottage. Sylvia Ross got out; Joe grabbed Melissa by the arm and pulled her behind a clump of blackberry bushes.

'What's the idea?' she demanded.

'That's Cynthia Thorne's car, right?' he hissed in her ear.

'So?'

'If she spots us, she'll make an excuse to hang around until we get back and then spend half an hour bending our ears about you-know-what.'

'Good thinking.'

They crouched out of sight, giggling like guilty children, while the two flower arrangers took their leave of one another. Polite farewells were exchanged, the words clearly audible in the still air. Just before the car moved off they heard Cynthia call, in her penetrating soprano, 'You'll be sure and tell your daughter, won't you, Sylvia? I'm sure she'll be interested.'

'What did I say?' said Joe gleefully.

They had been back indoors for only a few minutes when Sylvia tapped on the door separating her self-contained dwelling from the main part of the house and called, 'May I come in for a moment?'

'We're in the kitchen,' Melissa called back. 'I've just put the kettle on.'

Her mother's face was pink with excitement as she entered. 'You'll never guess what people are saying,' she began as she pulled out a chair and sat down.

'You wouldn't be talking about Aidan Cresney's death, by any chance?' said Melissa.

Sylvia blinked in surprise. 'However did you guess?'

'I'm just a natural psychic. Well, what are they saying?'

'You know we've been wondering whether there was a tear or a hole in Aidan's bee veil that let the bees in?'

'That seemed a fairly obvious explanation. What of it?'

'Well, it seems that Caroline – his widow – was asked to hand over the overall for the coroner to examine and they think that must be what he's looking for.'

'So where's the big surprise?'

'Well, someone suggested that if there is a hole, it didn't get there by accident.'

Melissa's eyes widened and her mouth fell open. 'Mum, you aren't seriously saying that someone tore it deliberately so that Aidan would get stung?'

'Well, everyone's saying what a difficult man he was, and what a hard time he gave his wife. Maybe she just wanted to teach him a lesson and it all went horribly wrong. And another thing,' Sylvia hurried on before either Joe or Melissa had a chance to put in a word, 'Caroline had washed the overall before handing it over. Doesn't that strike you as strange?'

Melissa shook her head. 'Not really. It was probably dirty; after all, he had been lying on the ground.'

'By the way,' said Joe, 'does this "someone" employ a cleaning lady called Mrs Wilson?'

'I've no idea,' said Sylvia. 'Why do you ask?'

'Because we've already heard the washing part of the story from Gloria, who got it from Mrs Wilson, who "does" for Caroline Cresney.'

'Oh.' Sylvia looked crestfallen for a moment before saying, 'Did you hear about the tear as well?'

'No, we didn't,' said Melissa, 'and even if there was one and Caroline made it deliberately – which I don't believe for a moment – she'd surely have the sense to mend it before handing it over.'

'I suppose so,' Sylvia admitted grudgingly, 'but Cynthia seems to think it's all a bit fishy.'

'Mum,' said Melissa, a little impatiently. 'I think it's very naughty of people to spread this sort of gossip and I hope you don't go repeating it to anyone else.'

'Of course not, how could I? I haven't seen anyone else since I got back from the flower club.'

'Then please don't. We don't want to have to defend you against an action for slander.'

Sylvia gaped in horror at the suggestion. 'My goodness, do you really think . . . I mean, it wasn't my idea, I'm only telling you what I heard.'

'And I'm going to forget you ever said it, and I advise you to do the same or you might find yourself in all sorts of trouble.'

The coroner having pronounced a verdict of 'death by misadventure', the funeral of Aidan Cresney was fixed for the following Wednesday. The small group of local residents who attended was supplemented by a handful of dark-suited men who, it was assumed, were former colleagues, together with their soberly but fashionably dressed wives.

'Not exactly an impressive turnout,' Joe whispered in Melissa's ear as they sat in the little church of Saint Andrew, awaiting the arrival of the cortège. 'It doesn't look as if he was universally popular, even with his own kind.'

'No, and I suspect most of the village people here have come out of sympathy with the family rather than through any sense of personal loss,' she whispered back.

'Probably.'

The service began. The Reverend John Hamley began by referring to the tragic and totally unforeseen misfortune that had brought Aidan Cresney's life to an end. He went on to speak of his distinguished career at the bar and his work on behalf of the community, in an address that had been largely composed – as his wife Alice later confided to Melissa – by his brother Quentin. 'John couldn't find anyone living locally who was prepared to say anything particularly nice about him,' she said, and Melissa replied that it was sad when a person with so much talent should be so short of friends. It also occurred to her, although she kept the notion to herself, that considering his supposed standing in his former profession, none of his former colleagues or associates had offered to pay a tribute to him.

As they filed out of the church to follow the coffin to the graveside, Melissa happened to glance over her shoulder. In the back row of pews a solitary woman remained kneeling. Her head was bowed and she held a handkerchief to her mouth in a gloved hand; unlike the other female members of the congregation she was dressed entirely in black and a small veil on her hat concealed all but the lower part of her face.

'Do you know who that is?' whispered Joe to Melissa as they stepped outside.

'No idea. His former secretary, perhaps?'

'She seemed distressed.'

'More so than his own family.'

The final prayers were said, the coffin lowered into the open grave, and one by one the principal mourners stepped forward to scatter their handfuls of earth. After a few moments of silence people began moving towards their cars for the short drive to the Manor, where it had been earlier announced that tea would be served.

'Are we going to join the party?' said Joe.

Melissa nodded. 'Yes, I think so. Caroline will appreciate our support.'

'I must say, she bore up pretty well during the service,' he observed.

'Better than the woman in black,' she agreed. She glanced round. 'I wonder where she is? I don't remember seeing her at the graveside.'

'She must have stayed in the church.'

'Or slipped away without anyone noticing.'

'I suggest we do the same as soon as we decently can.'

She gave his arm a squeeze. 'All right.'

Refreshments had been laid out in the drawing room overlooking the garden where a little over a week ago Melissa had sat drinking tea with Caroline. The clouds that hid the sun during the ceremony began to disperse; as if in response, the sombre atmosphere lifted and people began chatting and even laughing as they sipped their tea and nibbled their sandwiches. Quentin opened the French doors and with a beaming smile and a proprietorial gesture invited the guests to go out on to the patio. A number of them did so, but Melissa noticed that those members of the village community who had accepted the invitation kept apart from the rest of the company, whom Mrs Foster from the village shop later referred to as 'they posh city folks'. Several of the former, having exchanged a few polite words of greeting and sympathy with the family, were taking advantage of a rare opportunity to view the gardens while the latter clustered in small groups like guests at a cocktail party. Quentin circulated among them, pausing for a few minutes' chat with everyone as he offered to replenish teacups and plates, smiling graciously or nodding with studied solemnity in response to condolences.

'Anyone would think this was his house and he was the host,' Joe whispered in Melissa's ear.

'That's Quentin for you,' she whispered back. 'I don't see Caroline or Sarah, though.'

'Gone to make more tea, perhaps.'

Melissa put down her empty cup and saucer. 'I'll see you in a moment; I must go to the loo.'

On her way across the deserted hall to the toilet she noticed that the kitchen door was ajar. From the other side came the sound of women's voices; they spoke quietly at first, but as she walked past she heard one of them exclaim, 'I don't know how she had the nerve to show her face here!'

There was a pause before the other replied, 'Anyone who got into that kind of relationship with him needed nerve.'

'At least she had the decency to disappear. Let's hope that's the last we see or hear of the bitch.'

They had said nothing to identify the subject of their conversation, but as Melissa continued on her way to the cloakroom she had no doubt in her mind that they had been speaking about the woman in black.

9

'So the mystery woman was more than just a secretary,' said Joe as, after taking leave of their hosts, he and Melissa drove slowly home.

'Aidan's widow and sister-in-law obviously think so,' she replied.

'You're sure it was them?'

'I definitely recognised Caroline's voice and I assumed the other woman in the kitchen with her was Sarah although I couldn't swear to it. Still, it's hardly likely Caroline would be saying things like that to anyone outside the family.'

'No, I suppose not. Of course,' Joe added after a moment's reflection, 'there was nothing to prove that it was the woman in black they were talking about.'

'Who else could it have been?'

'One of the other members of the congregation maybe – someone we didn't happen to spot, who also slipped away after the service.'

Melissa shook her head. 'No, I'm sure it was the woman who was sitting behind us,' she said firmly. 'And she'd been crying, which would seem to confirm what they were saying about a relationship.'

'With Aidan?'

'They didn't actually mention him by name, but I assume that's who they were talking about. I must say, until Gloria put the notion into my head, I'd never have suspected him of having a lover. He always seemed so cold and distant.'

'We don't know for certain that this woman was his lover.'

'What other explanation can you suggest? She obviously cared about him and wanted to be here to say goodbye, knew she wouldn't be welcomed at the wake so hid herself away at the back of the church and then quietly disappeared.'

'It could have been unrequited love.' Joe gave his wife a sideways glance and added softly, 'I know how that feels.'

She put her hand on his knee and gave it a squeeze. 'It wasn't unrequited love in your case, it just took me a while to recognise my own feelings.'

'I know. Better late than never.'

They had reached the end of the lane leading from Cold Wells to the main road. As Joe waited at the junction to allow a farm tractor to pass, Melissa noticed a car parked a short distance away on the other side. A woman whose face was partially concealed by a veil was sitting behind the wheel.

'That's her!' she exclaimed. 'Whatever is she doing there?'

'Search me.' He turned out and drove slowly down the hill into the village. 'Maybe she's waiting for everyone to disappear before she goes to the house to find out if Aidan's kept his promise to include her in his will,' he suggested.

'Don't be daft.' Melissa glanced in the passenger door mirror. 'She's pulling out. I do believe she's following us.'

'It's probably coincidence. Maybe she needed time to compose herself before driving home.'

It seemed at first that Joe's guess was correct. The woman followed them at a discreet distance through the village, but drove straight on after he turned on to the track leading to their cottage. They had all but forgotten about her until, ten minutes or so later, just as they had settled down in the sitting room and switched on the television to watch their favourite quiz programme, there was a ring at the doorbell.

'Oh bother, who's that?' said Melissa crossly. It had been a trying afternoon and she was longing for a chance to unwind.

'I'll get it,' said Joe. There was a brief interval during which she heard a woman's voice saying something indistinguishable, followed by her husband's saying, 'What's it about?' and then, 'Just a moment.' He reappeared in the doorway and said quietly, 'It's her, and she wants to speak to you.'

'What about?'

'She won't say. She asked if you were Mel Craig the crime writer and I asked her who wanted to know, but she won't even give her name. She still seems a bit agitated. What do you think? Will you go and speak to her?'

'This is very intriguing.' By this time Melissa's initial irritation at the interruption had given way to curiosity. She picked up the remote control and put the television on stand-by. 'Why not ask her in?'

'All right.'

The newcomer entered hesitantly, pausing for a moment in the doorway and casting a timid look round the room as if seeking assurance that no one else was there. Melissa got to her feet and pointed to a chair. 'Good afternoon,' she said politely. 'Do sit down and tell me what I can do for you. Would you like a cup of tea?'

'Thank you.' The visitor's voice had a husky quality that might have been due to emotion. She had removed her hat; without the veil she appeared far younger than Melissa had expected and her eyes were bright with unshed tears. 'I am rather thirsty,' she said shyly. 'I didn't think the invitation to take refreshments in the house included me.' There was neither wry humour nor resentment in the remark, merely quiet acceptance.

In response to a glance from Melissa, Joe nodded and left the room saying, 'Tea coming up.'

The moment he disappeared, the visitor leaned forward in her chair and said urgently, 'Please forgive me for bursting in on you like this, but I recognised you as you left the church. I'm a great fan of your books, you see, and I've seen you on the telly and read articles about you.'

Melissa frowned. 'I don't want to sound rude, but this isn't exactly the right occasion to come looking for autographs,' she said.

'Oh, please, it isn't that. I don't normally do this sort of thing, but I simply didn't know which way to turn, and seeing you was a heaven-sent opportunity. I was afraid to hang around where people could see me so when everyone drove away I watched to see which car was yours and then followed to see where everyone went. Then I waited at the end of the lane until I saw you coming back.'

'Quite the little detective, aren't you? I presume you had plenty of fuel in your tank? For all you knew, we might have been going somewhere miles away.'

'Well, of course you might have been . . . but I knew you

lived somewhere round here so I took a chance you were going straight home.'

This piece of reasoning made sense. Although Melissa made a point of not allowing details of her address to be publicised, it was generally known that she lived in a Cotswold village.

'All right, take a Brownie point for initiative,' she said, 'but you still haven't explained why it's so important to talk to me.'

'It's because I've read about how you've helped the police solve real life mysteries and I'm hoping you can help me solve this one.'

'Hang on a minute!' said Melissa in some alarm. 'Who said anything about a mystery? And who are you anyway – and what's your interest?'

'I . . . my name doesn't matter. I'm just . . . someone who knew Aidan Cresney quite well.'

'I gathered that.'

At the hint of irony in Melissa's tone, the young woman turned her face away and her cheeks became pink. She had small, delicate features, striking blue eyes fringed with long dark lashes, and short, almost black hair cut in a nineteen-twenties bob. Her figure in the clinging black dress was soft and rounded. She was just the kind of woman an older man might be attracted to, Melissa thought – and, by the look of her, young and impressionable enough to be flattered by the attention of someone as eminent as Aidan Cresney.

'How well did you know him?' she asked more gently. The flush deepened, but there was no answer. 'Were you lovers?'

'No!' This time the blue eyes looked directly into hers. 'He was just very kind to us when we badly needed a friend.'

'Us?'

'Me and my mother. She's a widow.'

'And what has this got to do with me?'

'I couldn't think of anyone else who might help.'

'Help you to do what?'

'Find out whether his death was really an accident. I can see that shocks you,' she added.

Melissa, aware that her mouth had fallen open, found herself momentarily at a loss for words. She wondered what this earnest young stranger's reaction would be if she were to reveal that this was not the first time she had heard such a suggestion. She hastily pulled herself together and said, 'How could it have been anything else? Somehow or other the bees got inside his protective gear and stung him. The official verdict supported the medical diagnosis of anaphylactic shock brought about by an acute allergic reaction to bee venom that killed him almost instantly. What makes you believe otherwise?'

'Why should the bees attack him in the first place? He knew how to handle them; he often used to say how careful he was when attending the hives. He loved his bees . . . he spoke about them so affectionately, almost as if they were his children. Oh, I know it sounds stupid,' the girl hurried on, 'but he never had any children; he said he'd have liked them but his wife never wanted any. After he retired, the first thing he did was enrol on a course about beekeeping. He became quite an expert; he's been interviewed on the radio,' she added with a touch of almost child-like pride.

Joe's reappearance with a tray of tea-things provided an opportunity for Melissa to collect her thoughts and try to decide how to respond to this extraordinary outburst. The picture the girl painted of Aidan Cresney was so far at odds with her previous conception, based on the impressions of her neighbours plus her own limited personal contact with him and his family, that she hardly knew how to respond.

After handing round cups of tea and offering biscuits, which both women refused, Joe provided an opening by looking from one to the other and saying, 'So, have you managed to sort out the problem?'

'Not so far,' said Melissa. 'Before we go any further,' she went on, turning back to their visitor, 'I must insist that you tell me your name. This is much too serious a matter to discuss with someone who prefers to remain anonymous. Our young friend maintains that Aidan was too experienced a beekeeper to make a mistake in handling them,' she explained in response to Joe's questioning glance. 'She believes there was something suspicious about his death and wants me to enquire into it.'

Joe frowned and shook his head. 'If you have reasons for making such a serious allegation, you should have reported them to the coroner,' he said firmly.

'The coroner wouldn't have taken any notice of me,' the girl protested.

'He certainly wouldn't have done if you refused even to say who you were.'

'Aidan was always very anxious that his family shouldn't know about us. He said they wouldn't understand.'

Melissa checked the impulse to retort that they would have understood all too well. Her mind went back to the snatch of conversation she had overheard an hour or so earlier. She glanced at Joe and raised her eyebrows; he gave her a brief nod, as if the same thought had occurred to him. 'How can you be sure they didn't know?' she asked. 'Do you imagine they didn't notice you in church?'

'I might have been a complete stranger who happened to be there at the time and couldn't decently get away.'

'Dressed in deep mourning and crying?' Melissa could no longer control her impatience. 'Look, Ms Whatever your name is, you're either incredibly naïve or you've spun this improbable yarn in order to trick your way into our house.'

'No, that isn't true, you must believe me!'

'Why should we when you won't even tell us who you are and why Aidan Cresney's death is of so much interest to you?'

The girl's features crumpled; more tears welled into her eyes and spilled down her soft cheeks. There was a long silence. Then she said slowly, her voice shaking with emotion, 'I loved him very much. He was like a second father to me.'

10

Little by little, in a series of jerky, sometimes almost incoherent phrases, the story came out. The girl's name was Rosalie Finn; after her father died in an industrial accident her mother had brought a case for compensation against his employer, which Aidan Cresney had fought and won on her behalf. After everything was settled, Cresney began visiting the widow and her daughter at home. Rosalie, who was just seventeen when her father died, developed a strong affection for the man who had given badly needed support and friendship to her mother.

'It was so dreadful to read about his death in the paper,' she said tearfully, 'like being bereaved all over again.' Her voice all but failed on the final words.

'Yes, I suppose it must have been,' Melissa heard herself saying – rather feebly, she thought, but her mind was elsewhere, humming with questions she hesitated to ask.

'It knocked Mummy for six,' Rosalie went on when she was able to speak again. 'Aidan was so supportive; he went on helping her in all sorts of ways, even after the employers paid the compensation. She'd never had to deal with business or finance or anything like that, you see; Daddy did it all. I don't know how she'll manage now.'

'Hasn't she any relatives who could help?'

'There's Daddy's brother, but I don't know if he'd be

willing. He disapproved of her relationship with Aidan; he said rather . . . unkind things.' Rosalie's colour deepened again and she picked nervously at her handkerchief.

'He thought they were having an affair, I suppose?' said Joe.

'Yes, but it wasn't true!' the girl protested indignantly. 'He was just a very good friend.'

'But that's probably how it appeared to your uncle,' Melissa said gently. Rosalie shrugged, but said nothing. 'Just the same, he surely wouldn't leave her in the lurch if she really needed help?'

Again, there was no reply. Melissa felt herself torn between the innate curiosity that made her long to know more about the situation and reluctance to give the impression that she was prepared to accede to Rosalie's outrageous request for her to become involved in it. She cast a slightly despairing glance in Joe's direction and to her relief he took the initiative.

'Look, Rosalie,' he said kindly, 'we really do sympathise with you and your mother, but you must surely see that my wife couldn't possibly be expected to do as you suggest. If you have any proof of your claim that Aidan's death wasn't natural, then you should take it to the police. Otherwise–'

'But don't you see, that's just the point!' Rosalie protested. 'I don't have any proof, only this very strong feeling that something's badly wrong. Mummy feels the same way, but what could we have done without something more than that to tell the authorities?'

'You haven't said anything about a motive,' Melissa pointed out. 'Can you think of anyone who would want to kill Aidan?'

The answer came without any hesitation. 'His brother, of

course. He was always jealous of Aidan. It was so ungrateful of him, after all Aidan did for him and Sarah.'

Recalling the subtle change in Quentin's manner since the tragedy, Melissa found herself wondering for a moment whether the girl had a point, but dismissed the notion immediately as being too fanciful to be taken seriously. 'Whose idea was it to come to me – yours or your mother's?' she asked.

'Mummy doesn't know anything about this. I told you, it was only when I saw you in the church that I had the idea of approaching you.'

'But presumably she knew you were coming to the funeral?'

'Oh, yes. She desperately wanted to be here herself, but we agreed it would be too much for her . . . she's very emotional and losing Aidan so soon after Daddy–' The girl broke off, swallowed and dabbed her eyes. 'It was hard enough for me,' she went on. 'I was going to wait behind until everyone had left and then just go back to the car and drive home . . . and then I saw you and I thought . . . it seemed almost like a sign from heaven.'

There was an awkward silence. Rosalie looked at her watch. 'Mummy will be wondering where I am,' she said. 'I told her I'd be home by six and it's gone five already. I'll have to be going. What shall I tell her?'

'I think you'd better tell her what my husband has just told you.'

Rosalie's face fell and her lower lip trembled. 'You mean you won't help us?'

Melissa was reminded of her son Simon when, as a child, it had been necessary to deny him something on which he had set his heart. It had been on the tip of her tongue to answer with an apologetic but firm no. Instead she found herself saying, 'I mean there's nothing we can do on the strength of what you've told us, but there's no reason why we shouldn't keep our eyes and ears open. If you'd like to leave your telephone number, one of us will get in touch with you if we should learn of anything significant.'

'Only don't hold your breath,' said Joe, who plainly saw this as a somewhat futile offer, but Rosalie paid no heed to the caveat. Her smile of gratitude was like a burst of sunshine.

'Oh, thank you!' she said fervently. 'Thank you so much!' She fished in her handbag and brought out a pen. 'Have you something I can write on?'

'Here.' Melissa tore a sheet from a notepad and the girl scribbled on it and handed it back. 'That's our home number. I'm at work during the day so perhaps you'd be kind enough to call in the evening.'

'I'll bear that in mind.' Melissa slid the note into her personal directory.

Rosalie stood up and held out a hand. 'Thank you for listening to me,' she said. 'I hope I haven't taken up too much of your time.'

'Not at all. Drive carefully.'

'That was a bit rash,' said Joe as he closed the door behind their unexpected visitor. 'Don't you think it was unfair to raise false hopes? The poor girl will be dashing home every night in the hope of getting a call to say you've made a dramatic breakthrough.'

'I simply couldn't bring myself to turn her down flat.'

'You're just too soft-hearted, my love.'

'That's how we writers are,' she informed him with an impish grin, 'full of the milk of human kindness.'

'You mean, not like us hard-nosed agents,' he said, returning the grin. 'Seriously, though, what did you make of all that?'

'I may be doing the man a gross injustice,' she said, 'but I have a suspicion that Aidan Cresney was an even nastier piece of work than we've always thought.'

'You suspect him of using the mother to get at the daughter?' She nodded. 'I have to admit the same thought crossed my mind,' he went on, 'but then I remembered the make-up on the shirt and I noticed Rosalie wasn't wearing any. Maybe he was having an affair with the mother without her knowledge. She struck me as being quite naïve in some ways.'

'It would be interesting to know what prompted the uncle to say "unkind things",' Melissa said. 'Rosalie certainly looked embarrassed when she mentioned that.'

'She'd have been even more embarrassed if she knew what you overheard during the wake,' said Joe. 'I noticed you dropped a hint that the family had probably spotted her.'

'It seems pretty obvious they either knew or suspected that Aidan was having an affair and they must have assumed Rosalie was the other woman. It's not surprising they were pretty affronted at seeing her in the church.'

'His relationship with the Finns must have started some time ago, before he retired,' Joe observed. 'When was that, by the way?'

'I don't know exactly – he was still practising when they moved into Cold Wells, which was about five years ago. He got himself elected to the parish council after they'd been here a couple of years or so and soon started chucking his weight about.'

Joe was doing calculations on his fingers. 'Assuming the Finn case was his swansong, the affair would have begun, say, between two and three years ago. Perhaps he was amusing himself with the mother, with an eye on a more desirable prey in the longer term.'

Melissa screwed up her face in disgust. 'If that was the case he deserved his rather beastly end, but I can't for the life of me think of a way anyone could have engineered it. On the other hand, why should so many people feel there was something suspicious about it?'

'I don't think that's particularly significant; you know what nasty minds one or two of our neighbours have.'

'True, but what do you suppose Rosalie meant when she suggested Quentin had a motive for doing away with his brother . . . "after all he did for him and Sarah", as she put it?'

'Yes, I have to admit that struck me as a strange thing to say.'

'It might have something to do with Quentin's sudden, unexplained appearance on the scene.'

'Maybe.' Joe began clearing away the tea-things. 'Let's give it a rest and start preparing our dinner, shall we? I know it's a bit early, but I feel I need a drink after all that.'

'Good idea.'

They went into the kitchen. While Joe poured gin and tonics, Melissa stood at the window and looked out at the view along the valley. The sun was setting in a blaze of red and gold, kindling fiery reflections on the windows of the extension to Hawthorn Cottage where her mother was settling down to her new life. As Melissa watched, Sylvia appeared from the side of the building with a weeding fork and trowel in her gloved hands. She spotted her daughter and waved; Melissa waved back and said to Joe, 'There's Mum. Shall we invite her to join us?'

'Good idea, but whatever you do, don't tell her anything about Rosalie or she'll want to start an investigation on the spot.' Joe paused in the act of reaching for another glass and said, 'You weren't seriously thinking of taking up the case, I hope?'

'Don't be silly, of course I'm not.'

'That's a relief.'

The first thing Sylvia said when she joined them was, 'Who was the young woman in the black dress? The one I saw knocking at your door a little while ago? Has she gone?'

'One of your daughter's loyal fans who recognised her at the funeral,' said Joe quickly. 'She spoke to us after the service and Mel asked her back for a chat about her books. She didn't stay long.'

Sylvia gave her daughter an approving nod. 'That was kind of you, dear,' she said. 'It must be nice to meet people who enjoy your books.'

'Oh, yes, it is,' Melissa agreed.

'I suppose she's some sort of relation to the Cresneys,' her mother went on.

'No, just a friend.'

'Oh, I see.'

Although she made no further reference to Rosalie, the three words were accompanied by a questioning look that gave Melissa an uneasy feeling that her mother's curiosity had been aroused and that she would return to the subject at a more convenient time. Meanwhile, however, she merely asked a few general questions about the funeral before the conversation switched to other topics.

Melissa and Joe spent the next few days checking the revised version of her latest novel, provisionally entitled *A Long Way from Home.* She had completed what she had believed to be the final draft before their wedding; on their return from an idyllic honeymoon as guests of Melissa's friends Iris and Jack Hammond at their home in Provence, she had found to her dismay that her editor had requested some fundamental changes. The work had been delayed by the task of installing Sylvia in her new quarters but now, with the revised deadline looming, it absorbed most of their waking hours and became almost their sole topic of conversation, even during breaks for meals and the occasional restorative walk along the valley.

The first indication that a further chapter in the saga of the Cresney family was about to unfold came the following Sunday, when they failed to appear in church. This aroused considerable interest among certain members of the congregation, who lingered after the service to speculate on possible reasons for their absence. Sylvia also expressed some curiosity as she walked home with Melissa and Joe.

'They hardly ever miss church, do they?' she said. 'You'd think it would be specially important for them at a time like this.'

'Maybe they've gone away for the weekend,' said Melissa. 'They could probably use a break after all the trauma.'

'I suppose so.' A trace of disappointment in Sylvia's voice hinted that she would prefer a more dramatic explanation.

'You're joining us for lunch today, aren't you, Mum?' said Melissa as they reached Hawthorn Cottage.

'Yes, dear, thank you. I'm looking forward to it. I'll just pop home first to freshen up.'

When Melissa and Joe got indoors the light on the answering machine in the kitchen indicated that someone had left a message. It was from Caroline Cresney and she sounded distraught.

'Something terrible's happened,' she gasped. 'The bees have gone for Sarah. She's been badly stung . . . she's in hospital . . . they're not sure if she'll survive.'

11

Melissa jabbed the callback button; the number had barely started to ring when Caroline answered. 'Yes?' she said in a shaky whisper.

'It's Melissa. I've just got your message. What an awful thing! What's the latest news?'

'Oh, Melissa, thank you so much for calling back.' Caroline's voice was breathless and uneven as she fought to control her tears. 'She's . . . still hanging on as far as I know. I haven't heard any more.'

'It's absolutely unbelievable. How in the world did it happen? I thought one of Aidan's beekeeper friends has been attending to his hives since his death.'

'Yes, Colin Palmer's been coming to see to them – but Sarah wasn't anywhere near the hives. We were all ready to go to church but we had a few minutes in hand and she decided to go out into the garden to cut some flowers. All of a sudden we heard her screaming; Quentin and I rushed out and there she was, surrounded by bees. They were attacking her . . . she was flailing her arms around trying to get rid of them . . . it was horrible.'

'Whatever did you do?'

'I turned on the hose and drove them off. I managed to get her indoors; she was moaning and her face and arms had already started to swell so Quentin rang for an ambulance. She was unconscious by the time it got here.'

'Is Quentin there with you?'

'No, he went with Sarah in the ambulance. They wouldn't let me go as well and I'm too upset to drive. Melissa, could you possibly–?'

'You want me to take you to the hospital?'

'No . . . at least, not just yet. If you could just come and keep me company for a while, or if I could wait for news at your house . . .'

'It's almost lunchtime. Why don't you come and have some with us? I'll pop up in the car to fetch you.'

'That's really kind of you, but I'm not sure I could face food.'

'Well, come anyway.'

'If you're sure you don't mind. It's so awful, being here alone, especially after what happened to . . .' Her voice had become increasingly unsteady; on the final words it failed altogether.

'I'll be with you in a few minutes.' Melissa hung up and turned to Joe, who was checking the joint of lamb they had left in the oven. 'You aren't going to believe this,' she said.

His expression was grim as she relayed the news. 'There must be a jinx on that family that makes bees take a dislike to them,' he muttered. 'Let's hope they've managed to get her to hospital in time. Yes, of course bring Caroline back here for lunch. There's plenty of meat on the joint and we can easily do a few extra vegetables. Sylvia and I will hold the fort here.'

'Oh gosh, I'd forgotten Mum was joining us. I hope she won't be too upset.'

'Upset? You must be joking. She'll be thrilled to bits to have the solution to this morning's great mystery before Cynthia Thorne.'

'We were wondering why you and the others weren't in church,' Melissa remarked as Caroline settled in the passenger seat of the Golf and clipped on her seat belt.

'Yes, I can imagine some of the comments.' There was a hint of acidity in the reply. 'Oh, I'm not under any illusions about the way our neighbours feel about us,' she went on in response to Melissa's questioning look. 'Some of them haven't forgiven Aidan for bulldozing the parish council into approving the development at Darnley Farm when local people were against it. I don't imagine the rest of us are particularly popular either.'

'Oh, I'm sure there's no ill will towards you or Sarah,' Melissa assured her.

'I dare say people are sorry for us for being married to Cresneys.' Caroline's voice was bitter. 'You saw how many turned up at Aidan's funeral. That shows you how highly everyone thinks of us.'

'You mustn't think of that now. I'm sure everyone will be very concerned to hear of Sarah's mishap. Have you had any more news since we spoke?'

'I called Quentin to let him know I'd be at your house and he said there was no change. I didn't give him your number; he'll call me on my mobile if there's anything to report.'

'Fine.'

They had reached Hawthorn Cottage. As Melissa opened the front door they were greeted by the smell of roasting lamb. 'I hope you'll be able to eat something,' she began, but Caroline was inhaling with evident pleasure.

'Something smells wonderful!' she exclaimed. 'I suppose you'll think it awful of me in the circumstances, but I've just realised I'm hungry. I haven't had anything to eat today, you see, except a biscuit with a cup of coffee while I was waiting for news from the hospital.' As if she felt the need for further explanation, she went on, 'Aidan would never allow it before communion and we would have been in church if it hadn't been for the bees attacking Sarah, so—'

'There's no need to apologise,' said Melissa. 'Come into the sitting room while I see what's going on in the kitchen. We usually have a drink before Sunday lunch. Will you join us?'

'Thank you, that would be lovely.'

'Gin and tonic? Sherry?'

'Dry sherry, please.' Caroline dropped into an armchair, stretched out her legs and closed her eyes. 'Oh, it's so good to be out of that house,' she murmured. 'I sometimes feel I'm living in a museum.'

Recalling her own impressions during her first visit to Cold Wells Manor, Melissa fully sympathised with the sentiment. It reinforced her earlier suspicion that Caroline had had little say in the planning of the décor during her husband's lifetime.

'We're just dishing up,' announced Joe as she entered the kitchen. He was standing by the window with a half-empty glass in his hand while Sylvia, clad in a blue and white striped apron, her hands encased in matching oven gloves, transferred the joint from the roasting tin to a platter and slid it back into the oven alongside a dish of roast potatoes.

'We?' said Melissa pointedly, her eye on the glass.

'I was told to keep out of the way.'

'That's right.' Sylvia closed the oven door, took off the

gloves and picked up her glass of sherry. 'A man shouldn't be expected to take charge of a roast. Everything's done except the green vegetables,' she went on with an air of satisfaction. 'I thought I'd leave them until the last minute.'

'Mum, I do believe you've been enjoying yourself,' said Melissa.

'You're quite right,' her mother admitted. 'I've always enjoyed cooking a roast and it's been ages since–' Her expression grew serious as she remembered the reason for her presence in the kitchen. 'Is Caroline here? What's the latest news?'

'She's in the sitting room and there isn't any further news. She'd like a dry sherry. Joe, will you–?'

'Of course.' He went to the cupboard to fetch a glass. 'You go and keep her company and I'll be right with you.'

When Sylvia and Melissa entered the sitting room Caroline was sliding her mobile phone into her handbag. 'I've just had a word with Quentin. They say the next couple of hours will be critical, but they think she'll pull through.'

'Well, thank God for that,' said Sylvia fervently.

'He sounded pretty desperate,' Caroline went on. 'He begged me to go to the hospital to keep him company.' There was a hint of scorn in her voice, as if she considered this a somewhat wimpish request.

'What did you tell him?' asked Melissa.

'I suggested he got something to eat in the hospital canteen and I'd join him later. If I still don't feel up to driving I'll get a taxi. Oh, thank you,' she added as Joe appeared with her sherry. She took it and helped herself from the dish of crisps he offered her.

'Well, here's to Sarah's complete recovery,' said Melissa. They all raised their glasses and drank.

There was a brief pause before Sylvia remarked, 'We were all so shocked to hear about the accident. Whatever made the bees attack Sarah, I wonder? Joe said she was nowhere near the hives.'

'I've really no idea,' said Caroline.

'I read somewhere that there are certain chemicals that make them angry, and if they get angry they sting. Have you heard that?'

Caroline shook her head and took another sip from her glass. 'No, I haven't,' she said. From the way her mouth tightened, Melissa could tell that the subject was painful to her, but the signal was lost on Sylvia.

'Maybe,' she went on eagerly as a further possibility occurred to her, 'they took a dislike to Sarah's perfume, or maybe it smelled like flowers and when they found it wasn't they got upset–'

'Mum, I don't think this is a good time to go into all this,' said Melissa gently.

'I was only trying to think of a reason–' Sylvia protested, but Caroline interrupted almost sharply.

'I think what you suggest is very unlikely,' she said and then, as if fearing she might have given offence, 'Please forgive me, I don't mean to sound rude, but I am rather on edge.'

'Of course you are,' said Sylvia. 'You've had such a dreadful time lately, what with losing your husband so tragically–' she hesitated for a moment and then continued, 'but of course, you're comparatively young. I'm sure life still has plenty to offer you.'

'I suppose so, when I've had time to pick up the pieces.'

'It's hard at first, being a widow I mean, but after a while . . .' Sylvia put a hand on Caroline's arm. 'I don't want you to think I'm trying to interfere, and if you don't fancy the idea you must be sure and say so, but perhaps when this crisis is over and your sister-in-law is out of danger, you'd care to come and have a cup of tea and a chat with me one afternoon?'

'That's a very kind thought. I'd like that,' said Caroline, but Melissa found it difficult to tell whether she meant the words sincerely or was merely being polite.

After lunch Caroline left the room to call Quentin on her mobile. She returned a few minutes later to give her hosts the glad news that Sarah was responding to treatment, but would be detained in the hospital for at least another twenty-four hours. She thanked them all warmly for their hospitality and support, and said – with what Melissa felt was a slight lack of enthusiasm – she supposed she'd better go and give Quentin some moral support. She declined the offer of a lift, assuring them that she was feeling much better and was perfectly fit to drive. She went further and declared that she would go back to Cold Wells on foot to pick up her car because she felt in need of the exercise. Melissa's offer to keep her company on the walk was also politely refused.

'It really is extraordinary that two people in the same family should be attacked by bees,' Sylvia remarked as the three of them began clearing the table after Caroline's departure. 'And within a few days of each other as well.'

'At least, Sarah had enough time to scream for help,' said Joe. 'If she'd had the same acute allergic reaction as poor old Aidan it would have been a very different story.'

Melissa shuddered. 'It doesn't bear thinking about.'

'I still think it might have been the perfume Sarah was wearing that the bees didn't like,' said Sylvia.

'I think you're wrong there, Mum. Sarah always wore

Chanel Number Five. It's been on the market for years and I've never heard of any woman being stung by bees because she was wearing it.'

'However do you know what perfume Sarah used?'

'Because you could smell it a mile off whenever she and Caroline came on one of our WI jaunts. That was before Quentin appeared, of course.'

'I don't recall noticing it whenever I've been near her in church.'

'Well, maybe Aidan didn't allow such frivolities as perfume on the Lord's day,' said Joe flippantly.

Sylvia wagged a finger at him. 'You aren't taking me seriously,' she said reproachfully. 'I'm just trying to find an explanation for what happened to poor Sarah so she can be more careful in future.'

'She'll probably be scared to put her nose outside the door while those hives are in the orchard,' said Melissa. 'I imagine Quentin will be asking Colin Palmer to take them away before she comes home. If she should get stung again, it would almost certainly be fatal.'

But such precautions were to prove tragically unnecessary. A few hours later a distraught Caroline called to say that Sarah, weakened by the shock to her system, had suffered a massive heart attack and died within minutes.

12

Melissa was trembling as she relayed the grim news to Joe. 'What was that you said earlier about a jinx on the Cresneys?' she said.

'It makes you wonder,' he muttered.

'It's unnatural,' she went on. 'I've picked flowers in my garden any number of times while bees have been buzzing around and they've never shown any sign of aggression.'

'I wonder if fear had anything to do with it?'

'Fear? What gave you that idea?'

'I seem to recall reading somewhere that some creatures can smell fear. There's a theory that when people are afraid their sweat contains a chemical that signals aggression. No, now I come to think of it, I believe it was dogs the writer was referring to . . . but maybe bees don't like it either.'

'It's a possibility, I suppose,' she admitted. 'It's been a very warm day, so Sarah might have been a bit sweaty, and if she saw bees among the flowers it might have made her nervous after what happened to Aidan . . . but from what Caroline told us it was more than just a few bees that attacked her. Something must have made them seriously angry to make them go for her like that.'

'Whatever could it have been, I wonder?' said Joe.

'Perhaps there's a new, more aggressive strain of bees

around,' she suggested. 'Or bees from another colony trying to invade the Cold Wells bees' territory.'

He shook his head, frowning. 'We just don't know enough about the creatures to judge, do we? Maybe the inquest will shed some light on what happened. Is there anything we can do for Caroline or Quentin, by the way? He must be pretty devastated, poor chap. First his brother and now his wife–'

'I don't think we can be of any practical help tonight. Caroline just gave me the news and hung up before I could even offer. She drove to the hospital earlier so presumably they can get home all right. I'll give her a call in the morning.'

'Your mother will be dreadfully shocked. Do you think we should tell her?'

Melissa went to the kitchen window and peered out. 'Her place is in darkness so she's probably gone to bed. There's no point in disturbing her now; it would only upset her and spoil her night's rest. It can wait until the morning.'

Joe glanced at the clock on the microwave. 'I vote we do the same,' he said. 'It's getting late and there are still a few chapters of the book to check over tomorrow.'

Melissa yawned. 'Thank goodness we're nearly done with it.'

'Have you given any thought to the next one?'

She thumped him on the arm. 'Slave-driver!' she scolded, but he only laughed.

A little while later, as she was brushing the glossy shoulder-length hair that Joe said reminded him of sweet chestnuts, he came in from the bathroom in his dressing gown and stood behind her. He leaned over her and she caught the scent of mint on his breath. He put both arms round her and with parted lips gently brushed the nape of her neck. The familiar sweet tingle of arousal surged through her body as she leaned against him with a sigh of happy anticipation. Their eyes – hers a light hazel, his dark and deep-set beneath strong brows – met in the dressing table mirror. She half turned to face him; he drew her to her feet and took the hairbrush from her hand.

'You don't need that; your hair looks perfect,' he said. He tugged gently at her robe; it slid to the floor, followed by her loose nightdress. 'And so does the rest of you.'

She gave a little moan of pleasure as he threw off his dressing gown and held her close. He began running his hands over her body while his mouth explored hers; at first she responded eagerly, but after a few moments she put her hands on his shoulders and tried to pull away from him.

'What is it?' he whispered.

'I . . . nothing . . . that is . . . this seems almost indecent after what's just happened.'

'Nonsense. It's exactly what you need to take your mind off the horror.' His embrace grew tighter and her resistance crumbled.

'I suppose you're right,' she murmured.

'You bet I am.'

Melissa was the first to wake in the morning. She propped herself on one elbow and looked down at her man, still sleeping quietly beside her. For a few moments, as she contemplated the strong profile outlined against the pillow and the tousled hair, still thick but greying a little at the temples, she was aware of nothing but an overwhelming love for him. It had been a warm night and his half of the duvet was partially thrown back; she kissed his bare shoulder but he did not stir. She slid quietly out of bed, put on her robe and slippers and stole out of the room and into the bathroom. She took a quick shower and went down-stairs.

She filled a kettle and stood by the kitchen window while waiting for it to boil. Her mother's bedroom curtains were still drawn; she too was probably peacefully asleep, having gone to bed happy in the belief that Sarah was on the road to recovery. The thought gave her an uncomfortable jolt and she felt almost guilty at the recollection of the previous night's joy, as if she had no right to be happy when neigh-bours had so recently suffered such an appalling tragedy. Then she told herself not to be foolish. But while she was waiting for the tea to brew, still gazing out of the window, she found herself grappling with a question that rose unbidden to the surface of her mind and would not be put aside: was there a link between the deaths of Aidan and Sarah Cresney and, if so, had they been deliberately brought about by someone whose hatred of the family had driven them to murder?

'No, it's not possible!' she exclaimed aloud.

'What's not possible?' Joe had entered the kitchen unno-ticed.

'Gosh, you made me jump!' she said. 'I never heard you getting up.'

'You were too busy contemplating the impossible.' He came and stood next to her, sliding an arm round her waist. He smelled of soap and his hair was still damp from the shower. 'Well?'

With an effort, she forced her mind back to her un-answered question. 'I was wondering if there's any way Aidan and Sarah could have been murdered.'

She half expected him to be dismissive of the idea, but to her surprise he said, 'I'm sure you won't be the only person to be wondering the same thing.'

'You're thinking of Cynthia Thorne and co?'

'Among others.'

'What about you?'

'I haven't given it a great deal of thought, but it does seem almost too much of a coincidence.'

She gnawed her lip in frustration. 'But how could anyone make it happen? No one could have known about Aidan's allergy. Even if someone had hit on a way to induce the bees to attack him, they couldn't have known it would kill him.'

'You can't be sure of that,' he said. 'I knew someone who was stung by a wasp and reacted so badly that he had to be rushed into hospital. He had to have desensitising treatment and they warned him that any further attack would need immediate attention or it could be curtains for him.'

'You're suggesting that something similar once happened to Aidan and someone knew about it . . . and might have . . .' They exchanged glances; the same thought had occurred to them at the same moment. 'Caroline?' she whispered.

He nodded. 'If anyone knew, his wife would be the most likely.'

'But why?' Until that moment, Melissa had written off speculation by the village gossips, and more recently Rosalie Finn's wild allegations, as the product of over-fertile imaginations. Suddenly, they seemed horribly plausible. Could some dark secret from the past have come back to haunt the Cresneys? She experienced a rush of gooseflesh at the thought and sought relief in a practical task by picking up the teapot, saying, 'This should be ready by now.' Almost mechanically she filled two mugs; they settled at the table and drank their tea in an uneasy silence.

After a little while she said, 'It's just occurred to me, Caroline had a telephone call while I was at her house the day Aidan died. Someone was calling in response to a message she'd left earlier.'

'Yes, you told me. Can you remember exactly what she said?'

'She said, "Something terrible's happened; Aidan's dead."'

'Is that all?'

Melissa chewed her lower lip, trawling her memory. 'There was something about its being instantaneous and due to anaphylactic shock, and she'd call back later on because she had a visitor, me.'

'She didn't say what caused his death?'

'No. That's surprising, when you come to think of it. You'd have expected the caller to ask.'

'Maybe she mentioned the bees in the original message,' Joe suggested.

'Without saying they'd killed him?'

'If she was in an acute state of shock she probably left quite a garbled message,' he pointed out. 'I don't think we can read too much into that.'

'Maybe not.'

'Have you any idea whether it was a man or a woman on the phone?'

Melissa shook her head, but once again the same thought sprang into both their minds: did Caroline have a lover?

'It's pretty obvious from what I overheard on the day of the funeral,' she said, 'that both she and Sarah knew – or anyway suspected – that Aidan was having a bit of nooky on the side. Maybe she did see that shirt after all.'

'What shirt?'

'Don't you remember, Mrs Wilson reported via Gloria that the make-up on the shirt she found was a different colour from the one Caroline uses.'

'Huh!' Joe's snort was dismissive. 'I can see those two rumour-mongers will be making hay when they hear about Sarah.'

'Not just them,' she predicted.

'Whatever you do, Mel, keep out of it.' Joe stood up and put their empty mugs in the dishwasher. 'Come on, it's time we were getting dressed. There's a book to be finished.'

After breakfast Melissa said, 'I'd better pop across and see Mum before we start work. I don't want her to hear the news about Sarah from anyone else.'

'Right. I'll be in the study.'

She knocked on the connecting door before cracking it open and calling to her mother. Hearing no reply, she stepped into the short passage leading to the tiny entrance hall by the front door and called again. After a few moments Sylvia appeared, looking somewhat taken aback. She was still in her robe and held an empty cereal bowl in her hand.

'Oh, Lissie, you must think me very slovenly,' she said with a self-conscious laugh, 'but I was so hungry when I woke up and I thought I'd have breakfast in the garden before getting dressed. It's so lovely out there in the sunshine and—'

'There's no need to apologise,' Melissa began, but Sylvia seemed determined to justify herself.

'It was such a relief, knowing Sarah was going to be all right, that I fell asleep as soon as I got into bed and didn't wake up until after half past eight. Do you know—'

'Just a minute, Mum, before we go any further.' Melissa took her by the arm and guided her into the sitting room. 'I'm afraid I've got some bad news.'

'Oh dear!' Her mother's smile faded and she sank into a chair, still clutching the cereal bowl. 'Has Sarah had a relapse?'

'I'm afraid it's worse than that. She died last night from a heart attack.'

'Oh, no! How absolutely dreadful! When did you find out?'

'Caroline phoned from the hospital at about eleven o'clock.'

'Poor soul, she must be in a terrible state. Quentin too. As if they haven't suffered enough already. Are they back home yet?'

'Probably, but we haven't heard from them this morning.'

'Perhaps it would be nice if I were to go and see Caroline,' said Sylvia earnestly. 'I could give her a little comfort. We seemed to be getting on so well when she came to lunch yesterday–'

'Mum, I don't think–' Melissa began, but once again her interruption was ignored.

'I've thought several times I really should have gone to see her after Aidan died; after all, I've been through the same kind of experience . . . I mean, suddenly losing a husband in very tragic circumstances. Oh, I know you've been very supportive, Lissie, but unless it's actually happened to you it's not easy to understand how it affects you. I was the one to find your father's body, remember, so I know exactly how Caroline must be feeling.'

Melissa experienced an unexpected wave of irritation against her mother. 'It did happen to me, in case you'd forgotten,' she said through gritted teeth. 'But as I wasn't married to Guy at the time, I suppose losing the father of my unborn child in a car accident doesn't count.'

'Lissie! You know I didn't mean that,' said Sylvia in a hurt voice, 'but it was a very long time ago; things were different then.'

Melissa opened her mouth to make a stinging reply, thought better of it and said grudgingly, 'Yes, all right, I'm sorry. But I don't think it's a good idea to go rushing off to Cold Wells just yet. I'll let you know as soon as I have any further news. I must go back now and get on with some work.'

'Yes dear, of course.'

'Oh, and one other thing. Whatever you do, don't go telling Cynthia Thorne or any of her cronies. Wait until the news is announced officially.'

'If you say so dear, but why–?'

'Just do it, please.' She returned to her own house, restraining the impulse to slam the communicating door. She went storming upstairs to the study and sat down beside Joe, who was sitting at her desk with the final chapters of her novel in front of him. Her jaw was set and she was breathing heavily.

Joe eyed her in some concern. 'Something wrong?' he asked.

'Only Mum, being insensitive.' She relayed the exchange of words that had aroused such bitter memories. 'For her to sit there and play the grieving widow when we all know that her life has been immeasurably better since Father died is one thing; to claim that the experience gives her a greater empathy with Caroline than me because of it made me want to scream. When I think of how she just sat by and let Father kick me out after Guy's death, I could–' Melissa thumped her fist on the desk, her face flushed with anger.

Joe put an arm round her. 'Come on, love, don't upset yourself over it,' he said gently. 'You know how things were between her and your father and all the trauma she went through when she was suspected of killing him . . . and then she had brain surgery on top of all that. She's told you more than once how badly she feels about everything; you have to forgive her.'

'I thought I had, but every now and then it hits me.' She leaned against him, feeling her anger fade under the healing power of his love and understanding. After a moment she sat up and reached for a pencil. 'Right, I'm over it now. Let's get this book finished.'

They had barely begun their task when the telephone rang. 'Let them leave a message,' said Joe.

'No, I'd better answer it. It might be Caroline.'

It was Caroline, and she sounded distraught. 'Melissa, I desperately need someone to talk to,' she said. Her voice was shaking, her words separated by gasps for air. 'Could you possibly come and see me? I'm here on my own and I'm almost going out of my mind!'

13

There was no repetition of the outbreak of hysterical weeping that followed Aidan's death, but Melissa found Caroline's reaction to her arrival considerably more disturbing. She had to wait several seconds after ringing the bell before the door opened halfway and Caroline peered round it, white-faced and wild-eyed. On recognising Melissa she reached out, grabbed her by the arm and pulled her inside before slamming the door shut again and leaning against it for a moment as if fearing that a hostile mob was about to burst in. Her teeth were chattering and her entire body seemed to be shaking.

'Oh, dear God, I'm so frightened!' she muttered.

Melissa stared at her in bewilderment. 'What of? You knew I was coming.' There was no reply. 'Did you think I might be someone else?' Caroline continued to stare dumbly back at her. She seemed petrified, like a rabbit caught in a beam of light. By way of reassurance, Melissa took her by the hand; despite the warmth of the day, it felt like coming into contact with dead flesh. She led her into the kitchen and deposited her, still trembling, on a chair. 'You need a hot drink,' she said. 'What shall it be – tea or coffee?'

'Coffee, please,' Caroline whispered.

'With a shot of brandy, perhaps?'

'No thank you, just coffee.'

'Have you had anything to eat this morning?'

'I had some muesli a while ago, but I brought it straight up again.'

'I don't suppose you had anything last night, either?' Caroline shook her head. 'You should get something inside you. How about some toast?'

'I'll try.'

'Good girl. Just show me where to find everything and leave it to me.'

By the time Caroline had drunk a mug of strong coffee and nibbled half a slice of dry toast she had lost her deathly pallor but was still shivering. 'Are you cold?' Melissa asked.

'A little.'

'Can I get you a wrap of some sort?'

'That would be kind. I'll have my white cardie, please.'

'Where do I find it?'

'In my bedroom, that's the first room on the right at the top of the stairs. It's in the second drawer of the tallboy.'

'Right, I'll nip up and get it. How about some more coffee?'

'Yes, please.' Caroline held her mug aloft like Oliver Twist asking for more. Melissa replenished it from the cafetière and went upstairs on her errand.

The galleried hall was illuminated by a large stained glass window, to which Melissa had paid little attention on her earlier visit. This time she paused briefly and looked at it with more interest; it depicted an armoured knight offering a single red rose to a lady of pre-Raphaelite appearance who wore a flowing blue gown and a circlet of leaves on her head. It was a sunny morning and splashes of coloured light passing through the panes lay like glowing flower petals on the dull green carpet that covered the dark oak staircase.

The effect was not unattractive, but it seemed nevertheless an incongruous feature to find in a listed Cotswold dwelling.

She found the cardigan Caroline had asked for and was about to leave the room when her eye fell on an empty frame lying on its back on the dressing table. On the floor close by was a waste paper basket containing a heap of crumpled tissues and the torn-up remains of a coloured photograph. Melissa hesitated and cast a slightly guilty glance over her shoulder before stooping to pick up two of the fragments.

The picture appeared to have been of a group of people, taken on a formal occasion. One of the scraps in her hand showed a woman in an off-the-shoulder dress standing beside a man in a smart grey suit with a carnation in his buttonhole. The woman's face was missing and the only clue to her identity was a cameo brooch at her throat, similar to one Melissa had often seen Sarah wearing. The upper half of the man's face had also been torn away, but she recognised Quentin from the fleshy jaw and the slightly sullen set of the mouth. Whatever the occasion, he did not appear to have been enjoying himself.

Resisting the temptation to explore further, Melissa dropped the fragments back into the basket and hurried downstairs. Caroline was still sitting in her chair with her shoulders hunched and her head bowed, her small hands clamped so tightly round the half empty coffee mug that the knuckles stood out like little pearl buttons. Melissa draped the cardigan over her and she whispered, 'Thank you, you're very kind,' without looking up.

When she had emptied the mug for the second time, Melissa prised it from her fingers and put it in the sink. She squatted down in front of her and took her by both hands; they were no longer icy to the touch and the shivering had begun to subside.

'You said you needed someone to talk to, and here I am,' she said gently. 'Do you feel well enough now to tell me what this is all about?'

'I suppose so.' Caroline sounded reluctant, as if she was having second thoughts.

'Look, if you've changed your mind—'

'No, I have to confide in someone.'

'All right, I'm listening.' There was a long silence. Then Melissa said, 'When I arrived, you said you were frightened. What – or who – are you afraid of? And where's Quentin, by the way? I know he must be pretty upset himself, but he shouldn't have left you on your own in such a state.'

Caroline gave a short humourless laugh. 'Why should he give a toss about my feelings?'

'You are his sister-in-law.' Caroline shrugged. 'So where is he?'

'He's gone.'

'Gone where?'

'Back to his ex wife, I suppose.'

'You mean Sarah was his second wife?'

'His first, actually – and then his third.' A weak smile flitted over Caroline's pallid features. 'That surprises you, no doubt.'

'It does rather, but—'

'I suppose you were going to say there's no accounting for taste,' Caroline said as Melissa fell silent, temporarily lost for words. She had never thought of Quentin and Sarah as a particularly close couple, but she would never have dreamed that they might have such a complex relationship.

Her suspicion that Aidan's malign influence had been at work was about to be confirmed.

'You might think differently if you'd known him years ago,' Caroline went on, evidently misinterpreting Melissa's silence. 'Oh, I can't deny I've said some pretty hard things about him, and he doesn't have many friends these days, but if it hadn't been for Aidan, doing all his thinking for him, telling him what to do, who to marry, I'm sure he'd be a much nicer person.'

'There are some people who like to dominate the weaker members of their families,' said Melissa slowly. My own father was such a man, she thought to herself. Such people often had the best of intentions, but so often, as in her own and her mother's case, the effects could be disastrous. Aloud, she said, 'So what did Sarah do after her first marriage to Quentin ended?'

'She waited at home for Aidan to get him back for her.'

'I don't follow you.'

'No, of course you don't.' Caroline stood up and began prowling round the kitchen, fiddling aimlessly with various utensils and other items scattered randomly around. She was calmer now; she pushed her arms into the cardigan, fastened the buttons, pulled a tissue from one of the pockets and wiped her nose with it. Then she came and stood on the opposite side of the table to where Melissa was standing and for the first time looked her directly in the eye.

'Quentin married Sarah the first time round because Aidan thought she'd make a good vicar's wife,' she said.

'A *vicar's* wife?' Melissa repeated in disbelief. 'Quentin's a *vicar*?'

'He took a degree in theology and was ordained shortly before I met Aidan. I'm only speculating now, but after a childhood spent under Aidan's manipulative influence, being at university must have given him his first taste of freedom and at the same time shown him his vocation. When I met him he was a conscientious parish priest whose parishioners thought well of him, but at my wedding to Aidan I overheard two of his friends talking and one said something about "a blazing torch that had gradually died down to a steady, but uninspiring, glow". And the other one said, "I reckon that brother of his has had something to do with it. He should have gone to a parish as far away from his influence as possible." I couldn't understand what they were talking about at the time – Aidan had never shown me that side of his nature, you see.' Caroline returned to her chair and pointed to another. 'Sit down while I tell you the full story.' Still trying to digest yet another astonishing revelation, Melissa mutely obeyed.

'After he and Sarah had been married for a few years,' Caroline continued, 'he met Poppy. She was one of his parishioners and she was having some problems with her mother, who was getting senile and Poppy couldn't cope. Quentin helped get the old lady settled in a home, but soon after that she died. Anyway, while all this was going on Quentin and Poppy fell in love and eventually they ran away together. He was so besotted that he persuaded Sarah to divorce him, much against Aidan's wishes of course, so he and Poppy could get married. He resigned his living; I suppose he could have moved to another parish, but Poppy had inherited quite a lot of money from the widowed mother so there were no financial problems. Aidan was furious at first, but he managed after a while to find a way to turn the situation to his own and Sarah's advantage.'

'Let me get this straight.' By now Melissa was feeling

thoroughly bemused. 'Quentin married Sarah, then there was a divorce and he married Poppy . . . and then he divorced Poppy and married Sarah for the second time.'

Caroline nodded. 'That's right. And guess what? One of the first things Aidan did after the wedding was to put one of their photos in a fancy frame and insist that I have it on my dressing table. It was a kind of trophy, a symbol of his power over them. I've torn it up,' she added. 'It felt good, like breaking an evil spell.' For the first time since Melissa's arrival she smiled, and it was not a pleasant smile.

'So it was Aidan who put pressure on Quentin to return to Sarah? But how?'

Caroline gave another harsh, bitter laugh. 'The way he'd been doing it for years; he was like a bulldozer, no one could stand up to him. I at least managed to keep him out of a few small corners of my life, but poor old Quentin had been subjected to it from childhood, except for those few years of freedom at Oxford. He was totally under Aidan's thumb.'

'He managed to escape once,' Melissa pointed out.

'Only for a while. Aidan kept chipping away at him until in the end he agreed to leave Poppy and file for a divorce.'

'Quentin divorced Poppy?' Caroline nodded again. 'On what grounds?'

'I was never told, but Aidan knew all the tricks so no doubt he managed to concoct something that would stand up in court if Poppy contested the suit. Quentin didn't come back home immediately; Aidan set him up in a flat and paid him a small allowance while the divorce was going through, and then he and Sarah had a quiet wedding and they settled down here.'

'And Aidan's been keeping them ever since?'

'No, Poppy has. Not willingly, of course,' Caroline

added, seeing Melissa's eyes widen. 'When the proceedings began, she had three choices: contest the allegations, file a counter suit for desertion or agree to the divorce. Rather than go through the courts she chose the latter, but it meant parting with a huge chunk of her fortune. Quentin had no income, you see, so . . . '

'But that's monstrous!' Melissa exclaimed.

'It's the law,' Caroline said simply. 'In an uncontested suit, the combined assets are split down the middle, or as the court decides. Poppy couldn't stand the thought of a prolonged legal slanging match, so she paid up. Aidan had gambled on that, of course.'

'So now Quentin's a wealthy widower?'

'I suppose so.' Caroline had begun to show increasing signs of agitation; her voice became harsh and shrill and she clasped and unclasped her hands. 'You see now, don't you, why I'm scared? Oh, I know I over-reacted when you arrived, but–'

'You were overwrought; it was only natural.'

'But you understand what I'm trying to say?'

'I think so,' Melissa said slowly. 'You're afraid all this will come out and people will start saying there was something suspicious about Sarah dying in much the same way as Aidan?'

'There are whispers going round already. That Mrs Wilson, she's said one or two things like, "You seem to be bearing your bereavement remarkably well, Mrs Cresney" and Mrs Foster gave me a funny look when I went in to buy stamps the other day. Melissa, in spite of it all I do feel sorry for poor old Quentin. He's a fundamentally decent person who's been seriously damaged by an unbelievably manipulative brother. He deserves a bit of happiness, but if the gossips start whispering who knows where it might lead? No matter what he's been through, I can't believe he'd have harmed Sarah.'

'I'm sure you're imagining things. No reasonable person could believe the two deaths were connected in any way.' Despite knowing from other sources that Caroline had some cause to feel uneasy, Melissa did her best to sound reassuring.

Caroline gave a short, mirthless laugh. 'We aren't talking about reasonable people, are we? We're talking about petty-minded gossips. And I'm thinking of myself as well. Melissa, I like this house, I liked it the moment I set foot in it. Not the decorations and fittings, of course – Aidan knew I hated them and that's why he wouldn't have anything changed – but I want to stay here and make it the way I'd like it to be. Is that so unreasonable?'

'I'd say it was very reasonable. You need to take things a step at a time, of course–'

'I could have my mother and sister here to live with me,' Caroline went on. 'They could have the part of the house Aidan had converted for Quentin and Sarah. Mother's disabled and Jennie has to look after her – life would be so much better for them both if they were to come here. Aidan would never hear of it, of course; he didn't really like me keeping in touch with them.'

'That sounds like a very promising arrangement,' said Melissa. 'Once everything's been settled, you can start making plans.' She stood up, glancing at her watch. 'Look, Caroline, do you think you'll be all right on your own now? I have some rather urgent work to attend to.'

'Yes, of course, you go.' Caroline stood up and held out her hand. 'Thank you so much for coming.'

'Just let me know if you need anything else. Would you like to come to us for a meal this evening?'

Caroline hesitated, then shook her head. 'That's very kind of you, but I've got quite a lot of things to do, phone calls to make and so on.'

'Well, keep in touch.'

As they crossed the hall to the front door, Melissa noticed a patch of bright scarlet on the bottom stair. It was made by a shaft of sunlight passing through the red rose offered by the knight to his lady, but for a moment it looked for all the world like a patch of blood.

14

When Melissa returned to Hawthorn Cottage she found Joe in the study with the printout of the last three chapters of *A Long Way from Home* in a neat stack on the desk in front of him.

'I hope that woman isn't going to make a habit of this,' he remarked, looking pointedly at his watch. 'You've been gone over an hour.'

'Oh, Joe, don't be hard on her.' Melissa flopped on to a chair beside him, leaned back and clasped her hands behind her head. 'She's had so much to put up with, it's no wonder she gets into a state at times.'

'Hasn't she got anyone else's shoulder to cry on? It's not fair to expect you to be at her beck and call. Anyway, she should be giving her brother-in-law some support; he's the one who's been bereaved this time.'

'That was my first reaction, but guess what – Quentin has gone to find comfort elsewhere.'

As Melissa repeated Caroline's story, Joe's expression became increasingly incredulous. When she had finished, he said, 'Let me get this straight: Aidan pushed Quentin into marrying Sarah, after which he left Sarah and married Poppy, and then divorced Poppy and remarried Sarah. Is that it?'

'That's right.'

'Aidan seems to have been a total control freak.' Joe shook his head in disbelief. 'How in the world do people like that get away with it?' He gave a sudden chuckle. 'The old devil must have been spitting feathers when his little brother escaped from his clutches.'

'Only for a while – and he managed to turn it to his own advantage eventually,' Melissa pointed out.

Joe's smile faded. 'The man was a manipulative monster,' he declared. 'Whatever possessed Caroline to marry him?'

Melissa shook her head. 'He must have kept that side of his nature well hidden until it was too late. It's hardly surprising she isn't exactly prostrate with grief at his death.'

'Do you suppose he took control of the money he screwed out of Poppy, or did he hand it over to Quentin?'

'I've no idea. All Caroline said was that Quentin and Sarah were living – very comfortably, if appearances are anything to go by – on Poppy's money, but she didn't say whether Aidan or Quentin held the purse strings.'

'Maybe she doesn't know.'

Melissa shrugged. 'That's quite possible – unless she managed to lay her hands on the keys to Aidan's filing cabinet before Quentin. I'll bet there are answers to quite a few questions in there.'

'Has she been to see Digby Morrison?'

'Not that I know of.'

'Whatever will she do now?'

'She's hoping to stay on at Cold Wells and have her sister and widowed mother to live there with her after she's made some alterations – and got Aidan's affairs settled.'

'That sounds like a good arrangement. She'd certainly find it lonely living on her own in that big house. Going back to her and Aidan's courtship,' Joe continued more slowly,

'I'd like to know whether he showed her the same kindly face before they were married as he obviously showed to Rosalie and her mother. It would be interesting to know what the attraction was.'

Melissa unclasped her hands and sat bolt upright. 'The Finns! I'd forgotten all about them! I wonder where they fit into this saga. Joe, you don't suppose Rosalie might have some grounds for her suspicions? You did say something about two similar deaths being too much of a coincidence.'

'Yes, I did, didn't I? But I thought we agreed it's hardly likely anyone could have engineered one death in such bizarre circumstances, let alone two.'

'Unlikely doesn't necessarily mean impossible, though.'

Joe gave his wife a searching look. 'Mel,' he said, 'you have that look in your eye. Something tells me you're dying to do a little discreet sleuthing.'

'There are a lot of questions I'd like to find answers to,' she admitted. 'The trouble is, if I start looking under stones I might find something that justice demands I should mention to the coroner, or even the police. Caroline blurted out all the family secrets because she was desperate for someone to confide in, but she's terrified it might become generally known and she begged me not to tell anyone. If I start going round asking questions it might have exactly the effect she most dreads.'

'There'll be plenty of people asking questions when people notice Quentin's disappearance from the scene. Incidentally, doesn't it strike you as a little odd that she's so anxious to protect him?'

Melissa thought for a moment. 'Not really. She admits she finds him a bit of a pain, but she does have some sympathy for him after what his brother did to him.'

'So she tore up his wedding photograph?'

'That was probably in a fit of rage when she realised he'd skipped off and left her to cope on her own.'

'Or because she wanted to eradicate all traces of the Cresneys. I wonder,' Joe went on, 'if she suspects Quentin of having something to do with the deaths? Rosalie Finn thought so.'

'It's true she suggested he might have been responsible for Aidan's death, but there's no reason to suspect him of wanting to kill Sarah. Anyway, he's terrified of bees, according to Mrs Foster. He might have resented his brother, even hated him, for breaking up his marriage to Poppy, but if he wanted to do away with him he'd have found some other means.'

'I'm sure you're right. So where does that leave us?'

Melissa got up and went to the open window. It was a warm afternoon and only the faintest of breezes stirred the curtains. She stood looking out at the back garden, smaller now since the extension had been built, but still bright with late summer flowers. Next season, she thought, a little planning would enable them to find room for a few of the vegetable crops that had been sacrificed during the construction.

After a minute or two of contemplation she said, 'I'm not too bothered about Quentin's feelings, but it seems to me that Caroline has suffered enough and I honestly can't see anything to be gained by dragging the skeletons out of the Cresney cupboards.'

'So you're going to let well alone?'

'I think so.'

'Well, thank goodness for that!' said Joe. 'Now perhaps we can get on with the final run-through of this script?'

*   *   *

Melissa's prediction that questions would swiftly follow the latest tragedy was fulfilled even earlier than she had supposed. When, towards the end of the afternoon, she went to the post office to despatch the script of her novel, her heart sank as through the glass door of the shop she saw Cynthia Thorne, apparently engaged in animated discussion with Mrs Foster. The minute she entered they pounced on her.

'Here's Mrs Martin!' they exclaimed in chorus.

'We were just saying–' Mrs Foster began.

'You're sure to know what's happened because–' Cynthia chimed in.

'Seeing as you're so friendly with poor Mrs Cresney,' Mrs Foster wound up, with a certain air of triumph at getting in the last word. Her pale eyelids were fluttering wildly. 'Two bereavements in less than a fortnight! Who would credit it? It's enough to send anyone out of their mind.'

'Anyone but Caroline Cresney,' said Cynthia, with a touch of disdain in her voice and a meaning shake of her head. 'A very strong-minded lady, that one. A little too strong-minded, if you ask me.'

'I reckon she needed to be, poor thing, being married to *him*,' said Mrs Foster. The final words were uttered in a doom-laden voice, as if Aidan Cresney had been the prince of darkness.

Despite the seriousness of the situation, Melissa had difficulty in keeping a straight face as she said, 'I take it you've been discussing the death of Sarah Cresney?'

'Is it true she died in exactly the same way as her brother-in-law?' asked Cynthia.

'Stung to death by they dreadful bees?' Mrs Foster's tone

of horror was in sharp contrast to the gleam of excitement in her eyes.

'She was quite badly stung, yes, but she seemed to be responding to treatment,' said Melissa. 'Then she suffered a heart attack and was dead within minutes.'

'It all sounds very fishy, don't you think?' said Cynthia.

'Fishy?' repeated Melissa. She did her best to appear surprised, as if such a notion had never occurred to her. 'I don't understand what you mean,' she said frostily. Until now, she had managed to shrug off Cynthia's gushingly fulsome praise of her mystery novels and her zealous, almost morbid interest in the character and motives of the murderers. Today, she found it difficult to conceal her dislike of the woman. One of Joe's observations sprang to her mind. 'There's something phoney about her,' he had once remarked. 'Everything about her is just too perfect. I'll bet even her gardening clothes have designer labels.' Melissa knew exactly what he meant: never a hair out of place, nail-varnish blending perfectly with clothes that were always exactly right for the occasion: accessories carefully chosen for style and colour. 'I'm sure you're right,' she had agreed, 'no baggy jeans or scruffy T-shirt for her; she'd rather die than be seen putting out her dustbin in anything but pants and sweatshirt from Harvey Nicks.'

On that occasion they had a quiet laugh at Cynthia's expense, but there was no cause for humour now. There was something repellent about her greenish eyes, narrow with suspicion but alight with anticipation of another succulent morsel of gossip.

'You don't think there's something fishy about two people in the same family dying in almost exactly the same way?' she said. Her tongue made a series of darting, chameleon-like appearances between her glossy porcelain teeth.

'I think it's more likely to have been a terrible and very tragic coincidence,' replied Melissa. 'Excuse me, please.' She moved towards the counter and Cynthia, almost reluctantly, made way for her. 'I'd like this to go by special delivery please, Mrs Foster.'

Cynthia, however, had no intention of allowing the matter to rest. She tried a new angle. 'You would think,' she remarked while Mrs Foster peered at the scales, made some calculations and filled in the necessary form, 'that at least she'd have the consideration to stay at home and comfort her poor brother-in-law instead of going off to play bridge as if nothing had happened.'

'Is that what she's done?' said Mrs Foster. Evidently, this was a piece of information that had not been volunteered before Melissa's arrival. 'I wondered where she were going when I saw her drive past earlier on.'

'No, we're not playing bridge until tomorrow. This afternoon' – Cynthia's voice became even more censorious – 'she had an appointment with her hairdresser and beautician. Much more important than giving comfort to the bereaved.'

'Fancy that now. Did she tell you that's what she were planning?'

'Oh, no, she didn't see fit to confide in *me*.' It was evident that Cynthia considered the omission a personal affront. 'It was Davina Sheffield who told me when I spoke to her on the telephone just before I came out. She didn't know about the other Mrs Cresney's death and she was really *shocked* when I told her. "Well," she said, "Caroline never mentioned it, but I know for certain she's coming tomorrow because I phoned to remind her not ten minutes before you rang and caught her just as she was off to the hairdresser." A very strange sense of priorities, it seems to me.'

'Fancy that!' Mrs Foster repeated. 'It does seem a bit callous, certainly.'

'She probably felt a hairdo and a facial would give her morale a much needed boost after all she's been through lately,' said Melissa. Privately, while defending Caroline against Cynthia's spiteful attack had been an instinctive reaction, she too was surprised that she was prepared to face the bridge-playing sorority so soon. 'Just out of interest,' she added, 'how did you come to hear that Sarah Cresney was dead?'

'Roger told me when he delivered the post,' said Cynthia. 'I imagine he told everyone he saw on his way round. That's why he was late this morning; he said he found Mrs Cresney in quite a state when he called at Cold Wells. He said she was crying and saying something about bananas . . . he couldn't make head or tail of it.'

'That's right,' said Mrs Foster, not to be outdone. 'He were a bit worried about her and offered to make her a cup of tea or something, but she said she'd be all right because she had a friend coming. That would be you, perhaps, Mrs Martin?'

'I did go to see her, yes, but she didn't say anything about bananas to me. Perhaps she was saying she thought she was going bananas . . . you know, a bit crazy? She was certainly very distressed when I got to the house, but she was calm when I left.' Perhaps a little too calm, she thought to herself. Not for the first time she found Caroline's changes of attitude a cause for unease.

'You'd have thought it would be her poor brother-in-law

who was in need of comfort after losing his wife,' said Cynthia, reverting to her original theme.

'Ah, now there's a funny thing.' Mrs Foster's manner became mysterious; she leaned across the counter and lowered her voice. 'Roger never saw hide nor hair of Mr Quentin, although he rang the bell twice because he had something for him that wouldn't go through the letterbox. He had to go back and leave it with Mrs Cresney.'

At this point the two women looked directly at Melissa, as if expecting her to account for Quentin's non-appearance. She ignored them both, picked up the receipt for her parcel, checked her change and put it in her purse. 'I must be getting along,' she said briskly. 'Good afternoon, ladies.' She was conscious of resentful stares directed at her back as she left the shop.

15

The following day, by mutual consent, neither Melissa nor Joe made any reference to Caroline or to the twin tragedies that had befallen her family. Since *A Long Way from Home* was at last finished and despatched to the publisher, and the next book little more than a rudimentary idea that would need time to germinate quietly at the back of her mind before requiring any serious work, it seemed an appropriate moment for them to think about taking a short holiday. As Joe had no pressing business commitments for the next week or two they spent an agreeable morning considering the rival attractions of the Lake District, Pembrokeshire and South Cornwall, but without coming to any conclusion.

They were still undecided when Caroline rang shortly after lunch. 'No panic this time,' she said when Melissa answered. 'I just wanted to thank you for the support you gave me yesterday, and to let you know that I've been to see your nice Mr Morrison. He was very helpful and I'm sure he'll look after my affairs very efficiently.'

'I thought you'd like him,' said Melissa, mentally uncrossing her fingers and giving a thumbs-up signal to Joe, who had glared and shaken his head on hearing her greet Caroline by name. 'Did you find the key to the filing cabinet, by the way?'

'Oh, yes, it was hidden at the back of a drawer in Aidan's desk. I've handed all the papers over to Mr Morrison and he came across the name of a solicitor Aidan had dealings with, although he seems to have handled most of his – or rather, our – affairs himself.'

'Well, that's hardly surprising in view of his legal training.'

'No, I suppose not.' There was a pause before Caroline went on, 'His will was in the cabinet – or rather, a copy was there. Aidan's solicitor probably has the original in his strong room.'

'I believe that's quite usual.'

'That's what Mr Morrison said.' For a moment, Melissa had the impression that she was about to say something else, but after another brief silence she said, 'Goodbye, Melissa, thank you again for all your help,' and hung up.

'Does that mean you're off the hook?' said Joe after Melissa relayed the brief conversation.

'I suppose so.'

'You don't sound too sure.'

'I've no reason to think otherwise, except that I have this feeling–'

'No!' Joe threw up his hands in mock supplication. 'Mel, you promised!'

'I'm probably imagining things, but she hesitated for a moment before saying goodbye, as if she wanted to–'

'I don't want to hear any more,' he said firmly. 'We'll decide where we're going, find a good hotel and make a booking. Give me that directory and let's stop faffing about.'

In the event, their plans were thrown into disarray when they checked their emails and found a message from Iris.

Due to a cancellation at short notice, Elder Cottage, the property adjoining Hawthorn Cottage that she still owned and let out as holiday accommodation, had unexpectedly become vacant for the next few days. Iris had decided to take the opportunity of making a short trip to the Cotswolds before winter set in. She planned to arrive in Upper Benbury on Wednesday morning and stay until the following Monday before spending a short time in London, looking up a few friends and visiting some art exhibitions.

'Isn't that great news!' Melissa exclaimed on reading the message. 'She'll be here tomorrow! It seems ages since I saw her, and with the book out of the way, this couldn't have happened at a better time.'

Joe showed little sign of sharing her enthusiasm. 'She might have given us a bit more notice,' he grumbled.

'She sent the message on Sunday. This is the first time we've logged on since last Friday.'

'That's because we've been working flat out on the book, in between running around after Caroline Cresney.'

'Well, at least those are off our backs.'

'Which is why we're planning this trip,' he reminded her. 'Anyway, you saw Iris less than a month ago.' The Hammonds' generous wedding present had been a fortnight's use of a converted barn on their property. After days spent exploring the sun-drenched delights of the Côte d'Azur they had passed the evenings in blissful relaxation on their small private patio, drinking the local wine and marvelling at the beauty of the velvet, star-encrusted skies of the Midi.

'That's true.' Melissa gave a little sigh of pleasure at the memory of those halcyon days. 'I didn't spend much time with Iris, though.'

'That's hardly surprising; we were on our honeymoon.'

'Plus the fact that she was busy most of the time with the students.'

Joe was beginning to sound exasperated. 'Are you seriously suggesting we drop our own plans just because she decides to pay a flying visit at five minutes' notice?'

'We don't have to drop our trip, only postpone it for a few days.'

'Oh, yes, and probably miss out on this spell of fine weather.' Joe threw down the directory in a rare gesture of ill-humour. It missed the table and landed on the floor, but he made no move to pick it up. 'I know exactly what's going to happen. The minute she arrives you'll be telling her all about the Cresney saga and the pair of you will get your heads together to find some sinister explanation for what we've already agreed are coincidences.'

She slipped a hand through his arm. 'No, I won't, I promise,' she said. 'I'm just as keen as you are to keep our distance from the Cresneys. Iris will only be here for a few days and it would be a bit unfriendly to disappear the minute she arrives, after she and Jack made us so welcome. Anyway, you know you've always enjoyed her company. We did have several lovely evenings with her and Jack at Les Genêts.

'That's the point; I had Jack to talk to. I wasn't swamped by chattering women.'

She was about to make an indignant reply when she spotted the glint of mischief in his deep-set eyes and gave his arm a shake. 'Now you're winding me up,' she said, relieved that his momentary irritation had passed. She picked up the directory and put it in his hands. 'Here, darling – go ahead and sort out a few nice hotels for me to choose from. No, on second thoughts, I'll leave it entirely up to you.'

'You haven't decided yet where you want to go.'

'I don't mind in the least as long as it's near water, preferably the sea.'

Leaving Joe to his research, Melissa went to tell her mother about the plans to go away for a few days. 'You'll be all right on your own, won't you, Mum?' she said anxiously. 'I'll make sure you know where we are and I'll phone every day.'

'Of course I'll be all right,' said Sylvia. 'You mustn't fuss over me, Lissie. I'm not an invalid any more, you know. And you deserve a break, after all that extra work on your book. The change will do you both the world of good.'

'It has been a bit fraught for both of us,' Melissa admitted. To say nothing of all the hassle with Caroline, she added mentally. Keeping a shoulder permanently available for her to cry on had been pretty exhausting. 'Oh, by the way,' she went on, 'Iris is coming tomorrow and staying until Monday.'

Sylvia clapped her hands in delight. 'Oh, I am glad. It will be lovely to see her again; she's such a nice person. Perhaps you'd like to bring her round for tea one afternoon.'

'That's a nice idea, Mum, but until she gets here I don't know what her plans are. I'll have to let you know.'

'Yes, of course. As a matter of fact, Thursday would be a good day, if she hasn't planned anything else, that is, because I've invited Caroline Cresney. Does Iris know her?'

'Only by sight.' It dawned on Melissa as she spoke that, although during a recent exchange of emails with Iris she had mentioned Aidan's death and funeral, she had said nothing about the startling revelations that a distraught

Caroline had confided to her. Nor had she told Iris about Sarah's death. Remembering her promise to Joe, she resolved to avoid the subject if possible.

'She's very lonely, poor thing,' Sylvia went on. 'I do think it was inconsiderate of Quentin to go off like that and leave her all by herself. I suppose he feels the need to be alone with his grief and all that, but it's very hard on her. Do you know when he'll be coming back? She was very vague about it when I spoke to her yesterday.'

'I'm afraid I've no idea,' said Melissa. 'She rang yesterday evening, but she didn't mention him and I didn't like to ask.'

'No of course not, dear. It's not good manners to be nosy, is it?'

'No, Mum, it isn't.' Recalling the keen interest in the Cresneys' affairs that her mother had shown over the past few days, and the scraps of gossip that she had repeated with such relish, Melissa had difficulty in concealing a smile.

The Martins' resolve to avoid all reference to the Cresneys was severely tested the following morning when Gloria arrived on her regular Wednesday visit, bursting to impart her version of the latest development.

'Would you believe it!' she exclaimed the moment she was inside the house. 'Mrs Caroline's turned her poor brother-in-law out on the street, and his wife not yet cold in her grave!'

'How did you come by this information?' asked Joe. His expression was one of detached curiosity, but Melissa detected an edge to his voice that should have warned Gloria to be careful of her facts.

'Mrs Wilson told me. She said, "I never did trust that woman, hard as nails she be. Never shed a tear when her own husband died, and now this." '

'But that's not true,' said Melissa. 'You know I found Mrs Cresney in a very distressed state when I went to see her because I told you. I hope you made that clear to Mrs Wilson.' From the way Gloria avoided her eye, she immediately suspected that the talkative young woman had done nothing of the kind, but she decided not to labour the point since the damage had almost certainly been done by now. No doubt there were other recipients of Mrs Wilson's confidences and it seemed that more than one garbled version of the truth would soon be circulating in the village. 'By the way,' she said, 'where did Mrs Wilson get all this?'

'She heard Mrs Caroline talking on the phone. She heard her say, "I want the place cleared as soon as possible." And then she said, "I don't believe you, I think you planned it this way all along," and hung up. What do you make of that?'

'I think,' said Joe, 'that Mrs Wilson should attend to her own business and not go spreading unsubstantiated rumours. Jumping to conclusions on the strength of a few remarks heard out of context can cause a great deal of trouble.'

Judging from the look of perplexity that flitted over Gloria's mobile features, she had some difficulty in unravelling what was probably to her a somewhat complex statement, but there was no doubt that she caught the general drift of its meaning.

'I'm only telling you what Mrs Wilson told me,' she said defensively, 'and I haven't said nothing to no one else.'

'Then I strongly advise you not to do so,' said Joe sternly.

Gloria looked wounded. 'I thought it were only right you should know what folks be saying, seeing as you be friends with the Cresneys.' She tied on her apron, sorted out her cleaning materials and clattered upstairs without another word.

'Oh dear, I think I've upset her,' said Joe. 'I hope she won't give in her notice.'

'She'll get over it. It's not the first time she's been ticked off for gossiping.'

Their attention was distracted by the sound of a car on the drive. 'That sounds like a taxi,' said Joe.

Melissa flew to the sitting room window. 'It's Iris!' she said joyfully, and rushed out of the front door to greet her friend.

'What's up with Gloria?' asked Iris over the vegetable curry that Melissa had prepared for lunch. 'Never known her so quiet. Hardly said a word over coffee.'

'Joe ticked her off for repeating false rumours and now he's terrified she'll give us notice,' Melissa explained.

'Is that all? Got plenty of stick from me in the past for gossiping. Used to sulk for a while, then forgot about it.'

'It wasn't so much the ticking off as all the long words he used,' Melissa said. 'You should have seen her expression – she was totally bemused.'

'She got the message, though,' said Joe.

'What rumours, by the way?' Iris demanded when she had stopped laughing. 'Some village scandal I've not heard about?'

'Worse than that,' said Melissa, becoming serious again. 'You remember I told you about Aidan Cresney dying of shock after being attacked by his own bees?' Iris nodded. 'Well, his sister-in-law met a similar fate.' Melissa briefly recounted the further chapter of misfortune that had befallen the Cresneys, followed by Quentin's sudden departure from the house at Cold Wells. 'Their cleaning lady's telling everyone Caroline kicked him out and Gloria repeated the story to us. We happen to know the truth, but we couldn't put her right without betraying Caroline's confidence.'

'Unpredictable creatures, bees,' Iris observed. It was typical of her that she made no attempt to prise further details out of Melissa. 'Seem to get upset now and again for no particular reason,' she went on. 'Never bother me, but one of the students got stung recently. Luckily Jack got the sting out before the venom got into the bloodstream.'

'I'm afraid Aidan and Sarah weren't so fortunate,' said Melissa. 'By the way, my mother has invited us – you and me, that is – to have tea with her tomorrow afternoon. She's decided Caroline needs a bit of TLC so she's invited her along. I don't know how you feel about it?'

'I don't see why not.' Iris pushed back her chair and stood up. 'Better go indoors now and do a bit of unpacking. See you later.'

16

'Iris! I'm so pleased to see you!' Sylvia held out both hands to greet her visitor. 'I was thrilled when Lissie told me you were coming.'

'Good to be here. Pretty little house you have.' Iris cast an appraising glance over the exterior of the extension to Hawthorn Cottage. 'Nice choice of name, too,' she added as her eye fell on the enamelled plaque bearing the word 'Brambles' fixed to the wall beside the front door. After lengthy consultation with Joc and Melissa, Sylvia had christened her new home after the numerous tangled patches that lined the footpath along the valley and acted as a magnet to blackberry-pickers in the autumn.

Sylvia beamed. 'I'm glad you think so. Do come in and sit down – or perhaps you'd like to have a quick look round first?'

'Love to.'

'Lissie, Caroline's in the sitting room. Would you keep her company while I show Iris round?'

'Of course.'

Caroline was sitting in an armchair opposite the French window, which looked out on Sylvia's little patio garden. She was half turned towards the door and her eyes were closed, but when Melissa entered she opened them and sat upright with a start, almost as if she had been guilty of a breach of good manners. She was pale and drawn, with dark circles under her eyes.

Melissa sat down beside her. 'Caroline, how are you?' she asked. 'I've been thinking about you so much these past few days.'

Caroline gave a faint, tired smile. 'That's kind of you,' she replied. 'I'm all right, I suppose, but I've not been sleeping too well at night and I find myself dropping off at odd times during the day.'

'That's quite understandable. It'll take a while for you to settle down, after everything you've been through.' In the background, Sylvia's voice could be heard enthusiastically pointing out the virtues of her bijou kitchen while Iris made laconic but approving comments. Just the same, Melissa dropped her voice before saying, 'Have you heard from Quentin?'

'He's supposed to be coming to collect the rest of his and Sarah's personal effects in a day or two. I've told him to arrange for his furniture to be collected as soon as possible.'

'Has the date been fixed for Sarah's funeral?'

'She's to be cremated next Tuesday after a private ceremony. After that, I'm severing relations.' There was a rasp to Caroline's voice as she added, 'I want every trace of the Cresneys out of my life.'

'I suppose that's understandable.' It crossed Melissa's mind to warn Caroline against making her sentiments generally known and that a remark on similar lines, made on the telephone, had been not only overheard but misinterpreted; on second thoughts she decided this was not the moment to raise such a delicate matter. Instead, she asked, 'Have you spoken to your mother and sister about coming to live with you?'

'Oh, yes!' A smile transformed Caroline's sad countenance. 'They're over the moon about it, but I've warned them it can't be straight away. I've arranged with someone from social services to come and assess the place to see what needs to be done to accommodate Mother. I'll have to have some modifications made, like a ramp for her wheelchair and a stair lift and so on. It will all take time.'

'At least you have that to look forward to. Ah, here they come from their conducted tour.' Melissa stood up as Sylvia and Iris entered. 'Caroline, I'd like you to meet a very dear friend and former neighbour of mine – Iris Hammond, Caroline Cresney.'

'How do you do, Iris?'

'Delighted!' Iris took the small white hand that Caroline extended in both her own thin brown ones. 'Heard about your tragic loss,' she said gruffly. 'Many condolences.'

'Thank you.'

'Iris is a very famous artist,' said Sylvia with a touch of pride. 'She and her husband run an arts centre in the south of France.'

'How interesting,' said Caroline politely.

'Well, I'll leave you three to chat while I make the tea. It won't be a moment; the kettle's just boiled.'

'Nice little place you've built for your mum,' said Iris. 'Seems as happy as a sand-boy here.'

'Oh, she's taken to village life like a duck to water and made quite a few friends,' said Melissa. 'She's joined a flower club and goes off to lunch with the other members once a week. She said something the other day about learning to play bridge. I believe you play,' she added, turning to Caroline, who nodded without replying.

'Do you belong to a club?'

'It's not exactly a club, just a group of bridge fiends who meet every so often in one another's homes.'

'What's that about bridge?' asked Sylvia, appearing at that moment wheeling a tea trolley. 'I'm thinking of learning. They run classes at the local adult education college. Do you play, Iris?'

'Not me. No good at cards. Can never remember who's got what.'

Sylvia tittered. 'I'm not sure I'll be any good, but Cynthia is trying to persuade me to have a go.'

'Cynthia Thorne?' said Caroline.

'That's right. She's a member of the flower club as well. Do you know her?'

'Yes.' Something in Caroline's tone suggested to Melissa that the fact that Sylvia and Cynthia Thorne were acquainted was not to her liking.

Sylvia, busy pouring milk into the teacups, appeared not to notice. 'Caroline, do you take sugar?'

'No, thank you.'

'Right. Now, I've given everyone a little table for their tea.' She bustled around distributing cups of tea, paper napkins, plates and pastry forks before offering slices of cake from a silver dish. 'I do hope you like this cake. It's a new recipe I found in a magazine.'

'Looks delicious,' said Iris. She sampled a piece and nodded approvingly. 'Mm, scrumptious.'

Caroline lifted a piece of cake on her fork, but instead of putting it in her mouth she gave a sudden thin shriek, returned it to the plate and covered her mouth with her hands. 'Banana!' she exclaimed, her face contorted with disgust. 'It's got banana in it!'

'Oh dear, don't you like banana? There's shortbread if

you prefer it.' Sylvia reached for a second plate, but to everyone's consternation Caroline leapt from her seat and rushed out of the room. Seconds later they heard her throwing up in the toilet.

'How extraordinary,' said Melissa as they exchanged bewildered glances. 'She didn't even eat any of the cake.'

'Must have been the smell,' said Iris.

The vomiting subsided after a minute or two and was followed by the sound of a tap running. 'Perhaps I'd better go and see how she is.' Sylvia hurried out, returning after a short interval with Caroline trailing behind her, looking more washed out than ever.

'I'm sorry to have made such an exhibition of myself,' she said sheepishly.

'My dear, there's no need to apologise,' said Sylvia. 'I'm sorry too; I had no idea–' It was difficult to know which of the two was the more embarrassed.

'Of course you hadn't,' said Caroline. 'I'm quite all right now, but I think I'll go home and lie down, if you don't mind. I apologise for breaking up the party. It was nice meeting you, Iris. Perhaps I'll see you again before you go back.'

'Oh dear, that was unfortunate,' said Sylvia after Caroline's departure. 'She must be really allergic to banana for it to have such a violent effect on her.'

'It must be an allergy that's developed quite recently,' Melissa said.

'Why do you say that?'

'Because I've just remembered that she and Sarah once came on a visit to a stately home with a party from the garden club and we had lunch in the restaurant. There were banana splits on the dessert menu and I know Caroline and

Sarah both had them because I did as well and we agreed how good they were.'

'That must have been a long time ago,' said Sylvia. 'You said they stopped joining in things after Quentin appeared.'

'Who's Quentin?' asked Iris.

'Aidan Cresney's brother,' said Melissa. 'The one whose wife died of a heart attack over the weekend.'

'Thought you said it was bee stings.'

'She did get quite badly stung, but she seemed to be recovering when she had this massive coronary.'

'Not the luckiest of families,' Iris remarked. 'So now there's just Caroline and her brother-in-law rattling around in that big house.'

'Only Caroline at the moment. Quentin's gone away; no one's quite sure where. Do you know' – Sylvia turned to Melissa with a troubled expression on her face – 'Cynthia says Caroline ordered him out of the house, but I can't believe she'd do a thing like that just after the poor man lost his wife, can you?'

'No, I can't,' said Melissa. 'I warned you once before, Mum, that woman's a troublemaker. I hope you won't go repeating that.'

'I shan't, but I'm afraid it's going to get around,' Sylvia sighed.

'That's the down side of village life,' Iris commented. 'Always someone spreading tales. Usually get the wrong end of the stick.' She put down her empty teacup and got to her feet. 'Delicious tea, Sylvia, thank you. I'd better be going now; things to do.'

'Of course. You're only here for a short time. Thank you for coming.'

'I'll go as well,' said Melissa, 'unless you'd like a hand with the washing up.'

'No thank you, dear, I can manage. You two run along.' Sylvia shooed them out of the door as if they were children being told to go away and play.

As they made their way back to their respective cottages, Iris said, 'That cake that upset Caroline: the smell might have reminded her of when her husband got attacked by the bees.'

Melissa stared at her. 'How do you make that out?'

'When our student got stung, he said he smelled bananas. Maybe she did too, when she got close to Aidan.'

'Now I come to think of it, according to Mrs Foster the postman said Caroline was saying something about bananas when he called at the house. She was in quite a state and I thought he must have said she was going bananas, but perhaps you're right.'

'Jack said it was a chemical the bees release when they're upset and sting someone. Other bees get the scent and join in the fun.'

'That could explain why Aidan suffered such a murderous attack,' said Melissa. 'Sarah too, although Caroline and Quentin really thought they'd got to her in time. Of course, it still doesn't explain why the bees began stinging in the first place.'

Melissa got back indoors just as Joe was putting down the telephone. 'Who was that?' she asked.

'Selina Stitch, with her knickers in a twist.' The best-selling romantic novelist was one of Joe's most temperamental authors as well as the most successful. As Melissa had once remarked, not without a twinge of envy, her novels sold by the containerload.

'What's up with the old harpy this time?' she asked.

'Her American publisher is paying a flying visit to London and wants to meet her to discuss a new contract. She wants me to be there to take care of her interests.'

'When?'

'Tomorrow, would you believe? I'll have to leave this evening because the meeting's scheduled to start first thing in the morning. Knowing Selina, it could go on all day.'

'Why don't you stay in town a second night, then? Friday's a bad day to drive back because of the traffic. Maybe you could get in a round of golf with Paul.' Joe's son led a bachelor existence in London, but usually managed to find time in his busy social life to spend time with his father whenever he was in town.

'That's not a bad idea. I'll give him a call.' Joe went to the telephone while Melissa began preparations for their evening meal. After a brief conversation, he hung up and said, 'That's fine, he's picking me up on Saturday morning. Thanks for suggesting it, love.'

'There you are,' she said slyly, 'it's all worked out for the best. If Iris hadn't turned up unexpectedly, we'd have been away. As it is, you can mother-hen Selina and then see Paul, I'll have Iris for company and we'll still have our mini break to look forward to.'

After Joe left, Melissa sat down and leafed through the evening paper. An item on the list of local events caught her eye. The local beekeepers' association were holding their monthly meeting the following evening. The speaker was to be the well-known biochemist Doctor Harold Finn and the subject of his talk was 'The Chemistry of Beekeeping'. The brief announcement ended with the words, 'All welcome'.

'Well, what do you know?' she said aloud. Finn was

certainly an unusual name. Could the speaker be Rosalie's uncle, the man who had disapproved so strongly of the family's association with Aidan Cresney? She decided to go to the lecture and, if possible, snatch a quiet word with him.

It was, she thought, fortuitous that Joe would not be at home. She had a feeling he would not have approved of her plan.

17

A woman answered the telephone in a brisk cultured voice that held no trace of the Gloucestershire burr that Melissa had been expecting. Her request to be allowed to attend the forthcoming meeting of the Stowbridge Beekeepers' Association was greeted in a manner that was hardly consistent with the friendly wording of the press announcement.

'Are you new to the county?' was her first question. The information that Melissa had lived in Gloucestershire for over five years did not appear to impress her and she asked, rather condescendingly Melissa felt, how many hives she had. Evidently, in her book, only established apiarists were expected to show an interest in the meeting and she obviously had some difficulty in understanding why anyone outside the charmed circle should want to know about the chemistry of beekeeping. However, she 'supposed it would be all right', added that non-members would be charged a fee of three pounds at the door, gave her directions to a private house a couple of miles from the centre of Stowbridge and informed her that the meetings began at seven thirty *sharp*.

Melissa put down the phone and went next door to tell Iris of this new development. 'The woman sounds a real battle-axe,' she said, after repeating the conversation. 'I'll bet even her bees have to do as they're told.'

'She's queen bee of the association!' said Iris with a mischievous grin that gave her the appearance of a benev-olent witch. 'Probably suspects you of running a rival organisation. Watch out you don't get stung.'

'I don't think the queens actually sting, do they? I thought they left that to the workers.'

'I'll bet they do if they come across a rival queen,' Iris cackled. There was a provocative glint in her keen grey eyes as she added, 'Going to tell Joe what you're up to?'

'That depends. He gets all huffy if he thinks I'm going to get embroiled in any more mysteries.'

Iris, seated in her favourite position cross-legged on the floor, gave her a penetrating look and said shrewdly, 'Haven't told me the full story, have you?'

'Well, no, I suppose not,' Melissa admitted. 'There are a few skeletons in the Cresney cupboards I haven't mentioned.'

'Can't say I'm surprised,' Iris remarked.

'Of course, I was forgetting. They came to Cold Wells while you were still living here. How come you never met them?'

Iris shrugged her thin shoulders. 'Our paths never crossed. Used to exchange polite greetings in church, that's all. Only three of them then.'

'That's right. Quentin appeared later, after you and Jack got married and moved away.'

'And now his brother and his wife are both dead, he's sloped off again. Any idea where? Don't tell if you don't want to,' she went on without giving Melissa time to think of a reply, 'but it sticks out a mile something about this busi-ness is bugging you.'

Melissa thought for a moment and then said, 'I know I

can rely on you to keep it to yourself, and I would like to know what you think.' As accurately as she could, she recounted the chain of events that began just over a fortnight ago with the terrible death of Aidan Cresney and ended with Quentin's return to his former wife after Sarah's death in similar circumstances. Iris listened with a look of intense concentration on her sharp tanned features; when Melissa had finished she sat for several minutes without speaking while fiddling abstractedly with one of the tortoise-shell slides that secured her short mouse-brown hair.

'So,' she said at last, 'you reckon there's more to these two deaths than meets the eye?'

'Let's say I'm not convinced there isn't. In fact, I don't believe Joe is either, but he's dead set against my getting involved.'

'And that's why you're going to this meeting tomorrow, to see if Doctor Harold Finn is any relation to Rosalie?'

'Partly that, but mainly to see if he's got anything to say about what makes bees sting.'

'Suppose he is her uncle, what then?'

'In the first place, it would be interesting to know what he had against his sister-in-law and her daughter associating with Aidan Cresney, and how strongly he felt against the man.'

'Think he's likely to tell you?'

'You never know, I might get some idea.'

'And in the second place?'

'I suppose, to find out if he thinks it's possible for someone with a knowledge of bee chemistry to induce the creatures to attack a particular person.'

Iris looked dubious. 'Sounds a bit fanciful to me. Oh, excuse me.' She put her hand over her mouth to stifle a yawn and then rose to her feet in one swift, effortless movement of her supple body. 'Mel, if you don't mind I'd like to push off to bed now. Let me know how things go tomorrow.'

'Will do.'

The house, an imposing building of Cotswold stone, was perched on a hillside overlooking the ancient town of Stowbridge, once an important centre of the woollen industry that in past centuries had brought prosperity to the Cotswolds. The parish church, like so many in the region, had been built with money donated by a wealthy wool merchant and was famous for its stained glass.

Mindful of the insistence on punctuality, Melissa made a point of arriving in good time. She drove slowly up the drive, followed a temporary sign reading 'Car Park' that directed her round the back of the house, and parked alongside half a dozen others. A warm and cloudless day was ending in a spectacular sunset. Other early arrivals were standing about in small groups chatting or strolling on a wide, manicured lawn admiring the display of trees, shrubs and late summer flowers against the flaming backdrop of the sky. No one seemed in any hurry to go into the house, although the double French doors to a large Victorian-style conservatory, its windows screened by lowered blinds, stood open to reveal a number of chairs arranged in a semicircle. Inside, an elegantly dressed woman was engaged in conversation with a short, balding, bespectacled man whom Melissa assumed to be the speaker. She wondered if the woman was the 'queen bee' who had subjected her to an interrogation on the telephone. She hesitated, uncertain whether to go and introduce herself or wait until there was a general move indoors. A short distance away, two women were discussing comparative honey yields. One of them appeared to be disputing the weight claimed by the other, and Melissa was listening with some amusement to claim and counter-claim when a pleasant-looking man of about fifty with sparse sandy hair and a ruddy complexion came over to her and said, 'Good evening. I think you must be our visitor.'

'That's right. Melissa Martin. I spoke to your secretary after seeing the notice in the *Gazette*.'

'I'm Colin Palmer. I'm treasurer of this outfit for my sins.'

'Colin Palmer? The gentleman who's been looking after Aidan Cresney's hives?'

'You know the Cresneys?'

'They're my neighbours – should say, neighbour. There's only Caroline there at the moment.'

'Oh?'

'Perhaps you hadn't heard that Aidan's brother's wife Sarah died at the weekend?'

'No, I hadn't. I've been away for a few days. I'm very sorry to hear that; what happened?'

Palmer's eyes widened and his almost invisible eyebrows rose in astonishment as she told him the story. 'But that's appalling!' he exclaimed. 'Quentin must be devastated. I can't say I ever took to the man – or to his brother, come to that – but you couldn't wish that sort of double tragedy on your worst enemy. You said Caroline's there on her own now?'

'Yes. Quentin's . . . gone away for a while.'

'I see.' Palmer sighed and shook his head. 'Terrible business. Aidan's death came as a shock to us all. You may have heard that the family called on me to help drive off the bees.

Of course, it was too late by then to save him.' He shook his head again and made tutting noises. 'Dear oh dear! And now his sister-in-law,' he went on gloomily. 'I suppose the coronary was brought on by her body's reaction to the venom. It makes you think . . . it's made all of us think.'

'Actually, that's the reason why I'm here this evening,' said Melissa. 'It occurred to me that it might help Caroline if she had some explanation for the way the bees suddenly turned on Aidan. I don't know much about the creatures, but it does seem strange that someone as experienced as he was should come to grief.'

Palmer raised his eyebrows again and seemed to be on the point of asking a question, but all he said was, 'If you see Caroline, tell her I haven't forgotten my promise to remove Aidan's hives. It's just a question of finding a new location for them. Ah, we're being summoned.'

The woman Melissa had observed a few minutes ago stepped out on to the lawn and announced, in a voice that she immediately recognised, that the time was seven twenty-five and would everyone please come and take their seats so that Doctor Finn could start his lecture promptly at seven thirty.

'A bit like being back at college, isn't it?' Colin Palmer whispered in Melissa's ear as they followed the others into the conservatory. His voice held an undercurrent of mockery as he added, 'That's our chairman, or chair*person* as she insists on being called. The Honourable Mrs Frederica Cardew. One of the oldest families in the county,' he added.

'I thought she was the secretary.'

'She combines the two roles. She moans about how difficult it is to get people to take on responsibility nowadays, but the real reason is no one's prepared to serve under her.'

'That reminds me,' Melissa said, 'I understand you make an admission charge of three pounds.' She fished the coins out of her purse and offered them to him.

'Oh, yes, I suppose so.' He looked faintly embarrassed as he took them, saying in a low voice, 'I don't really see the need for it; it's not as if we get swamped with visitors and we're not short of funds. I voted against the charge when it was proposed, but I was over-ruled.' It was not difficult to deduce from the way his mouth crimped after the final words where the veto had come from. 'Come along and be introduced.'

The Honourable Mrs Cardew, clad in a simple but beautifully cut sage green trouser suit with a double row of pearls round her neck, greeted Melissa with a gracious smile and held out a blue-veined hand loaded with diamonds.

'How do you do, Mrs Martin?' she said in a carefully modulated voice. 'It's always nice when newcomers to the county take an interest in our activities. Mr Palmer is our treasurer, by the way, so perhaps you'd settle your little debt with him.'

'I have already done so,' said Melissa, trying not to mind being referred to as a newcomer.

'Splendid. Do go in and sit down. Doctor Finn is ready to begin. There will be refreshments after his lecture and the opportunity to ask questions.'

As Melissa later reported to Iris, he was a fluent and at times humorous speaker, and although a large proportion of the lecture went over her head she found it entertaining nevertheless. The rest of the audience appeared to find it fascinating and applauded enthusiastically when it was over. Mrs Cardew gave a fulsome vote of thanks, there was more applause and then, in response to an invitation that sounded like a royal command, everyone moved into the house. In a sumptuously furnished sitting room a small, grey-haired woman in a black dress appeared with a tray of glasses of wine while another followed with bowls of nuts and crisps.

Doctor Finn was quickly surrounded by eager questioners, and it was some time before Melissa found an opportunity to approach him and introduce herself.

'I'd better begin by admitting that I'm not a beekeeper,' she told him.

'But you're thinking of getting some hives?'

'Actually, no. My interest is more academic.'

'Are you a biochemist?'

'Nothing so distinguished, I'm afraid. It's just that I've recently heard of a case of an experienced beekeeper being attacked whilst attending to his hives and I wondered if you could offer an explanation of why it should happen.'

'Who was this beekeeper?' he asked. 'Someone you know?' She had not expected the question, and was momentarily floored. Before she had time to decide how to reply, he said, 'I understand that you live in Upper Benbury?'

'Well, yes, but–'

'How do I know? Our hostess informed me that there would be a visitor from a neighbouring village. As a matter of fact, she seemed to think your motive in being here was somehow suspect.' He had open mobile features and a pair of light brown eyes that held a humorous twinkle.

She found herself warming to him and decided to abandon her attempt at dissimulation. 'Yes, I had the same impression when I spoke to her on the phone,' she admitted with a chuckle.

'So?' He gave her a keen look. 'Are you talking about Aidan Cresney?'

'As a matter of fact,' she said candidly, 'I am. I take it you knew him.'

'I most certainly did.' His expression hardened. 'Forgive me if I'm speaking out of turn, but you don't seem to me the type of woman who would be susceptible to his brand of charm.'

Once again, she was taken aback by his directness. 'Whatever put that idea into your head?' she said. It was his turn to appear nonplussed and hers to press home the advantage. 'Could it be on account of the way he won the confidence of your sister-in-law and her daughter?'

'How in the world do you know about that?'

'Rosalie told me. I don't know if she's mentioned it to you, but she and her mother are both convinced Aidan's death was due to foul play and she came to ask me to try and find out how it happened.'

'Why on earth should she come to you?' To Melissa's astonishment, when she explained he burst out laughing. 'Miss Marple in the flesh!' he exclaimed. 'I don't believe it!'

'I'm not surprised. I was astounded when she suddenly turned up on our doorstep with such a bizarre request. My husband wants me to have nothing to do with it.'

There was a hint of condescension in his smile as he said, 'But you can't resist having a nosey round?'

'I'd decided to forget about Rosalie's notion until I saw the piece in the paper about your talk. Finn is an unusual name and . . . well, I have to confess that I'm a bit of an elephant's child.'

'With an insatiable curiosity? I see.' There was a further hint of condescension, this time in his voice, that had

Melissa revising her earlier impression. 'Well, what would you like to ask me?'

'First of all, there have been several references to the smell of bananas. Does that mean anything to you?'

'Indeed it does. A substance called isopentyl acetate is released when a bee is alarmed or agitated. I've never smelled it myself, but I'm told it has a sweetish, banana-like smell.'

'Is it a constituent of the venom?'

'No. Its purpose is to alert other bees to what it perceives as a threat to the colony.'

'So they smell it, and join in the attack.'

'That's right. I imagine that is what must have happened to Aidan Cresney.'

'It would be interesting to know what caused that first sting.'

Harold Finn shrugged. 'Who knows? One bee might have got trapped inside his veil and become angry and stung him whilst trying to get out.'

'And the smell would attract other bees?'

'It's quite likely.'

'Supposing someone found a way to reproduce that substance you mentioned – something or other acetate – synthetically, could that induce any bees within range of the smell to sting?'

'It would need access to some sophisticated laboratory facilities, but it would hardly be necessary. The stuff is readily available commercially.' He gave her a penetrating stare. 'Are you seriously suggesting someone might have used it to induce Aidan's bees to sting him?'

'All I'm asking you is, is it feasible?

Finn hesitated as though reluctant to commit himself.

Then he said, 'If you want my frank opinion, the whole notion is unreal and my niece and my sister-in-law are clutching at straws. That man had an almost hypnotic effect on them . . . in their eyes he could do no wrong. What they hope to achieve with this insane notion I simply can't imagine.'

'I take it you didn't share their admiration?'

Finn's light brown eyes, that had earlier been warm, gentle and full of kindly humour, became as hard as lumps of amber as he replied, 'I most certainly did not.'

18

There was an awkward pause, relieved by the arrival of the Honourable Mrs Cardew, who bore down on them with a purposeful expression on her aristocratic features and her hand on the arm of a timid-looking grey-haired woman.

'Mrs Martin, you have monopolised Doctor Finn long enough,' she pronounced in ringing tones. 'This lady has several questions she is simply *dying* to put to him before he has to tear himself away.' She took her hand from the woman's arm, put it in the small of her back and gave her a gentle push, like a teacher urging a reluctant pupil to step forward and recite a poem.

Melissa hastily fished out one of her business cards and offered it to the biochemist. 'I realise you're much in demand,' she said, 'but there are one or two other things I'd like to ask you. Would you be kind enough to give me a call . . . or perhaps let me have your phone number so that I could call you?'

'I'm not sure I can be of any further use in your quest, but I'll give it some thought,' he replied a little stiffly. He took the card and put it in his breast pocket, but did not offer one of his own in return.

'Thank you, I'd appreciate that,' she said, and moved aside to allow Mrs Cardew to introduce her protégée.

Having done so, the lady withdrew without a glance in Melissa's direction. Feeling a little lost, and realising that she was unlikely to learn anything else of interest, she decided she might as well go home. She was heading for the exit through the conservatory when Colin Palmer appeared with a bottle in one hand and a glass of wine in the other.

'How about a refill?' he said, waving the bottle in the direction of the empty glass she had just put down on the windowsill.

'No thanks, I'd better not as I'm driving,' she said.

'Fair enough.' He put the bottle down beside the glass. 'Were you thinking of leaving?'

'To be honest, I don't see any reason to hang about. I don't know anyone here and I'm not going to be allowed anywhere near Doctor Finn again.'

He grinned. 'I noticed the green dragon casting disapproving looks in your direction.'

'She decided I'd been monopolising the learned doctor for too long when someone else is *dying* to meet him,' she said in a fair imitation of their hostess's cut-glass accent.

Palmer gave an appreciative chuckle. 'She can't figure out why a non-beekeeper should want to attend one of our lectures,' he said. 'I explained that you're a neighbour of the late Aidan Cresney, but she didn't seem to consider that a valid reason.'

'Perhaps she suspects me of being a spy from a rival association,' Melissa suggested, and they both laughed.

'Did you learn anything useful, by the way?' he asked.

'Not really.' She repeated the gist of her conversation with Doctor Finn. 'I'd have liked a bit more time with him, but when her ladyship interrupted our *tête-à-tête* I had no option but to move over. Anyway, I gave him my card and said I'd

like to talk to him again if he'd be kind enough to call me.
I'm not holding my breath, though.'

'I'd be interested to know if he does come up with
anything.' Palmer finished his drink and held out a hand. 'I
think I'll push off now. It's been a pleasure meeting you,
Mrs Martin. Perhaps I'll see you again when I come to
collect Caroline's hives.'

'That would be nice,' she said. 'I've enjoyed talking to you
– and please call me Melissa.'

'Thank you, Melissa. I'm Colin.' He gave a polite little
half salute and moved away. Moments later, she too made
her escape.

'You gave him your address?' Iris pursed her lips and shook
her head in disapproval. 'Shouldn't have done that. Don't
think Joe would like it.'

'Why not? I'm not trying to start a relationship with the
man.'

'Don't be a goose. Didn't mean that.'

'What then? All I'm trying to do is find out whether
someone with the right expertise could–'

'That's the point,' Iris interrupted, 'the right expertise.
Someone like him, for example.' Her expression was
serious. 'I don't think you've been very bright, Mel.'

'You're saying . . . oh, good heavens!' Melissa clapped a
hand over her mouth. 'He didn't like Aidan; maybe he
distrusted his motives towards his niece and her mother the
way Joe and I did and decided to do something about it. If
anyone could do it, he could.'

'Exactly. Not like you to miss that.'

'You're right, especially as I knew beforehand that he
wasn't particularly well disposed towards Aidan Cresney.

But what about Sarah? Surely, he couldn't have had anything against her. She didn't even know the Finns.'

'She might not have known them by name, but she knew there was another woman in Aidan's life and so did Caroline. *And* they recognised Rosalie, or thought they did. Remember that snatch of conversation you overheard?'

'That's true,' Melissa admitted, 'but it would hardly be a motive for murder.'

Iris shrugged. 'Suppose not. Just a thought.'

Melissa fell silent, her brain working furiously.

'Penny for 'em,' said Iris after a few minutes.

'I was just thinking, if Sarah was killed because she knew about the Finns and started putting two and two together, then the same would apply to Caroline. She could be in danger as well.'

'That's a bit far-fetched. No reason to suppose they know about Uncle Finn and his chemistry set.'

'Just the same, it wouldn't do any harm to—'

Iris slapped her forehead in an exaggerated gesture of dismay. 'Why don't I keep quiet?' she lamented. 'Now you'll be even more determined to go on playing the detective. Look, Mel, why not drop it? It's no concern of yours. You've already admitted it could be coincidence, two deaths in similar circs.'

'I know, but that was before I met Doctor Finn. I'll have to think about it.' Melissa finished her drink of herbal tea and stood up. 'I must go now. Shall I see you tomorrow? Joe won't be home until the evening so we could go out somewhere if you like.'

'There's an exhibition of wild life paintings in the Cheltenham art gallery. French artist, neighbour of ours. I promised I'd try and get there.'

'Then let's do that. And how about a matinée at the Theatre Royal in Bath afterwards? They're doing a season of Restoration comedies.'

'Good idea!'

They arranged a time to set off in the morning and made their way to the front door. Just before she closed it behind Melissa, Iris said mischievously, 'If you get an unexpected package, listen for buzzing before you open it.'

When she returned to Hawthorn Cottage Melissa checked the answering machine and found a brief message from Joe to say he'd had an exhausting but profitable meeting with Selina Stitch and her American publisher and was looking forward to relaxing on the golf course with Paul the next day. She called him back at his hotel to tell him of her and Iris's plans. 'I'll get something out of the freezer for our dinner before we go. If you get back first, would you make a start on the veg?'

'Of course, love. Have a nice day.'

'You too.' She put down the phone feeling vaguely guilty at not having mentioned her visit to the beekeepers' meeting. She would have to tell him about it when he got home and it was not difficult to imagine his reaction.

She got ready for bed and tried to read for a while, but found it impossible to concentrate. She switched off the light and tried to sleep, but was unable to relax. Instead, she went over her conversation with Harold Finn again and again, seeing in her mind's eye the way his expression had hardened as he virtually admitted his dislike of Aidan Cresney. It should not have caused her any surprise; Rosalie had told her as much, and yet to hear it from the man himself seemed to bring it home much more forcefully. Was it possible that he had such a strong antipathy towards the man, such an obsessive fear of his malign influence on his sister-in-law and her daughter, that he had devised a particularly fiendish way of disposing of him? He undoubtedly had the scientific expertise . . . but it was one thing to know of a substance that would have the desired effect, quite another to make sure it reached its target. He would certainly have needed an accomplice.

Caroline? There seemed little doubt that her marriage was far from happy, but to bring about such a terrible end would call for a destructive, bitter hatred of the intended victim. She was certainly liable to sudden flashes of rage – witness the torn photograph – but was she capable of conniving in such a cold-blooded plot? Even if she was, would she be likely to enter into some kind of unholy alliance with a relative of a woman she suspected of being her husband's lover? And if Finn was indeed Aidan's killer, was it likely that he would go on to murder the brother's wife? Which led to yet another question: was Sarah indeed murdered, or was her death in a similar manner to Aidan's a grotesque coincidence? And finally, was either death a case of murder, or were they both merely tragic accidents?

The questions revolved ceaselessly in Melissa's head until, in desperation, she switched on the light, reached for the notepad and pencil that she kept permanently on her bedside table and made a detailed list of possible lines of enquiry. Only then was she able to settle down to sleep.

After spending an hour at the exhibition, Iris and Melissa set off for Bath. They had lunch before the matinée and afterwards went to the Pump Room for tea. On the way back, traffic on the A46 was heavy and it was a little after seven o'clock when they reached home.

'Want to join me for a veggie burger?' said Iris as she unlocked her front door.

'Thanks, but I've taken something out of the freezer and Joe will have already got things on the go for dinner. Why don't you come round for a drink and coffee later on? Say about eight thirty.'

'Thanks. Will do.'

Joe greeted Melissa with a hug and a kiss to which she eagerly responded. 'Had a good day, darling?' he asked.

'Lovely, thanks. How about you? And how's Paul?'

'He's fine. We had a good game of golf and guess what, I did a hole in one!'

'Brilliant! Iris is coming for a drink after dinner. Why don't we crack a bottle of bubbly to celebrate?'

'Why not? By the way, there was a call for you just before you got home. A Doctor Harold Finn. He'd like you to call him back; I've made a note of the number.'

'Ah!' Melissa hesitated and then said, 'He's a biochemist. I met him yesterday evening at a meeting of the Stowbridge Beekeepers' Association.'

'What on earth were you doing there?'

'I saw a notice in the paper that said he was going to give a talk on the chemistry of beekeeping. I wondered if I might learn something that could explain why the bees attacked Aidan.'

'So that's what you were up to when I phoned last night. I might have known you wouldn't be able to leave it alone. Did you learn anything useful?'

'Not a lot, because we were interrupted. That's why I gave him my phone number and asked if he'd be kind enough to call me.'

'Well, you'd better call him back while I get on with the dinner.'

'Right, I'll do it from the study.'

When Doctor Finn answered the telephone Melissa was immediately struck by a change in his attitude. From being stiff and aloof, he sounded positively cordial and at the same time apologetic.

'Mrs Martin,' he said, 'I have spoken to my niece and she confirms that you are indeed Mel Craig, the crime writer and that she asked you to carry out some kind of investigation on her behalf. It's quite a preposterous notion, of course, as I've impressed on her. I think she's now prepared to accept my advice and forget about it.'

'That's good news,' Melissa said. 'I have to admit I thought at the time it seemed a bit ridiculous, but the poor girl was so distressed I didn't have the heart to turn her down flat. I couldn't for the life of me see how I could help, but when I saw your name and the subject of your talk in the paper, I couldn't resist taking the opportunity of meeting you. I'm still curious to know whether you think there's any possibility that . . . well, that anyone could actually induce bees to sting someone to death.'

'I dare say you had some notion of using the idea in a plot?' Doctor Finn said with the familiar touch of condescension.

'I have been considering it,' she said, mentally crossing her fingers.

'To be honest, I think it would be virtually impossible to create a credible story out of such a situation,' he said emphatically. 'I'm sorry to disappoint you, but you did seek my professional opinion, and I have given it to you.'

'Well, thank you very much anyway. I find it's always as well to get expert advice about feasibility before becoming too involved in a plot.'

'Very sensible. I'm sure you'll soon think of another one.'

'I hope so. It was good of you to call.'

'Not at all,' he replied and put down the phone.

When she went back downstairs Joe said, 'So what was that all about?' He listened intently while she brought him up to date. When she had finished he said, 'I can't believe you're seriously thinking of using Aidan's death in a plot.'

She burst out laughing. 'Of course I'm not, silly. It was Finn, thinking he'd uncovered my true motive in asking all those questions. It seemed to make sense to let him run with it.'

There was no answering laughter from Joe. 'I just hope you'll keep it that way,' he said earnestly. 'If there is anything suspicious about either of those deaths and it becomes known that you're going round asking leading questions, you could be at risk yourself.'

'So you do think there's something fishy about Finn? Oops, sorry! No pun intended.'

This time he could not restrain a smile. 'All I'm saying is we still don't know, and I'd rather you didn't stick your neck out. Just the same,' he added resignedly, 'knowing you, I can't see you being put off as easily as that.'

19

Later that evening, while Joe was in the kitchen opening the champagne, Melissa took the opportunity of telling Iris about Finn's telephone call and his assumption that her attendance at his talk and subsequent questions were part of her programme of research for a possible crime novel.

'So after you buttonholed him on Friday he went and checked with his niece,' Iris commented. 'That's interesting.'

'Why do you say that?'

'Could be he found your questions disturbing and wanted to know what she'd been saying to you.'

'It's more likely he was concerned on her behalf. He said he hoped he'd been successful in allaying her suspicions over Aidan's death. I think he's been seriously worried about her and her mother.'

'Or worried about himself? If he has been up to no good, the knowledge that the Sherlock Holmes of Upper Benbury is on his tail might interfere with his sleep.' Iris's flippant words were at odds with the serious expression in her eyes. 'Think you should still be on your guard, Mel.'

'Oh, for goodness' sake, you're getting paranoid,' said Melissa in exasperation.

'Just don't want you to come to any harm, that's all,' her friend said gruffly.

'I know, thanks.' Melissa touched her on the arm in a gesture of appreciation of her concern. 'That sounds promising,' she added as a loud 'pop' came from the kitchen. 'By the way, I've already talked it all over with Joe and he's had it up to here, so please don't refer to it again for now.'

Iris opened her mouth as if to say something further, but closed it again as Joe appeared with a tray of glasses in one hand and a bottle of champagne in the other. 'I hope you're not dying of thirst,' he said. 'It was rather an obstinate cork.'

The three spent a convivial evening, toasting Joe's hole in one, his profitable negotiations with Selina Stitch's American publisher, the continuing success of Jack and Iris's enterprise and anything else they could think of. By tacit agreement, there was no further reference to the Finns or the Cresneys.

When Caroline turned up in church the following morning she glanced hopefully towards the pew where Joe, Melissa, Sylvia and Iris were sitting. She looked disappointed on seeing that it was full, but gave a shy smile in response to their greeting and sat down in the empty pew in front of them. It was noticeable that no one else looked in her direction, and although the church was fairly full, no one came to sit beside her. As usual after the service, a number of people stood in groups chatting in the warm September sunshine but, apart from the rector and his wife, no one gave Caroline more than the briefest of greetings. A few glanced her way and then averted their eyes rather than meet hers. It was left to the Martins' little party to walk with her along the path to the church gate.

'How's the tum?' asked Iris. 'No more upsets I hope?'

'Oh, no, thank goodness.' Caroline spoke hesitantly. Her eyes were cast down and Melissa had the impression that she was hurt by the coolness of so many of her neighbours. 'I don't know what you must have thought of me,' she said. 'I felt so ashamed of myself.'

'No need. We all have our *bête noire*,' said Iris. 'Mine's meat; can't stand the beastly stuff. One whiff of it makes me want to puke.'

'You must come to tea again soon,' said Sylvia, 'and I promise I won't offer you banana cake.'

At the mention of the word banana, Caroline winced. She was plainly still embarrassed by the memory of the incident, but she managed a smile and said, 'Thank you, I'd like that.'

As they parted at the church gate, Melissa said casually, 'How are things going? Is Digby Morrison looking after you properly?'

'He's being very helpful, but there's a bit of a delay. He's waiting to hear again from Aidan's solicitor – something to do with probate, he said, but I don't really understand legal matters I'm afraid.'

'Well, these things always take time. I'm sure he'll do his best for you.'

'That's strange,' Sylvia remarked after they separated from Caroline.

'What is?' asked Joe.

'All that talk about delay and waiting for probate. When Frank died, Mr Bell had it all settled very quickly. He said it's always straightforward when a husband leaves everything to his wife – or the other way round, of course.'

'It doesn't follow that Aidan left everything to Caroline,' Melissa pointed out.

'Oh, but he did, she told me so the other afternoon when she came for tea, before you arrived. She said Aidan made a will doing just that before they were married. Her father was alive at the time, and he insisted on it.'

'He must have been a pretty tough egg to be able to stand up to Aidan,' Melissa commented. 'Did she actually see the will?'

'Oh, yes, and there was a copy in his filing cabinet. I imagine his solicitor has the original.'

'Maybe Aidan added a codicil, or even made a new will, without telling her?' suggested Joe. 'He was something of a law unto himself, by all accounts, and we know they weren't exactly a close couple.'

'But why would he do that, I wonder?' For the rest of the walk home, Sylvia was silent. It wasn't until they were back in the kitchen of Hawthorn Cottage, where it had already been arranged that the four of them would have Sunday lunch, that she suddenly said, 'Do you suppose he might have left anything to that young woman who called on you after the funeral?'

Melissa was so startled by the question that she almost dropped the tray of ice she had just taken out of the freezer, while Joe paused in the act of pouring pre-lunch drinks and said, 'Whatever gave you that idea?'

'Well, you said she came to see you after the service because she wanted to tell you how much she liked your books, but what was she doing there in the first place?'

'I told you, she was a friend of the family.'

'You didn't say anything about the family. If I remember rightly' – here Sylvia fixed her daughter with an accusatory gleam in her eyes – 'you managed to change the subject very quickly.'

'I don't remember doing that,' Melissa protested weakly. 'Anyway, what are you suggesting?'

'I thought perhaps' – here Sylvia turned a little pink – 'maybe it's rather naughty of me to think of it, but do you suppose she's his daughter . . . I mean his illegitimate daughter?'

'Actually, she isn't,' said Joe. 'She told us she came to the funeral to pay her respects on behalf of herself and her mother because Aidan had been very helpful to them over a claim for compensation following the death of her father. He was still a practising barrister at the time. Then she recognised Mel and couldn't resist taking the opportunity of talking to her about her books.'

'So why did she have to come here? You could have had your chat when you all went back to the Manor.'

Melissa was trying to think of a convincing reason when Iris came to the rescue. 'Don't suppose Mel thought it was quite the thing in the circs,' she suggested.

'No, perhaps it wouldn't have been.' It was hard to tell from Sylvia's tone whether she accepted the explanation or was hurt at not having been taken into her daughter's confidence in the first place. She thought for a moment and then said, 'Why didn't her mother come as well?'

'According to Rosalie, she was too upset,' said Joe. 'She told us that she didn't have much grasp of practical matters and had been relying pretty heavily on Aidan to look after her affairs.'

'In that case, it could well be that he left something to the widow and her daughter without saying anything to Caroline,' Sylvia went on, reverting to her original idea.

'Yes, I suppose so,' said Joe, handing her a glass of sherry.

'I wouldn't worry about it, Sylvia. Digby will sort it all out for her.'

The next morning Iris left for London, leaving the Martins to deal with some paperwork that had accumulated while they were working on the final version of *A Long Way from Home.* They had arranged to set off for Pembrokeshire on Thursday and it was a relief that the intervening days passed without any call from Caroline. Melissa suggested, a little diffidently, that it might be kind to let the young widow know that they would be away for a short while, but Joe was adamant that she should do no such thing.

'Sylvia can be her mother hen while we're gone,' he said firmly. 'She'll enjoy that.'

'So long as Caroline doesn't tell her anything she doesn't want passed on,' she replied. 'You know how thick Mum is with Cynthia Thorne and co.'

'That's up to Caroline. You can't go on propping her up indefinitely.'

'I suppose not.'

'In any case I get the impression, give or take the odd wobbly when there's a crisis, that she's quite a strong character. She's probably inherited some of her father's genes.'

Accordingly they set off as planned for five blissful days in Pembrokeshire, walking the magnificent coastal paths, lazing on the beach and returning each evening to their hotel to enjoy the 'superb meals prepared from fresh local produce' of which it boasted in the brochure.

'That was like a second honeymoon,' said Melissa with a sigh of content as they got into the car to set off for home.

'And only just over a month after the first,' Joe replied.

'You know what, you're getting thoroughly spoilt. But as I'm feeling magnanimous, you can have another week or two pottering about at home before you write the next book.'

'Slave-driver!' she retorted in mock indignation. 'I'm not Barbara Cartland, you know, churning them out in a couple of weeks.'

'Can't have you sitting around indefinitely not earning your keep,' he said cheerfully.

'Now you're winding me up again.'

They had an uneventful drive home. Sylvia was working in her little front garden when they arrived; the minute she caught sight of them she dropped her trowel, pulled off her gloves and hurried over to greet them.

'I'm so pleased to see you back!' she exclaimed, giving each a quick hug. 'Did you have a lovely time? Hasn't the weather been gorgeous? I was just thinking about making a cup of tea,' she rattled on as she changed into her indoor shoes. 'Do come and have one with me before you start unpacking. You must be tired after your journey.'

'A cup of tea would be lovely,' said Joe. 'Give us five minutes to get our stuff indoors and then we'll be round.'

While Joe put the car away, Melissa checked the answering machine. The first message was from Caroline, who said in a slightly tremulous voice, 'Melissa, I hate to keep bothering you with my woes, but I've had some very disturbing news and I'd like your advice. Could you possibly call me back?'

'Bother!' said Melissa aloud. She gave the 'delete' button a vicious jab before listening to the rest of the messages. After a couple of non-urgent calls there was a further one from Caroline. 'Sorry, just learned that you're away. I'd still like to speak to you, but there's no rush.'

Melissa made a mental resolution not to mention either message to Joe, but any notion she had of responding to Caroline's request without letting him know was scotched very shortly after they sat down in Sylvia's sitting room.

'Do you remember what we were saying about that girl Rosalie, after church the Sunday before last?' Sylvia said as, having handed out cups of tea and home-made chocolate sponge, she settled in her favourite armchair. 'And how I suggested Aidan Cresney might have left her some money?' she went on without waiting for a response. 'Well, I was right! He did. Quite a lot, in fact.'

'How do you know all this?' asked Melissa.

'Cynthia Thorne told me.'

'How in the world did she find out?'

'She heard it from her cleaning lady.'

'That Mrs Wilson again! I swear she listens at keyholes. I thought I'd warned Caroline to be very careful when she's around. Now it'll be all over the village in no time.'

'We'll get the details tomorrow, when Gloria comes,' Joe observed dryly. 'The local cleaning ladies have their own bush telegraph; nothing seems to escape them.'

'Did you see Caroline while we were away, Mum?'

'Yes. She rang me up . . . she said she'd called you and you hadn't returned her call. Then Roger the postman told her you were away so she came to see me. She said she'd had some news from her solicitor that had been a bit of a shock.'

'Did she say what it was?'

'No, she backtracked as if she wished she hadn't mentioned it, and of course I didn't press her. I think she just wanted a friend to talk to.'

'I take it you didn't let on you'd heard about the legacy?'

'No, of course not. I invited her round for tea and we had a nice chat about her plans for the house. She'd cheered up a bit by the time she went home.'

'Well, I'm sure Digby will sort it out for her,' said Joe. Melissa, recognising the touch of impatience in his voice, guessed that he was becoming a little tired of hearing about Caroline's problems.

'I do feel sorry for her,' said Sylvia. 'The poor girl doesn't seem to have any close friends. You will let her know you're back, won't you, Lissie? I know she wants to have a proper talk with you.'

'I suppose I'll have to,' said Melissa, ignoring the negative signals coming from Joe's direction and at the same time trying not to sound too eager. She felt sure that there was more to be learned than the bare fact of the unexpected legacy, but she had no intention of letting him know just yet that her curiosity was rapidly coming back to the boil.

20

'You'll never guess what!' said Gloria as she took off her jacket and donned a brightly coloured, close-fitting overall that showed her generous breasts to maximum advantage. Her round cheeks were pink with excitement. 'That Mr Cresney what got stung to death by they bees has left half his fortune to his lady friend!'

Melissa and her husband exchanged resigned glances. 'And how did you come by what is doubtless a highly confidential piece of information?' asked Joe.

As usual, Gloria was momentarily nonplussed by his phraseology, but having grasped the meaning behind it she was quick to deny any suggestion of indiscretion on her part. 'It were Mrs Wilson what told her Billy and he told my Stanley in the Woolpack the other night.'

'And what was the source of Mrs Wilson's information? You surely don't believe that Mrs Cresney confided in her personally?'

After taking a moment to figure this out, Gloria said, 'Don't know how else she could've known, Mrs Wilson I mean. Maybe Mrs Cresney were so upset she had to tell someone.'

'I think it's more likely that Mrs Wilson has been eavesdropping, and I strongly advise you not to repeat anything she tells you,' said Joe severely. 'I know my wife has warned you before against spreading unsubstantiated rumours.'

'It weren't me she told, and I haven't said nothing to no one else,' Gloria asserted with an air of slightly pained virtue. 'I just thought, seeing as you're a friend of hers, Mrs Craig . . . sorry, Mrs Martin, you should know what folks be saying.'

'Thank you, Gloria.' Despite the seriousness of the situation, Melissa found it difficult to conceal her amusement at such artlessness. 'But you must promise me not to tell anyone else,' she went on. 'Mrs Cresney's having a difficult enough time as it is.'

'Cross my heart,' said Gloria earnestly. 'Well, I'd best be getting on. Bathroom first as usual?' Without waiting for a reply, she gathered up the cleaning equipment she had been assembling and disappeared upstairs.

The minute she was out of earshot Melissa said, 'Joe, you are naughty to baffle the poor girl with all those long words!' She tried to sound reproachful but could not restrain a giggle.

'Sorry, can't resist it,' he chuckled. 'It's worth it just to see the look on her face while she's working it out. Not much point in extracting that promise, was there?' he added, turning serious again. 'The damage has already been done.'

'I'd like know how that woman found out,' she said. 'I think I'll give Caroline a call, and maybe pop up and see her. Don't look like that,' she pleaded, seeing his expression of disapproval. 'She did say she wanted to talk to me, and it would look very rude if I didn't respond. Besides, it's only fair to warn her what's being said.'

'I suppose so,' he admitted. 'I just don't want her on your back all the time.'

'You mean you don't want her distracting me when I'm

supposed to be thinking about the next best-seller,' she retorted as she picked up the phone and tapped out Caroline's number.

He pulled a face at her and she blew him a kiss in return.

'It's so good of you to come, Melissa,' said Caroline. 'Would you like some coffee?'

'No, thank you. I really can't stay long, but you sounded a bit wound up when we spoke on the phone, so I–'

Caroline cut her short with an impatient gesture and said, 'Well, at least come in for a few minutes.' Melissa followed her into the sitting room; as they sat down in the two armchairs facing the window she recalled her first visit, when the young widow had been distraught with an emotion that she had at first assumed to be grief.

'I expect your mother has told you I've had some surprising news from Mr Morrison?' Caroline began.

'Yes, but she didn't say what it was.'

'I didn't tell her because, well, I know she's friendly with Cynthia Thorne and–' Caroline broke off and looked uncomfortable.

'I'm sure Mum would never repeat anything she learned in confidence,' said Melissa, hoping it was true.

'No, I'm sure she wouldn't, but . . . anyway, I'd like to tell you.' Without waiting for Melissa to say anything she went on, 'I had a letter telling me Aidan had made another will that I didn't know about, leaving quite a lot of money to another woman.'

'Really?' said Melissa, hoping that her tone of surprise sounded convincing. 'That must have come as a shock. Is it anyone you know?'

'Oh, yes, at least, someone I know *of*.' Caroline gave a

short, bitter laugh. 'It's a woman he'd been having an affair with for at least a couple of years.'

'Good heavens!' Melissa's mind went racing back to Gloria's tale of the make-up stains on the shirt. 'Did you know about it?' Caroline nodded. 'Did Aidan know he'd been rumbled?'

'Oh, yes, but he didn't care. I'd had my suspicions for some time, so I hired a private detective to keep an eye on him. When I faced him with it, he wasn't in the least put out. All he said was, "You may as well accept that I've no intention of ending the relationship and I wouldn't even think about a divorce if I were you. It would not be to your advantage."'

'What do you suppose he meant by that?'

Caroline stood up and began moving restlessly round the room, aimlessly fiddling with ornaments and straightening the magazines on the coffee table. Then she went to the window and stared out at the garden. Eventually she said in a low voice and without turning round, 'Like a fool, I'd given him control over most of my financial affairs. I still trusted him in those days, you see, and I was quite happy to sign any piece of paper he put in front of me. I was even still in love with him, although I find that hard to believe now. Anyway, he took great pleasure in explaining that he'd tied everything up so effectively that it would cost me more than the money I still had control over to get it unscrambled.' She swung round, dropped back into her armchair and dabbed her eyes with a handkerchief. 'He was determined to keep his precious reputation unsullied no matter what he got up to on the quiet.'

'Is that what he said?'

'More or less.' Caroline gave a helpless shrug. 'I fretted

about it for ages, but in the end I decided I had no choice but to make the best of the situation. He didn't make many physical demands on me, I had a comfortable lifestyle, I had my bridge-playing friends, and quite a lot of freedom to do what I liked, provided it didn't interfere with anything he wanted me to do. Sarah and I were, well, not exactly close, but we had quite a lot in common . . . in addition to having Aidan rule our lives, that is.' Her lips twisted in an ironic smile on the final words.

'Yes, I remember how the pair of you used to come on some of our WI outings to the theatre and so on,' said Melissa. 'You always seemed to enjoy them.'

'Oh, yes, we did – until Aidan put a stop to it. He hated us "hobnobbing with the villagers" as he called it. And he was determined that news of Quentin's matrimonial escapades remained a secret once he was reunited with Sarah.' Fresh tears welled into Caroline's eyes. 'I'm really going to miss Sarah.'

'I'm sure you are.' Melissa leaned forward to put a consoling hand on her arm. After a pause she said, 'I assume her funeral went off all right?'

'So far as I know. I was given to understand that my presence would not be welcome. I'm not surprised you find that shocking,' she went on as Melissa's jaw dropped. 'Quentin and Poppy have made it quite clear that they share my wish to sever relations, but I never expected them to go that far.'

'You've met Poppy?'

Caroline bit her lip and hesitated for a moment before replying and Melissa sensed that for some reason she had touched a raw nerve. 'She was a member of Quentin's congregation, before we moved down here.'

'So you and Aidan used to attend his church?'

'Of course. I don't know how many people were aware of it, but Aidan was the power behind the pulpit, so to speak.' She gave a fleeting smile at her own witticism. 'He even used to vet all his brother's sermons.'

'It's a wonder Quentin ever plucked up enough courage to break away.'

'That was Poppy's doing, of course. She's a very strong character.'

But not strong enough to keep him when Aidan decided otherwise, thought Melissa. Aloud, she said, 'So, what are your immediate plans – I mean, apart from getting the finances sorted out? Will you be able to go ahead with the alterations to the house to accommodate your mother and sister?'

'Oh, yes, that won't be a problem. Mother will help to pay for them. Actually, I'm going to spend a couple of days with her and Jennie so that I'm out of the way when Quentin comes to collect the rest of his stuff. Some of the things in the other part of the house belonged to Aidan, so I've moved them out. It's not that they have any sentimental value for me; I just want to make sure he doesn't pinch anything he's not entitled to.' Caroline was practically grinding her teeth in suppressed fury as she muttered, almost under her breath, 'I can't believe that creature and I were ever friends.'

'It seemed to everyone that after Quentin appeared on the scene you all sort of retreated into your shell,' Melissa remarked. 'I think everyone assumed that now you were one big happy family you had no further need of outside contacts.'

Caroline gave another staccato, mirthless laugh. 'If you only knew!'

There was a slightly awkward silence before Melissa said, 'Anyway, have you decided what you're going to do about this bequest Aidan's made? What does Digby say about it?'

'I haven't made up my mind yet. He says if I contest the new will there's a fifty-fifty chance of getting the amount of the legacy reduced, but the reduction could well be swallowed up in costs. Knowing Aidan, he's quite likely ring-fenced it pretty effectively to make sure that's exactly the situation.'

'What do you know about the woman he's left the money to?'

'Not a lot, except that she's a widow with a daughter – I wouldn't be surprised if he's got his eye on the girl as well. He always fancied younger women; that's why he married me, but of course I'm not so young any more.'

'You've met her?'

'She actually had the cheek to turn up for his funeral. You might have noticed a woman in black sniffling into her handkerchief at the back of the church.'

'Yes, we did notice her,' Melissa said guardedly. 'Are you sure that's who she was?'

'Who else could she have been? There can't be many people who shed tears at his passing.' Her voice throbbed with such intensity that Melissa felt a prickle of gooseflesh. Once again the possibility of collusion between Caroline and Harold Finn came back to mind. If that were indeed the case, how had it come about? Just how detailed had the private detective's investigation been? She would have given a lot to know the answers to these and many other questions.

She glanced at her watch and stood up. 'I really must go now, Caroline, but please let me know if there's anything more I can do.'

'You can go on being my friend,' said Caroline earnestly. Impulsively, she gave Melissa a hug and kissed her on the cheek. 'Thank you for listening.'

'No problem.' As Caroline opened the front door, Melissa said, 'Speaking of listening, I think it's only fair to tell you that your cleaning lady seems to have overheard some of your phone conversations. I did warn you, didn't I, that she has rather an inventive mind and a tendency to gossip.'

'You certainly did and I've been very careful ever since.' Caroline looked suddenly anxious. 'What has she been saying?'

'I'm afraid she's found out about the legacy.'

Caroline's face registered a mixture of horror and disbelief. 'But how could she possibly–' she began, and then put both hands over her eyes. 'The letter!' she groaned. 'She must have seen thc letter!'

'What letter?'

'The letter from Digby Morrison.'

'The one about the legacy to Aidan's mistress?'

'It didn't actually mention a name, just that Aidan had added a codicil to his will leaving a legacy to another person and suggesting I make an appointment to go and see him to discuss it. I'd just been reading it when a delivery man came to the front door with a parcel. I was about to sign for it when I realised it was for Quentin, not for me, so I went into the study for a piece of paper to write down his new address. I must have left the letter on the kitchen table.'

'Was Mrs Wilson in the room?'

'No, she'd gone upstairs. The nosey old bitch must have come back to fetch something, spotted the letter and read it. I suppose she's gone round telling everyone . . . and no doubt embroidering it in the telling.' Caroline clenched her fists and pressed them to her eyes. 'Now everyone will think it was my fault that Aidan got stung by those accursed bees,' she moaned. 'Oh, dear God, what am I going to do? They'll say I killed him out of jealousy, but how was I to know?'

'Know what?'

Caroline's only answer was to burst into tears.

21

When Melissa returned home a little after midday she found Joe in the kitchen, washing his hands at the sink.

'I thought I'd take a morning off from being a literary agent to do a spot of gardening,' he remarked as she entered. 'Gloria left early, by the way. She had to take one of her kids to the dentist.'

'Fair enough. I put her money in the drawer – did you find it?'

'Sure.' He gave her a questioning look. 'You're looking very serious; is Caroline all right? You've been a heck of a time.'

'I didn't mean to stay so long, but she threw another wobbly and it took me ages to calm her down. She was reasonably controlled at first, although she didn't attempt to hide her fury at what Aidan's done.'

'So it's true he's left a legacy to Rosalie?'

'So it seems.'

'No wonder she's upset; it must have been a shock to find out what he'd been up to.'

'It's not the affair that upset her; she already knew about that.' Joe listened in astonishment as Melissa related the latest chapter in the saga of manipulation and deception behind the façade the Cresneys had presented to the world.

'No wonder it came as a shock to see Rosalie at the funeral,' he commented.

'She was practically incandescent when she got to that point. She said he's always fancied young girls.'

'That bears out what we were saying about him, doesn't it?'

'And explains Uncle Harold's hostility.'

'Do you think Caroline knows the background to the relationship?'

Melissa shook her head. 'I wouldn't think so. She certainly never referred to the death of Rosalie's father or Aidan's part in getting compensation for the mother.'

'I take it you didn't let on that Rosalie had paid us a visit?'

'What do you think?'

'So what happened to bring on another outburst?'

'In a way, it was my fault. Just as I was ready to leave I told her that news of the legacy had got out, probably via Mrs Big-mouth Wilson.'

Joe looked dubious. 'Do you think that was wise?'

'I hated doing it, but knowing that sooner or later someone like Cynthia Thorne was bound to make some sly comment in her hearing, I thought it best that she should be forewarned.'

'How did she take it?'

'She practically went berserk, saying everyone would think it was her fault Aidan got stung and she'd killed him out of jealousy. And then she said, "How was I to know?" and "What am I going to do?"'

'How was she to know what?'

'She didn't say. She was really quite beside herself; I was afraid for a moment she was going to pass out or have a fit or something. In the end I gave her a slug of brandy and stayed with her until she'd pulled herself together. Incidentally, it seems Mrs Wilson got hold of the story by reading a letter Caroline had left lying about, but the interesting thing is, it didn't mention any names, only that Aidan had added a codicil to his will leaving a legacy to someone Digby referred to very discreetly as "another person".'

'And the old witch put her own spin on the story when passing it on, I suppose.'

'Something like that.'

'How come Caroline knew nothing about the codicil?'

'Probably because Aidan was crafty enough not to have it added to the copy he kept at home. The original was probably with his solicitor.'

'Well, you can understand Caroline being upset, can't you? Do you think she's all right to be left on her own?' Joe's earlier reservations over Melissa's involvement gave way to neighbourly concern. 'She won't do anything foolish, will she?'

'I hope not. I was a bit hesitant about leaving her, but once she'd stopped crying she started looking at the clock and saying she'd taken up too much of my time already and wouldn't you be wondering where I'd got to.'

'Why don't you ask her round for a meal this evening? She'd be better for a bit of company.'

'What a nice idea. I'll do that right away.' She called Caroline's number; it rang several times and then the answering service cut in. Melissa issued the invitation and hung up. 'I wonder why she didn't reply,' she said with a worried frown.

'Well, there's not much we can do for the moment.' Joe glanced at the clock. 'I'm getting peckish after all that manual labour. What are we having for lunch?'

'How about quiche and some salad?'

'Fine.'

Melissa had only just finished preparing the salad when the telephone rang. It was Caroline, responding to her message.

'I gather she's accepted,' said Joe when she put the phone down.

'Oh yes; she sounded a bit shaky, but quite keen to come.'

'Good. Now let's get on with our food.'

When they had finished eating, Melissa cleared the table while Joe brewed coffee. At his suggestion, they drank it while strolling round the garden so that she could admire the result of his morning's work. As she watched the honey bees busily taking nectar from the runner beans for which, despite the loss of a sizeable chunk of her vegetable plot, she had managed to find a space, Caroline's insistence that she return home came back into her mind.

'I wonder,' she said slowly, 'whether Caroline wanted me out of the way so that she could make a phone call.'

Joe gave her a slightly puzzled look. 'Do you have someone in mind?'

'That call I overheard the day I went to see Caroline to offer condolences.'

'What about it?'

'I still think it's odd there was no mention of the cause of Aidan's death.'

'We went over all this at the time. She may have said in her earlier message that he'd been badly stung, without actually saying it was fatal.'

'I suppose that must have been it,' Melissa said, but she was only partially convinced. 'There's no doubt she's been terrified of what people will think, ever since Sarah died.'

'But isn't that because she didn't want the story of Quentin's multiple marriages to get out and let the world know what a hard-nosed, Machiavellian character she'd married?'

'It was also because she was afraid people would think there was something suspicious about a second death,' she reminded him. 'And now the secret of Saint Aidan's bit on the side is as good as out, she probably wanted to tell this person about it as soon as possible.'

'There you are then. Why should it be significant? Maybe it's an old friend, or a relative? After all, we really know hardly anything about the woman. It could be anyone.'

'That's true, but I'd like to know why, if she's that close to whoever it is, it's me she turns to every time for comfort, as if she's got no one else to confide in.'

'Because you're on the doorstep?' Joe suggested. 'The other person may live miles away. Abroad, even. Anyway, this is pure guesswork. You don't know that was the reason she wanted to be on her own.'

'I suppose not.' Melissa continued to wander round the garden, but the flowers no longer held her attention. She found herself once more mulling over the sequence of events that began with Aidan's death. Whilst recognising that each separate example of apparently irrational behaviour on Caroline's part was capable of a perfectly reasonable explanation, she could not help seeing them as part of a sinister chain. Was it possible that Caroline, after her discovery of Aidan's affair – or supposed affair – with Rosalie, had somehow learned of her uncle's objections to the liaison and made contact with him? Had the two of them then conspired to rid their lives of someone they both had cause to hate?

Harold Finn had confirmed that the chemical contained in the stinging pheromone was readily available. Whilst not showing any particular unease at the reason she gave for her enquiry – on the contrary, he had appeared to find it amusing – he had taken the trouble to check her story and, after concluding that it was part of some research she was carrying out for a mystery novel, telephoned her to say that her supposed plot was not feasible. There had, too, been a noticeable change in his manner, which had become quite amiable instead of somewhat supercilious. Was this his genuine opinion, or an attempt to put her off the scent?

Joe broke into her reflections by relieving her of her empty coffee mug. 'I have a feeling that you're still having serious doubts about this business,' he said after she declined his offer of a refill.

'I suppose I am,' she admitted.

'Are you sure you're not being influenced by all the gossip and innuendo that's flying around?'

'Of course I'm not. I have this feeling that in spite of the way Caroline keeps saying how much she values me as a *confidante*, there are things that she isn't telling me. It's as if she's carrying a burden of guilt that she daren't reveal, even to me. I'd give a lot to know what she was referring to when she blurted out, "How was I to know?" She must have something on her conscience.'

'You're thinking of that stuff that induces bees to sting?'

'Stinging pheromones? Yes. How about this for a scenario?' Suddenly, Melissa found a theory taking shape in her brain. 'Aidan decides he wants to take up beekeeping as a retirement hobby. Caroline hates the idea; she's scared stiff of bees and tries to talk him out of it. From what we've recently learned about Aidan, that would simply add to his determination to go ahead. In the meantime she's found out about Rosalie Finn. Maybe she was covering up when she led me to believe that she accepted the situation. Maybe she's learned through her private eye about the rift the affair has caused in the Finn family. She makes contact with Uncle Harold, maybe to enlist his help in putting a stop to it. He doesn't hold out any hope on that score, but when she learns he's a scientist with an extensive knowledge of bee chemistry it sets her mind working in a different direction: can he suggest a way of giving Aidan the fright of his life by inducing his bees to attack him so that he'll be only too ready to get rid of his hives? She asks Finn about it and he gives her some stuff that will do the trick if she manages somehow to get it on him or his clothes. What she doesn't bargain for is that the multiple stings will actually kill him. That could account for her saying, "How was I to know?" couldn't it?'

Joe looked doubtful. 'I suppose so, but it sounds pretty far-fetched. After all, no one could have known that Aidan would suffer such a violent and immediate reaction to bee venom.'

'But you reckon it could happen?'

'I suppose it could, but why would Finn be so ready to play ball with Caroline? Making Aidan give up beekeeping wouldn't be of any advantage to him.'

'No, but maybe he calculated that if he were to die of the stings it would rescue Rosalie from his clutches. And remember,' Melissa went on, warming to her theory, 'Rosalie was absolutely certain that Aidan would never take any risks when handling the bees.'

'I don't think we can attach much importance to Rosalie's opinion. And anyway, where would Caroline have got the idea? She's hardly likely to have known anything about these what d'you call 'em . . . stinging pheromones, is she?'

'We can't be sure of that. Aidan probably had loads of books on beekeeping; she might have got it from reading one of them. It might even have been one of Harold Finn's own books – he's sure to have written some. That would explain how she came to contact him in the first place.' Once again, Melissa felt a surge of adrenalin. 'She'd already discovered that Aidan was having it off with a girl called Rosalie Finn; then she comes across a book by someone with the same name and makes the same con-nection as I did.'

Joe thought for a while before saying, 'Like I said, it seems pretty far-fetched, but if it were true it would certainly explain a lot. Yes, it might have happened like that, but I don't suppose we'll ever know.'

'Unless we can find some proof.'

'We?' Joe looked alarmed. 'Hang on a minute! You weren't thinking of taking this a stage further, were you?'

'Er, yes, I suppose I was,' she admitted. 'It's almost like a problem I've had with one of my mystery novels. Now and again I'd find my plot thickening so much I couldn't see my way forward and I'd spend ages trying to get it moving again. I've got the same feeling about this.'

'Mel, you promised–'

'I didn't actually *promise*.' She sidled up to him, put her arm through his and gave it a squeeze. 'Just give me a few days to ferret around,' she coaxed. 'You did say you weren't expecting me to start on another book for a week or two.'

Despite his attempt to look severe, his face relaxed into a smile. He dropped a kiss on her forehead and said softly,

'You are the most infuriating woman, but . . . all right. Tell you what,' he went on, 'why don't we do a spot of sleuthing together? At least it would enable me to keep tabs on you!'

'Great!' She tugged on his arm and dragged him back to the house. 'Come on, let's work out a plan of campaign.'

The click of the front door as she closed it behind Melissa reverberated in Caroline's head like a funeral knell and then died away into a deathly silence that permeated the empty house. She stood with her hand on the latch, black despair filling her mind. She tried to think, but shock and fear had numbed her brain.

She had no idea how long she had been standing there when the telephone rang. The sound made her jump and tremble; was this first of a series of abusive, probably anonymous, calls? She remained motionless while the ringing persisted for what seemed an eternity before it ceased as the answering machine cut in and she heard Melissa's voice saying, 'I hope I'm not disturbing you if you're having a lie down. I just wanted to check you're okay and to ask if you'd like to have a meal with us this evening, say about seven o'clock. Bye.'

A sob of relief almost choked her; at least there was one person – no two, three if she counted Sylvia – who did not judge her. The thought restored the power of movement to limbs that had felt paralysed; she went slowly up to her room and sat down on the edge of the bed. After a while she went into the bathroom to wash her face and tidy her hair before picking up the telephone to respond to Melissa's call.

'Yes, please, I'd love to come,' she said, aware that her voice was weak and unsteady, and added, 'you're all so kind to me,' before putting down the phone as another gush of emotion overwhelmed her.

She lay down on the bed and closed her eyes. After a while, she became calmer and her brain began to function again. She sat up and reached once more for the telephone.

22

Joe fetched a notebook from the study and they sat down at the kitchen table. 'So, where do we start?' he said, pencil poised over a blank sheet.

'I was hoping you had some ideas,' said Melissa. 'It was your suggestion that we join forces.'

'All right, let's begin by eliminating the things we can't do.'

'Such as?'

He drew a vertical line down the page to divide it into two columns and wrote a plus sign at the top of one and a minus sign on the other. He wrote 'Talk to Caroline' in the minus column. 'You can't very well question her without letting on that you think there's something fishy about Aidan's death, can you?' he said.

'That's true. What about Rosalie . . . or her mother?'

He shook his head. 'Not a good idea. If, as it appears, the family breach has been healed, it would almost certainly get back to Uncle Harold, and if he's mixed up in all this he's the last person we want to know what we're doing.' He added 'the Finn family' to the minus list. 'Right, let's think of some people we can talk to.'

'What about Colin Palmer? A beekeeper friend of Aidan's,' she explained as he raised an eyebrow. 'I got chatting to him at the meeting I went to while you were away.

He's been looking after Aidan's hives so it's possible he's known the family for quite a long time.'

'What were you thinking of asking him?'

'We know Aidan was always very meticulous about wearing his protective outfit when tending the bees. I was wondering whether he had ever mentioned having been stung at some time in the past and suffering a strong reaction to it.'

'You're suggesting that if that was the case then Caroline would have known about it as well?'

'Why not? It might have put the idea into her head.'

'But would he be likely to choose beekeeping as a hobby if he'd already had a bad experience with bees?' Joe looked doubtful. 'It seems a very long shot, but I suppose it wouldn't do any harm to ask.' He wrote Colin Palmer's name in the plus column.

'And I could ask Doctor Charman the same question,' Melissa went on.

'Ye . . . es.' Joe added the name with a question mark beside it. 'Don't you think, though, that if he knew Aidan was allergic to stings it would have come out at the inquest?'

'Maybe the coroner didn't ask him. Anyway, if it had happened before the family came to live here he might not have known about it.'

'Probably not, but I'll leave him on the list for the time being.'

Melissa looked over his shoulder and frowned. 'It's not a very promising list, is it? I mean, even if we got positive answers from them both, it wouldn't get us any further forward. I know!' she added in a flash of inspiration. 'What about Caroline's private detective?'

'The one she hired to tail Aidan when she suspected him of having an affair?'

'That's right.'

'You know who he is?'

'No, but I can ask her. I'll say it's for some research I'm doing for a new mystery novel.'

'But you've given up writing mysteries. Everyone knows that.'

'All right, so I tell her I've changed my mind and decided to do another one. I can say it's by popular demand. You can back me up; say you've advised me to do it in response to a stream of requests from frustrated fans. Well, there have been quite a few, haven't there?' she added, seeing his eyebrows lift.

'Let's say, a trickle,' he conceded. 'Anyway, your idea's worth a try, I suppose.' He added 'private eye' to the plus list. 'What do you hope to get out of him?'

'For a start, how much he learned about the Finn family in the course of his enquiries, whether he had any contact with Rosalie's Uncle Harold and if he got any idea of the strength of his antagonism towards Aidan.'

'And supposing he's prepared to share such confidential information with you, which I'd have thought pretty unlikely, where will that get you?'

Something in her husband's voice made Melissa give him a sharp look. 'Joe,' she said, 'I've got a feeling your heart isn't really in this.'

He put down his pencil and met her gaze frankly. 'To be honest, love, it isn't. After our chat in the garden I became quite fired up, but now we're getting down to practicalities I feel as if we're chasing shadows. Even if we get positive answers to our questions, it won't give us a shred of proof that anything untoward actually took place.'

'It would be a pointer in the right direction, though.'

'Okay, so what would you do next?'

'If I could establish that several people would have liked to see Aidan out of the way, and that one of them was in a position to supply the means of disposing of him to one of the others who had the opportunity of using it, it might be sufficient to persuade the authorities to look a little more closely into the case.'

'By "the authorities" I presume you mean the coroner?'

'No, I mean the police.'

'Oh, come on, love, the police would surely want something a bit more substantial to act on than a vague hypothesis.'

'If I went to them officially, yes. What I had in mind was to run it past Matt Waters and get his reaction.' Detective Sergeant Waters was an old friend in the local CID with whom Melissa had had regular contact over the years.

Joe picked up the pencil again and began doodling, his brow wrinkled in thought. 'You referred just now to "*one* of the others",' he said after a moment. 'Did you have someone else in mind besides Harold Finn and Caroline Cresney?'

She nodded. 'I was thinking of Quentin. He was Rosalie's number one suspect, remember? She claimed he'd killed his brother out of jealousy. And everyone noticed how his persona changed quite dramatically after Aidan's death. And then, not long after that, his current wife suffers a similar fate and he goes scuttling back to the previous one, leaving his brother's widow alone in the house.'

'She's not exactly a sorrowing widow, is she? Are you thinking of a three-way conspiracy?'

'Maybe.'

'But I thought you said Caroline had hardly a good word to say for her brother-in-law. If she had such a low opinion of him, would she be likely to join forces with him in such a fiendish plot? And in any case, there was no need to kill Sarah. Once he was free of big brother's influence, there was nothing to stop him simply walking out on her.'

'Of course there isn't. And in any case, it's quite possible that Sarah's death was a hideous coincidence and totally unrelated to Aidan's.'

Joe completed the elaborate pattern in which he had encircled his plus sign and began to do another round the minus. For several minutes he sat in silence, apparently absorbed in his task, while Melissa, knowing from experience that to interrupt his train of thought would be counter-productive, waited patiently for him to speak.

'All right,' he said eventually, 'let's start with Caroline's private eye. You can ask her for his name this evening.'

'Gosh, I'd clean forgotten we'd invited her to dinner.' Melissa jumped to her feet. 'I'll have to pop down to the shop for a few more potatoes and things.' She pointed to the list. 'Better make sure we keep that out of sight.'

'Caroline's not likely to come in here, is she?'

Melissa grinned. 'I wasn't thinking of Caroline. I don't think it would be a good idea to let Mum know what we're planning.'

A customer leaving the shop politely held the door open for Melissa, enabling her to enter without activating the bell. Cynthia Thorne and Mrs Foster were deep in conversation on opposite sides of the counter and showed no sign of being aware of her presence. It was, as she insisted to Joe afterwards, in the hope of avoiding being drawn into their conversation rather than a deliberate attempt to eavesdrop that she moved quickly to the far corner of the little shop where a display unit hid her from view. She picked up a basket and was concentrating on selecting the items she needed when a remark by Cynthia made her hand freeze in the act of reaching for a tin of tomatoes.

'We all know she keeps saying she's not writing her detective books any more, but I don't believe it,' Cynthia asserted in the slightly acid tone that she habitually used when making some critical comment about one of her neighbours.

'Oh, why do you say that?' said Mrs Foster.

'Can you think of any other reason why she should keep on hobnobbing with Caroline Cresney? I mean, they were never particularly friendly when her husband was alive.'

'That's true, but the Cresneys weren't particular friends with anyone, were they?'

'That's got nothing to do with it,' said Cynthia flatly. 'I think those two deaths have given Mrs Martin an idea for a new book.'

'You reckon?'

'Oh, yes. I have made a few suggestions myself from time to time, but none of them seems to have appealed to her.' The last words were spoken with a hint of resentment. 'Of course,' she went on, 'I seem to remember reading that some writers don't like to base their stories on real life mysteries, but since the latest news got out, maybe she can't resist it.'

'You mean the news about Mr Aidan Cresney's will?'

'What else? I reckon there's more to that than meets the eye. If he was looking elsewhere the wife almost certainly knew about it, and who's to say she wasn't doing the same?'

Before she realised what she was doing, Melissa stepped forward and confronted them. Two pairs of eyes grew round and two mouths fell open in consternation. The effect was so comical that she had difficulty in keeping a straight face. 'I had absolutely no intention of eavesdropping,' she said before they had time to recover from the shock of her sudden appearance, 'but I couldn't help overhearing what you were saying, and from what I know of the law I'd say that last remark was little short of slanderous. As a friend of Caroline Cresney, I think you should know that she is already deeply distressed by the fact that her private affairs have become a topic for public discussion.'

Cynthia was the first to recover. 'I'm sure I would never dream of slandering anyone,' she said with an attempt at dignity. 'I was merely repeating what a number of people are saying.'

'Including Mrs Wilson, I suppose?' Melissa gave her a direct, slightly scornful look. 'The biggest mouth in Upper Benbury?'

'Well, really!' Cynthia's colour rose, but she stared defiantly back at Melissa. 'I'm surprised to hear you speak like that of a very respectable hard-working woman, Mrs Martin.'

'And I'm surprised that a young widow who has suffered a very traumatic experience should be the subject of malicious gossip by neighbours who profess to be Christians,' Melissa retorted. 'She's in need of friendship and support, which is what *we* are trying to give her.' She took a lemon cheesecake from the freezer, put it with the other items she had already selected and dumped the basket on the counter. 'How much does this come to, please?'

In silence, a subdued Mrs Foster totalled the items on her cash register while Melissa, who had deliberately turned her back on Cynthia, transferred them to her shopping bag. 'That'll be four pounds seventy-five,' she said. As Melissa handed over the money, there was a 'ting' from the door-bell. Cynthia Thorne had departed without uttering another word.

'You should have seen their faces when I popped out from behind the tins of soup and confronted them!' said Melissa gleefully as she described the incident to Joe on returning home. 'Wait till I tell Mum – it's time she knew what a nasty-minded creature her friend is.'

'Nasty-minded maybe, but she may have a point about Caroline having an affair,' said Joe.

'I don't believe she is, but in any case, who could blame her after what Aidan put her through?'

'I'm sure there'll be one or two ready to cast the first stone,' said Joe dryly. 'It's interesting, isn't it, that Cynthia came to the same conclusion as Doctor Finn?'

'About my intention of writing a new mystery novel, you mean?'

'Yes. When it gets about, it'll strengthen your cover.'

'I'm not too bothered about that, so long as Caroline swallows it.'

It had been Melissa's intention to wait until they had finished dinner before she raised the subject of her supposed new mystery novel, but in the event the matter resolved itself without any effort on her part. Caroline arrived punctually; at first she appeared nervous and ill at ease, but as the evening wore on she began to relax and talk with growing enthusiasm about her plans to spend a few days with her mother and sister.

'I'd like Jennie to come back with me so that the two of us can discuss the proposed alterations to the house with the social services people, but it will mean making arrangements for someone to take care of Mother while she's away. Jennie would love to meet you, Melissa,' she added. 'She's read lots of your books, especially the detective stories. She was saying only the other day how sorry she is that you aren't writing any more.'

'Funny you should say that!' It was exactly the lead-in Melissa needed. Caroline expressed her delight at the prospect of another Mel Craig mystery and had no hesitation in revealing the name of the private detective she had engaged to spy on Aidan. She rummaged in her handbag and took out a small address book. 'I've got his details here.' She jotted them down on a scrap of paper that Melissa gave her. 'I can thoroughly recommend him,' she said as she handed it over. 'He's very discreet and his charges aren't too outrageous.'

'I don't think Mel is thinking of hiring him,' said Joe with a chuckle. 'At least, I hope not,' he added with glance of mock concern in his wife's direction.

When Caroline had gone home, thanking them effusively for their hospitality and also for their friendship and support, Joe turned to Melissa and said, 'I noticed your reaction when Caroline gave you the name of her private eye. You recognised it, didn't you?'

'Yes, I did. He's a former detective sergeant, a chap called Mike Mellor. I met him once at a crime scene after I'd found a rather gruesome corpse.' She shuddered at the memory.

'It wasn't a pretty sight . . . but no, it didn't come about as a result of my doing a spot of private sleuthing,' she added, suddenly afraid that the remark might give Joe second thoughts about the current enterprise.

To her relief, the idea did not seem to have occurred to him. All he said was, 'Perhaps your previous acquaintance might encourage him to be less discreet than if you were a complete stranger.'

'Let's hope so.'

23

'Mel Craig! Fancy seeing you!' Ex-Detective Sergeant Mike Mellor's broad features were practically carved in two by his smile of mingled surprise and pleasure as he held out a hand to greet her. 'It's been a long time. Come into my office.'

Thank you.' She followed him into a small room sparsely furnished with a desk, some chairs, a bookshelf and two filing cabinets. 'And thanks for giving me an appointment so quickly.'

'No problem. Glad I had a slot free – but I wasn't expecting you. I was told it was a Mrs Martin.'

'That's right,' she said. 'I am Mrs Martin now.'

'I see,' he replied, but it was clear from his tone that he did not see.

'I know what you're thinking,' she said, 'and yes, you're right, DCI Ken Harris and I were once an item. He decided to go into partnership with a friend who runs a successful enquiry agency in New York and he asked me to go with him. He's a great guy, but it would never have worked. I married my agent, Joe Martin, at the beginning of August and Ken sent us a lovely wedding present to show there were no hard feelings.'

'That's great! Congratulations!' Mellor beamed again.

'Do have a seat.' He indicated a chair facing the desk. 'Would you like some coffee?'

'Thanks, that would be nice. Milk but no sugar, please.'

Mellor cocked his head round the door and called to the quietly spoken middle-aged woman in the outer office who had greeted her on her arrival, 'Did you hear that, Judy?'

'I did,' she called back. 'The kettle's just boiled. I take it you'll be wanting another one as well?'

'What do you think?'

'I think you drink far too much coffee,' she retorted.

Mellor gave Melissa an embarrassed grin. 'That's what comes of employing the wife as secretary,' he said. 'It's just till I build up enough business to afford to pay someone. It's been slow at first, but we're getting there.'

'I'm glad to hear it,' she said. 'It seems quite a popular enterprise for ex-CID people to take up after they retire.'

'Why not? We're still active and we've got the experience and know-how to offer a good service to people with problems the police can't help with. Ah, thanks, love,' he said as Judy entered with two mugs of coffee, which she placed on the desk. 'Meet Mel Craig, famous crime writer and amateur sleuth. She used to help us with some of our trickiest cases.'

'That's not the kind of attitude I encountered at the time,' said Melissa with a smile. 'Mostly I was told in no uncertain terms to keep my nose out of police business . . . especially when a certain DCI Holloway and his sergeant were dealing with the case,' she added with a sly glance at Mellor. 'I'm pleased to meet you, Judy.'

'I didn't realise . . . I mean, you gave your name as Mrs Martin,' said Judy. She clasped the hand Melissa held out to her and shook it warmly. 'I'm thrilled to meet you; I love your books.'

'Thank you. I hope Mike doesn't make you work too hard.'

'I'd like to see him try!' said Judy, glaring with mock severity at her husband, who responded with a shrug and a smile of resignation. 'Oh, excuse me,' she added as the phone rang in the outer office. 'I'll leave you two to talk business.' She went out and closed the door behind her.

'Well, this is an unexpected pleasure!' Mellor sat down at his desk and raised his mug of coffee in salute. 'It must be several years since our paths crossed. Remember that time just after Ken retired when you and he found that old woman dead in her bed? I thought Ken was going to blow a gasket when DCI Holloway more or less elbowed him aside!' He chuckled at the recollection.

'It didn't seem funny at the time,' she said with a shudder. 'That was a horrid case.'

'Yes, it was rather. Anyway, I don't suppose you came here to talk over old times, so what can I do for you? Research for a new book, is it?'

'As it happens, it isn't, but if any more people jump to that conclusion I'll begin to believe it myself.'

'What then?' His eyes twinkled at her over the rim of his mug. 'Don't tell me you suspect your new husband of going off the rails already?'

She laughed. 'No, but if I ever do, I promise you'll get the business. As a matter of fact, I may be here on a wild-goose chase,' she went on, turning serious again, 'but both Joe and I have reason to believe – or rather, to suspect – that at least one and possibly two particularly nasty murders have taken place in our village.'

'Murders?' Mellor was clearly taken aback. 'That's hardly my field. Why don't you take your suspicions to the police?'

'Because there's nothing concrete to go on, only some rather strange coincidences which may in fact be just that, but they keep bugging us.'

'So why do you think I may be able to help?'

'Because one of our suspects is a former client of yours, Mrs Caroline Cresney. She recommended you, by the way; she said you're very discreet and won't rip me off!'

Mellor smiled, then frowned and looked thoughtful. 'Ah, yes, Mrs Cresney,' he said after a moment's deliberation. He got up, went to a filing cabinet and took out a folder. 'She was one of my first clients,' he said. 'A very charming, very beautiful lady. I was surprised that any husband would cheat on her . . . especially with—' He checked himself as if realising he had been about to reveal confidential information, closed the folder and put it on his desk. 'So who do you suspect her of murdering?'

'Her husband.'

'Aidan Cresney's dead? I had no idea. When?'

'About four weeks ago.'

'How?'

'Multiple bee stings. It's all in here.' Melissa took some sheets of paper from an envelope and passed them to him. 'This is a résumé of events, beginning with Aidan's death.' She drank her coffee while he read the notes she and Joe had prepared together. When he had finished he placed both hands palm downwards on the desk and looked across at Melissa. 'Well?' she said.

'It's certainly a rum kettle of fish,' he agreed. 'That business with the will surprises me. I'd have expected him to leave money to his mistress, but here you're suggesting it's her daughter.'

'I admit Joe and I sort of assumed that . . . are you saying

Rosalie was telling the truth when she said she wasn't having an affair with him?'

'Oh, yes, it was definitely the mother he was shagging, sorry, I mean–'

Melissa smiled at his embarrassment, which she found rather endearing. 'I assure you I've heard far stronger expressions than that without blushing,' she said, 'but can you be certain?'

'Oh, yes, he always made sure the daughter was out of the way before going to the house. The man you say is her uncle, by the way, this Doctor Harold Finn. It could be him I once saw calling at Mrs Finn's house one evening when I expected to see Cresney. He – Cresney, that is – had his regular times for visiting, but on this occasion another bloke turned up, a man I hadn't seen before. When she opened the door and saw him she didn't look best pleased, but he didn't wait to be invited in, he just barged past her and she shut the door behind him. It wasn't long before it opened again and it was obvious they'd been having a furious argument. It continued for several seconds more and then she slammed the door in his face. He came storming down the steps, got into his car and drove off like a maniac.'

'Could you hear what they were saying?'

'I'm afraid not. As luck would have it, a crowd of youngsters came past with a ghetto-blaster at the crucial moment. All I heard were Mrs Finn's final words, which were something like, "Next time you want to come, ring first to find if it's convenient."'

'She obviously didn't want him there if she was expecting Cresney.'

'I thought he might have been someone she was running in tandem with Cresney, but it could have been her brother-in-law trying to persuade her to stop seeing him. Rosalie seems a really shy little innocent, but her mother's exactly the opposite. Very sexy and vivacious, but quite a tough old bird.'

'That surprises me. Rosalie implied that her mother was a rather sensitive soul, easily moved to tears.'

'Maybe that's a trick she uses to keep the girl under her thumb.' Mellor thought for a moment. 'Now you mention it, she did act differently when the girl was with her.'

'You've seen them at close quarters?'

'Once Cresney took them both out for a meal and I followed them into the restaurant and sat at a nearby table. I was hoping to catch something useful from their conversation, but there was too much background noise. Once or twice, though, when the mother's attention was elsewhere, I noticed him eyeing the girl in a way that I can only describe as lecherous. If I caught a man looking at my daughter like that I'd do my best to make sure he never got her on her own.'

'Ah!' Melissa exclaimed. 'Joe and I wondered about that after Rosalie came to see us. We didn't mention it in our notes because we thought it better to stick to facts and leave you to draw your own conclusions.'

Mellor gave a nod of approval. 'Good thinking.'

Melissa thought for a moment and then said, 'If the nearest you got to seeing Aidan and his fancy woman together was in a restaurant, it would hardly have been enough evidence for Caroline to start divorce proceedings.' She was about to add, 'even if Aidan hadn't made sure she'd be unlikely to', but remembered that Caroline had given her this information in confidence. 'What's the joke?' she went on, seeing him smile.

'I didn't tell you everything I observed, and I'm not going to,' Mellor chuckled. 'On the strength of the evidence I gave her she could have divorced him all right, if she had a mind to, but I gather from all this that she didn't.'

'No, and I'm not going to tell you her reasons, either,' she retorted. 'Going back to what you said a moment ago, it seems that what you admit to observing confirms our impression about Aidan's intentions towards Rosalie, and it also ties in with something Caroline said when she told me about the legacy.'

'What was that?'

'She said, "Aidan always fancied younger women; that's why he married me." Joe and I both felt Rosalie was a bit naïve, so if Aidan wanted to have it off with her mother as a way of preparing the ground it would be easy to keep it from her until he was ready to move in for the kill, so to speak.'

'It adds up. He seems to have been a thoroughly nasty piece of work.' Mellor scratched his nose and looked thoughtful. 'I gather Caroline confides in you quite a lot,' he said after a moment. 'If she really played some part in her husband's death, would she be so forthcoming?'

'I've asked myself that more than once. She's very highly-strung and emotional, and I suppose I just happened to be around at times when she needed to get something off her chest. I must say, though, that several times I've had a suspicion that she's keeping something back. I think there's guilt there as well, and when she came out with that remark about people saying she killed him out of jealousy, but how was she to know, it seemed to confirm that feeling.'

'Yes, I see what you mean.'

'What do you advise me to do? Go to the police?' When

he did not answer immediately, she said, 'Supposing you were still in the force and someone came to you with this story, how would you respond?'

Mellor played the piano on the desk with the fingers of both hands for several moments before replying. 'In the first place I'd refer it to a senior officer,' he said at last. 'He of course would ask for my opinion about the informant. Nine times out of ten I think we'd conclude that someone had let their imagination run away with them . . . but if it was someone whose judgment we knew to be pretty sound–'

'Someone like me, for example?' Melissa suggested, as he broke off with his wide mouth puckered in a mischievous smile that gave him a boyish look. 'Then you might take it a bit more seriously?'

'I think perhaps we might.'

'So what do you advise me to do?' she repeated.

He picked up her notes and said, 'Okay if I keep these for now?' Without waiting for a reply he slipped the pages into the file and closed it. 'Leave it with me for a day or two and I'll see what I can find out about Doctor Harold Finn.'

'He didn't say in so many words, but it's obvious he agrees there might be something fishy about it,' said Melissa when she got home.

'It'll be interesting to see what he comes up with,' said Joe.

'I'd love to know how he plans to set about his enquiries into Harold Finn's activities,' she said, a shade wistfully.

'With your experience of police work, I'd expect you to have a good idea–' he began, but broke off as the communicating door to Brambles flew open and Sylvia burst into the room. 'Oh dear,' she began in a breathless voice before they had time to speak, 'I'm sorry to barge in without knocking, but I'm terribly worried about Caroline. I'm afraid she's ill and I think someone should go to her at once.'

Melissa's throat tightened as if a hand had closed round it. Was yet another tragedy about to happen? 'What's wrong with her?' she asked in a voice made hoarse by dread.

'I don't know, but I'm afraid she may have done something silly and I think we should go immediately. It could be urgent; I'll explain on the way.'

24

The three of them hurried from the house and scrambled into Melissa's car. On the short drive to Cold Wells, Sylvia told her story in a series of jerky half-completed sentences.

'I rang to invite her for tea . . . I thought she might have been upset by all the talk at the bridge club . . . and her voice on the phone sounded strange, almost as if she was drunk . . . then she sort of sighed and there was a bump . . . and then another bump and after that, nothing.'

'Was it a heavy bump, as if she'd fallen over?' asked Joe.

'The second one was. The first time it sounded as if she'd dropped something, the phone perhaps. I was worried and I rang again and got the engaged tone. That's when I came to you.'

'You did the right thing,' he assured her. 'Just keep calm; we'll soon be there.'

'Oh, I do hope nothing dreadful's happened. Can't you go a little faster, Lissie?'

'Not if you want to get there in one piece, Mother dear,' Melissa replied. She deliberately kept her tone light to conceal her gnawing fear that Caroline might indeed have 'done something silly'. Fortunately, the lane into the village, and the village street itself were almost deserted and within less than ten minutes of leaving they pulled up outside Cold

Wells Manor. Sylvia was the first out of the car; she rushed up to the front door, put her finger on the bell and kept it there for several seconds. They could hear it ringing; when she released it they held their collective breath while listening for sounds of movement within the house. Nothing stirred. She tried again, jabbing the bell push in short regular bursts and muttering, 'Come on, come on,' repeatedly while the insistent jangle echoed through the house. At Joe's suggestion, she began pounding on the knocker. There was still no response. They peered through the ground-floor windows, but could see no sign of Caroline or of anything untoward. They returned to the front door and tried the bell and the knocker again, without success.

'Oh dear, whatever shall we do?' said Sylvia. She looked helplessly at Melissa and Joe. 'I don't suppose you know anyone who has a key?'

They shook their heads. Joe did another circuit of the house to check the upstairs windows. 'They're all tightly shut, and anyway we've no ladder,' he reported. 'If we're going to get into the house it looks as if we'll have to break a downstairs window.'

'Just a moment.' Melissa had been taking a closer look at the small window of the downstairs cloakroom. 'This one's very badly fitting. Have you got your Swiss knife on you, Joe? I reckon, if you could slide the blade between the window and the frame, you might be able to lever the handle up.'

'I'll have a go.' Melissa and her mother watched in a tense silence as he took the knife from his pocket, opened out one of the blades and set to work. He succeeded in prising up the handle until it was almost clear of the catch, but it refused to go any further and the minute he withdrew the knife it fell back into place.

'Damn,' he muttered under his breath. 'Hang on, I'll try a bigger blade.' This time he was successful; the handle rose to its furthest point and the two anxious women gave a muted cheer as the window swung open. 'Right,' he said as he put the knife away, 'who's going to make the illegal entry?'

'I'll do it,' Melissa volunteered, 'but you'll have to give me a lift.'

'Okay.' He took her by the waist and hoisted her up to the sill. She swung her legs over, dropped on to the floor and hurried to the front door. Moments later, they were all standing in the hall.

Sylvia was the first to hear the faint, high-pitched warbling note that seemed to come from a distance. 'Listen!' she exclaimed excitedly. 'That sounds like a siren. Perhaps she knew she was ill and managed to call for an ambulance before she passed out.'

'No, it isn't an ambulance, it's coming from a phone that's been left off the hook,' said Melissa. She was halfway up the wide staircase as she spoke, with Joe close behind her, while Sylvia followed more slowly. The noise became louder as she flung open the door to Caroline's bedroom. For a moment, she thought it was deserted; there was no one on the bed, although the duvet was slightly rumpled, as if someone had been lying on top of it and got up without bothering to straighten it. The insistent warbling came from the other side of the bed; as she went round to pick up the phone she saw Caroline sprawled face down on the floor. On the bedside cabinet was a glass tumbler and beside it a small brown bottle. Both were empty.

Melissa quickly replaced the receiver, lifted it again to check for dialling tone and jabbed the buttons for 999, at the same time yelling, 'Mum! Come quickly! It looks as if she's OD'd on something . . . see if you can . . . yes, ambulance please, it's urgent,' she said into the phone while making frantic gestures as Sylvia hurried into the room. 'Someone's taken an overdose at Cold Wells Manor, Upper Benbury . . . just a minute.' She picked up the bottle. 'Codeine, according to the label. We don't know exactly whcn, but we think she passed out about half an hour ago. Yes, I'll stay on the line.'

Meanwhile Sylvia, who had trained as a nurse before her marriage, dropped to her knees beside Caroline and gently moved her head to one side. 'There's a pulse, but it's slow and her breathing's irregular,' she reported. 'Tell the ambulance driver to be as quick as he can.'

'Anything I can do?' said Joe from the doorway, while Melissa relayed the message.

'Yes,' said Sylvia, 'come and give me a hand.'

'Do you want to get her on to the bed?'

'No, she's better where she is until the ambulance gets here. Her blood pressure's probably dropped so we need to keep her head as low as possible. Just help me turn her on her side. Thank God she fell on her face; if she'd landed on her back she might have swallowed her tongue or choked on her vomit.'

Between them they put Caroline into the recovery position while Melissa continued to pass information to the ambulance crew. The minutes ticked past as they waited, the anxious silence broken only by her response to requests for directions, until the approaching siren brought spontaneous exclamations of relief. Joe hurried to open the front door and within minutes Caroline was on her way to the hospital, with Melissa promising to follow shortly to help with any necessary formalities.

'What do we do about locking up?' said Joe.

Melissa picked up Caroline's handbag, which was lying on the dressing table. 'I wouldn't normally do this, but in the circumstances–' A brief search yielded a bunch of keys; they went downstairs and made sure that one of them fitted the front door before closing it behind them.

On the way back to Hawthorn Cottage Melissa said, 'Mum, what was all that about the women at the bridge club? What have they been saying?'

'You know I decided to have some bridge lessons?'

'Yes, you did mention it.'

'Well, I went along yesterday evening with Cynthia. She introduced me to a lady who teaches beginners. Caroline was there with some other women I didn't know – don't think they live in our village. Anyway, after the play was finished the hostess for the evening served drinks and nibbles and some of them started talking about that woman who stabbed her husband with a carving knife when she found out he'd been having an affair and had given a lot of money and a fancy car to his other woman. It's been in all the papers lately, you must have read about it?'

'I'm afraid we haven't; we didn't buy a newspaper while we were away,' said Joe. 'We decided to cut ourselves off from the world for a few days.'

'Oh well, never mind. The point is that while they were talking about it one or two of them made what I thought were rather sly remarks that seemed to be directed at Caroline.'

'What sort of remarks?' asked Melissa.

'About wives who've been deceived by their husbands and the things they do to get their own back. I could tell it was making her uncomfortable. I managed to change the subject by asking a question about bidding, but she left soon after without saying goodnight or anything.'

'I'm surprised she was there in the first place.'

'Why do you say that? She enjoys her game of bridge. She told me the other day it helps to keep her sane.'

'When I saw her earlier in the day she was very upset about the legacy. I wouldn't have thought–'

'She told you about the legacy?' Sylvia interrupted. 'All she said to me was that she'd had some disturbing news from her solicitor, but she didn't go into details. I only heard about it later, when Cynthia told me. Did she say who he'd left the money to?'

'Mother, that really isn't any concern of ours.'

'Lissie, I hope you're not implying that I can't be trusted to keep a secret?'

'All I can say is,' Melissa said, ignoring her mother's aggrieved tone, 'that she rather carelessly left a letter from her solicitor where Mrs Wilson could see it.'

'Ah!' Sylvia drew in a sharp breath. 'So that's how Cynthia got to know about it.'

'Yes, but the interesting thing is that the letter didn't contain any information about the legatee. Either Cynthia or Mrs Wilson – or quite likely both of them; when it comes to dishing the dirt they're as bad as one another – put their own interpretation on it without a scrap of evidence.'

'You mean the money isn't going to Mr Cresney's lady friend?'

'Mum, I've already made it clear that I've no intention of telling you any more. And just to let you know what a spiteful busybody your dear friend Cynthia is,' she went on, her anger rising by the minute, 'I'll tell you what I overheard her saying to Mrs Foster in the shop yesterday afternoon.'

Sylvia listened in a subdued silence until Melissa had finished. 'Oh dear,' she said in dismay, 'this is dreadful! Lissie, do you think Caroline took that overdose because she believes people think she killed her husband?'

'I think those jibes may have been the last straw,' said Melissa sadly. 'In a way I'm afraid I'm partly to blame.'

'I don't see how.'

'I was the one who told her the news of the legacy had got out and she immediately guessed that Mrs Wilson had read the letter. If it hadn't been for that, she might not have taken all those remarks personally. How I wish I could get my hands on that poisonous old bat!' she added in a fresh wave of indignation.

'You mustn't blame yourself, darling,' said Joe. 'Caroline shouldn't have left the letter lying around. After all, you did warn her the woman's a nosey-parker and given to tittle-tattle.'

'I know, but I feel bad about it just the same.'

They had arrived back at Hawthorn Cottage. Melissa switched off the engine and was about to get out of the car when Joe said, 'Mel, didn't you promise the ambulance crew to follow Caroline to the hospital? They'll be wanting to know who her doctor is and so on, and she can't answer their questions while she's unconscious.'

'Oh gosh, yes! I was so exercised over the school for scandal that it went right out of my mind. I've got her handbag; let's hope it contains the personal details they need. If they decide to keep her in overnight I can pop back and pick up some toilet things for her.'

'Do you think we should let her mother and sister know?'

'If the worst happens, of course they'll have to be told, but if, please God, she pulls through, it'll be up to her to decide.'

'There's her brother-in-law as well,' he reminded her.

'Oh, him!' Melissa pulled a face. 'From the way things are between them, I think it's unlikely he'd come rushing to her bedside,' she said scornfully. 'I suggest we let that one stew for the time being. Can you two organise yourselves some lunch? I'll grab a sandwich in the hospital canteen while I'm waiting for news.'

'Are you a relative?' asked a staff nurse when Melissa, having finally found her way to the ward where Caroline had been taken, begged to know how she was.

'No, but I'm a close friend and neighbour,' she explained. 'My husband and I found her and my mother gave her some emergency treatment while we were waiting for the ambulance.'

'I see. May I have the patient's full name and address? And yours?' The nurse noted the replies on a form. 'What about her next of kin?'

'She's a widow and so far as I know her only relatives are her mother and a sister who live together, but I don't know where. I've brought her handbag with me; there may be an address book in it.' She was rummaging in the bag as she spoke. 'Yes, here it is.' She began turning the pages. 'The trouble is, I don't know their surname. Nurse,' she pleaded while she searched, 'can you give me some idea of how she is? Is she going to be all right?'

The woman shook her head. 'I'm sorry, I haven't any information at the moment. She's having emergency treatment now, that's all I can say.'

'Do you mind if I stay and wait for news? I'm really the only person she's got at the moment and I'd like her to know I'm here when she comes round.' *But supposing she doesn't come round?* she thought. *Then we may never know what really happened.* She sent up a fervent prayer and pushed the awful possibility to the back of her mind.

'Stay by all means,' she heard the nurse saying. 'I dare say the doctor would like to ask you a few questions anyway. Have you found anything?' she asked with her eye on the address book.

'I think this may be what we're looking for.' She had found an entry that read, 'Mrs Helen and Miss J. Blackley' with 'Mum and Jennie' beside it in brackets. 'They live in Surrey. The trouble is, Caroline's mother is disabled so it may be difficult for them to get here. Do they have to be told now, or could it wait until we know how she is?'

'We'll have to ask the doctor,' said the nurse. A buzzer sounded and she turned to check who was calling. 'I'm sorry, I have to leave you for the moment.' She pointed to a chair. 'Sit there. I'll let you know as soon as there's anything to report.'

25

'Mrs Martin?'

'Yes?' Melissa looked up from the out-of-date copy of *Cotswold Life* that she had been scanning to pass the time while waiting for news of Caroline. A black-haired, dark-eyed young man in a white coat with a stethoscope round his neck was standing in front of her. She threw the magazine aside and jumped to her feet.

'You are a friend' – he consulted a clipboard – 'of Mrs Caroline Cresney?'

'That's right.'

He held out a hand and said, 'I am Doctor Constantine.'

He smiled, showing a row of even teeth that gleamed white against smooth skin the colour of dark honey. The analogy, which sprang spontaneously into her head, gave her a momentary *frisson*, but she hastily pulled herself together, took his hand and said, 'Please, how is she?'

'I suggest we talk somewhere a little more private. Will you please follow me?' He led her to a small room behind the nurses' station and invited her with a gesture to sit on one of two chairs placed on opposite sides of a wooden table. Then he sat down on the other before taking a small brown glass bottle from his pocket and handing it to her. 'I understand this was in the room where Mrs Cresney was found?'

Melissa studied the label, which read, 'Codeine Phosphate 60 mg. 30 tablets, to be taken as directed' and underneath, 'not more than 4 tablets in 24 hours'. There followed Caroline's name, the name of the pharmacist and the previous day's date. She gave the bottle back to him and said, 'I presume it's the one we gave to the ambulance crew. I didn't examine it closely at the time, although I did notice the word "codeine".'

'Thank you.' He put it back in his pocket and referred once more to his clipboard. 'Is it true that Mrs Cresney has no immediate relatives living in the area?'

'So far as I know.' It did not occur to Melissa to mention Quentin. 'Please, Doctor Constantine,' she repeated, 'can you tell me how she is? Will she pull through?'

'In cases of this nature we normally give detailed information only to a patient's next of kin,' he replied.

'But I explained to the nurse–' she began.

'Yes, I understand there are special circumstances of which you, as a close friend, have some knowledge. First of all, can you tell me the name of Mrs Cresney's doctor?'

'I believe she's registered with Doctor Charman.'

'Thank you.' He made a note. 'Has Mrs Cresney said anything to you recently about severe headaches or back pain, or anything of that kind?'

Melissa shook her head. 'No, nothing like that. Her problems have been of a more personal nature. Both her husband and her sister-in-law have recently died in very shocking circumstances.'

'The poor lady,' said Doctor Constantine. 'She has certainly suffered considerable psychological and emotional distress.' His voice had the attractive, undulating rhythm particular to people from the Caribbean, with an underlying note of sympathy that Melissa found encouraging. 'The danger is,' he went on, 'that two such devastating experiences in quick succession can lead to clinical depression. Have you noticed anything to suggest that might be the case?'

'She has certainly become very emotional on several occasions. I and my family – that is, my husband and my mother – have been giving her what comfort we can, but . . .' Melissa hesitated, wondering how much she should reveal of Caroline's private, half-disclosed fears. She decided for the time being to keep them to herself, merely adding, 'since Mr Cresney's death she has had to spend quite a lot of time on her own in a large house with no immediate neighbours.'

'I see. Well, she has obviously consulted Doctor Charman recently, so he may be able to tell us more about her state of mind. Do you know if she has been in touch with her family since the double tragedy?'

'Oh, yes; in fact she has been telling me of her plans to visit her mother and sister in the near future. The long-term intention is for them to move in with her.' Melissa outlined the situation and Doctor Constantine nodded in approval.

'It sounds an excellent arrangement,' he said. 'It makes it difficult to understand why she should try to take her own life.' He made a further note and then said, 'Perhaps we shall know more when she is well enough to answer some questions.'

'So you do think she'll recover?'

'She appears to have responded well to the antidote,' he said and she almost wept with relief. 'We shall keep her under close observation for the next twenty-four hours, longer if we think her mental state requires it.'

'Do you think I should get in touch with her mother and sister?'

Doctor Constantine drummed on the table with long, delicate fingers while he considered the question. 'Perhaps,' he said after a moment, 'in view of the fact that her mother has a disability, it would be as well to wait, say, until tomorrow when I hope you will be able to give her re-assuring news. Of course, if there should be an unexpected change in the patient's condition it would be necessary to advise her of the situation right away, but in my opinion . . .' He lifted his hands and tilted his head in a way that seemed to confirm his previously expressed optimism.

'Well, that's really encouraging,' she said. 'I imagine she'll need some toilet things and a nightdress and so on. I'll go back to her house and fetch them.'

'Excellent.' He gave another brilliant smile as he stood up and opened the door for her. 'She is very fortunate to have you as a friend. Try not to worry; we are taking good care of her and she is a healthy young woman.'

She restrained an urge to hug him. 'Thank you, thank you very much,' she said warmly. 'I'll be back later.' She returned to her car and called Joe.

'Well, that sounds encouraging,' he said when she had put him in the picture. 'Have you had anything to eat, by the way?'

'Oh Lord, I'd forgotten all about food,' she said, suddenly aware that she was hungry. She glanced at her watch. 'The canteen probably stopped serving lunch ages ago. Will you make a sandwich I can grab before I go to collect Caroline's things?'

'I'll make you something more substantial than a sand-wich, and you'll sit down and take your time eating it,' he said firmly. 'If Caroline wants to brush her teeth, she'll just have to wait.'

'Yes, sir.' Her smile as she switched off her mobile was a mixture of amusement at his pretence of bossiness and relief at being able to relax. She drove home, repeated the gist of her conversation with Doctor Constantine for the benefit of her mother, who was naturally eager for news, and ate the omelette that Joe made for her before setting off for Cold Wells. On arrival, she was surprised to see Gloria's Mini parked on the drive. Moments later, Gloria herself emerged from the back door of what had been Quentin and Sarah's part of the house, carrying two plastic bags that appeared to be full of rubbish.

'Gloria, what on earth are you doing here?' Melissa exclaimed.

'Mrs Wilson asked me to come . . . Mrs Cresney asked her to tidy the place up a bit after her brother-in-law moved out, but she's hurt her leg – Mrs Wilson, I mean – and she can't work for a while, so I said I'd do it,' Gloria explained.

'Well, it's kind of you to help out, Gloria, but how did you get into the house?'

'Mrs Cresney gave Mrs Wilson a key. I'm to return it to her when the job's done.'

'I see.' The thought ran through Melissa's head that she wouldn't trust Mrs Wilson with a key to a rabbit hutch, but she kept the sentiment to herself.

'Funny business, innit, Mr Quentin going off like that?' Gloria said as she dumped the bags in the wheelie-bin and went back to collect a third that she had left just inside the door. 'Wonder where he's gone?' Her expressive toffee-coloured eyes were full of questions that Melissa had no intention of answering. 'Got a lady friend, most like,' she

went on, not in the least discouraged by the lack of response.
'Never did think he and his wife was, well, you know, right
for each other. You come to see Mrs Caroline, no doubt?'

'As a matter of fact, I've come to collect a few things that
she'll be needing while she's in hospital.' There was no point
in dissimulating; it was certain that someone had noticed the
ambulance tearing through the village and it would not be
long before its destination became known.

'Hospital?' Gloria's eyes nearly popped out of her head.
'She ill, then?'

'Not ill. She had a fall,' said Melissa in a moment of inspiration. It was perfectly true; Caroline had fallen off the bed
and there was no necessity to reveal the cause. 'They don't
think she's done any serious damage,' she went on, fore-
stalling the barrage of questions Gloria was obviously dying
to ask, 'but they're keeping her in for tonight, just in case.'

'Poor lady,' said Gloria, unconsciously echoing Doctor
Constantine's sentiments. 'She do have some bad luck.' She
pulled the door to and deposited the third bag in the bin.
'Well, that's that. Perhaps I could leave this with you?' She
handed Melissa the key. 'If you'd be kind enough to give it
to Mrs Cresney – and please give her my best wishes for a
speedy recovery.'

'Thank you, I'll do that.'

'Must dash; time to pick up the kids from school.' Gloria
got back into her Mini, started the engine and then got out
again. 'Silly me, got a head like a sieve!' she exclaimed.
'There's another bag of rubbish in the kitchen; I left it till
last 'cos it's leaking and needs putting in another bag. If
you'd just give me back the key–'

'Oh, don't worry, Gloria, I'll see to it. You go and fetch
your children.'

'That's very kind of you, Mrs Martin. It's a bit smelly, I'm afraid. I've left it in the sink and there's a plastic carrier on the draining board. See you next week then!' She scrambled back into the car, slammed the door and shot off down the drive, scattering gravel in all directions and leaving Melissa wondering, for the umpteenth time, how she had managed to avoid a serious accident.

The door through which Gloria had emerged led into the kitchen. Everything moveable had been taken away, leaving only the fitted units, which were of more recent design than those in the main house. All the work surfaces were bare and the cupboards and shelves empty. She picked up the bag of rubbish that Gloria had left with the intention of transferring it bodily into the spare supermarket carrier, but before she could do so the bottom gave way and deposited the contents in the sink.

'Damn!' she muttered, surveying the unsavoury-looking heap with disgust. Having no intention of disposing of it with her bare hands, she decided to leave it for the time being and went to carry out her original task. A quick search in Caroline's bedroom and en suite bathroom was sufficient to find everything the patient would need for one night; if a longer stay was deemed necessary she could always return for more. She found a small holdall in the wardrobe, put everything inside and carried it downstairs. Then she went into the kitchen and took a pair of rubber gloves that she found draped over one of the taps. She went out of the house, closed the door behind her and put the holdall in the car before going back to deal with the debris in Quentin's kitchen.

Among the empty tins and polystyrene containers that had once contained pre-prepared meals, and the fruit and vegetable remains that had decomposed into a semi-liquid mass, was a small round pot made of transparent plastic containing the remains of some pale yellow cream. On the side of the pot was a label; the wording was partially obscured by tomato sauce from a baked bean tin and out of curiosity Melissa rinsed it under the tap. A closer inspection informed her that the pot had contained a free sample of Fruit and Herb Skin Cream with the compliments of Holistic Health Laboratories.

She lifted the pot to her nose, unscrewed the lid and sniffed. Then she pulled off the gloves, scooped up a minute quantity of the remaining cream on one finger, spread it on the back of her other hand and sniffed again. The temperature in the kitchen seemed to drop by several degrees as she caught the distinctive, unmistakable smell of banana.

26

Melissa hastily put the lid back on the pot and screwed it up as tightly as she could without splitting the flimsy plastic. She stood staring at it for several minutes, holding her hand with the smear of cream on it a few inches from her nose, while her mind slowly absorbed the possible significance of her discovery. Then she put the pot on the draining board and washed her hands under the tap as thoroughly as she could without the aid of soap. There was no towel; she went in search of one elsewhere, but both the downstairs toilet and the first-floor bathroom had been stripped of everything removable. She hurried back to Caroline's part of the house, let herself in and washed her hands again using plenty of soap and rinsing them repeatedly long after she could no longer detect the smell of banana. For all she knew, bees could recognise scents indiscernible to humans and she had no intention of taking any chances. She might be making a completely false assumption, but it was better to be safe than sorry. After disposing of the last bag of rubbish, her final act before leaving was to wrap the pot in several layers of cling-film from Caroline's kitchen before putting it into her pocket. Even then she kept a wary eye open for bees as she jumped into the car and made sure all the windows were closed.

Instead of going straight back to the hospital, she called in at home. Joe was in the study; he looked up in surprise as she entered. She sat down beside him, unwrapped the pot of cream, unscrewed the lid and held it under his nose. 'Have a sniff of that and tell me what it reminds you of, but whatever you do don't touch it.'

He obeyed and without hesitation said, 'It smells like bananas. Where did you find it?'

'In Sarah and Quentin's kitchen.'

'What were you doing there?'

'Never mind that now. Doesn't it suggest something to you?'

'Not especially.' He looked at her in concern. 'Mel, you're shaking. Whatever's the matter?'

'Surely you remember? The substance that's a constituent of the stinging pheromone smells of bananas. Iris mentioned it and Harold Finn confirmed it.'

'So he did. I'd forgotten.'

'And it was the smell of bananas in Mum's cake that made Caroline throw up,' she went on. 'Don't you see what this means?'

'I see what you're driving at, but if this cream contains a genuine extract of bananas it's unlikely to fool bees into thinking it's the stinging thingummy.'

'But supposing it isn't genuine banana? Incidentally, I put a tiny smear on my hand and after a few seconds the smell got stronger. Supposing bees could smell it from a distance? Give me that pot a moment.' He handed it over and she looked closely at the label. 'Look,' she said excitedly, 'there's no address or phone number.' She dropped the pot on the desk, reached for the telephone directory and began flicking through the business pages for names beginning with H. 'It goes from Holidays to Holland,' she said after a rapid search. 'There's no listing for Holistic Health Laboratories. Joe, this could explain why the bees attacked Sarah, and maybe Aidan as well.'

'Steady on, love,' he said. 'It doesn't have to be a local firm. Why don't we see if we can find them on the internet?'

'Good idea.' She caught sight of the time and said, 'Will you do it while I take Caroline's things to the hospital? If I leave it any later I'll get caught in the rush hour. And be sure to keep the lid on that pot and the windows closed,' she added as she hurried from the room.

It was a full half-minute after Melissa sat down beside the bed and took one of the hands lying limply on the covers before recognition dawned in Caroline's dull eyes. Her mouth flickered in a smile that died almost before it was born and her voice was little more than a whisper as she said, 'Hullo, Mel. I suppose you know why I'm here?'

'Oh, Carrie, whatever made you do it?' Melissa felt her own voice threatening to break at the sight of the misery etched on the pale features. 'Why couldn't you confide in me? You know I'm your friend; you know you can trust me.'

'It was the guilt, you see.' Caroline's eyes looked through rather than at her. 'It would have been so unfair. To tell or not to tell, that was the question.' She gave a weak laugh that held the threat of tears. 'Hamlet thought he had problems.'

'Carrie, I can't help you if I don't know what the problem is.'

'I know.' Tears gathered, overflowed and trickled slowly down the colourless cheeks. Caroline made no attempt to brush them away and Melissa gently dried them with a paper tissue from a packet on the bedside cabinet. 'No one can help. That's why I–' Her weak grasp of Melissa's hand suddenly tightened and she said, almost fiercely, 'I should have died. Why didn't you leave me there to die?'

'I'm sure you know the answer to that one. And I'm sure also that it isn't true that no one can help. You mentioned guilt just now,' Melissa went on as Caroline's only response was to turn her head away. 'Would you like me to ask John Hamley to come and see you? Perhaps you could confide in him better than a lay person.'

This time Caroline laughed aloud, a hollow sound that held no hint of mirth. 'Secrets of the confessional and all that? Lay your burden at the feet of the Lord? If only it were that easy.'

'Well, at least think about it. It's up to you of course, but if you should change your mind, remember I'm here. And think of your mother and sister,' Melissa went on. 'How do you think they'd feel if they knew what you've done?'

'You haven't told them? Please, Mel, don't tell them. It would be a terrible shock for Mother.' More tears began to flow, tears that Melissa suspected were partly caused by self-pity.

'You might have thought of that before,' she said gently. Caroline nodded without replying. 'I've brought your handbag, a few toilet things and a nightie and so on,' she went on, putting the holdall on the bed. 'There's some make-up in here as well; I thought it might do your morale good to put a face on. I hope it was all right to go and rummage in your bedroom, by the way?'

'Of course. That's really kind of you.'

'Incidentally, Gloria Parkin was there when I went to the

house. That is, she was in Quentin's quarters. She was doing the bit of tidying up that you'd asked Mrs Wilson to do.'

Caroline gave a little gasp. 'Oh Lord!' she exclaimed. 'I'd forgotten I'd asked her to do that. Whatever was I thinking of to let that woman have a key?'

'It was only to clear out rubbish after all the furniture had been removed,' Melissa reminded her. 'There can't have been anything confidential left lying around in that part of the house, surely?'

'No, I suppose not.' Caroline appeared only partly re-assured.

'Anyway, in the event it was Gloria who did the job because Mrs Wilson's hurt her leg. She might be a gossip, but she's as honest as the day and she certainly doesn't go poking and prying. By the way, I thought I'd better tell her you were in hospital before anyone else did. I didn't give the real reason; I said you'd had a fall. Well, you had, hadn't you?' Melissa hurried on in an effort to forestall further anxiety. 'You'd fallen off the bed; there was no need to say what caused it. She was very concerned and asked me to give you her best wishes for a speedy recovery.'

'Thank you. And please thank Gloria for stepping into the breach. I'll settle with her when I get home.'

'The key to Quentin's place is in your handbag, in there.' Melissa pointed to the holdall. 'Shall I hang on to the key to your house for the time being, just in case you need anything else?'

'Yes, you might as well.' Caroline's voice took on a dreamlike quality and then trailed away. Her eyes began to close.

Melissa stood up. 'You're tired. I think I've stayed long

enough. I'll ring the hospital in the morning and if they say you can come home I'll pick you up.'

Receiving no response, Melissa tiptoed away.

'What do you suppose she meant by guilt?' asked Joe when Melissa returned home and told him of her conversation with Caroline.

'Do you remember my telling you how she blurted out something like, "How was I to know?" and "Now people will think I killed Aidan out of jealousy" when I told her about Mrs Wilson finding out about the legacy to Rosalie? It made me think at the time that she might have done something that contributed to Aidan's death.'

'That's what we both thought.'

'The problem was, we couldn't figure out what it could have been. Then Harold Finn came on the scene and we had the idea about the something or other acetate, the so-called stinging pheromone.'

'And you think that little pot of cream holds the key?'

'Supposing he sent it to Caroline and somehow she contrived to get it on to Aidan or his clothes in such a way that the bees would detect it and attack him?'

'But without meaning to kill him?' Joe looked dubious. 'What other motive could she have?'

'To put him off beekeeping, perhaps. We know she wasn't that keen on it. Or maybe just to scare the hell out of him as a kind of reprisal for all the grief he'd put her through in the past.'

'That still doesn't explain what the pot was doing in Quentin's kitchen. Or why Harold Finn should be involved in the scheme. I can't see an eminent man of science conniving with a discontented wife to help her achieve a result that couldn't have been of any benefit to him.'

'Unless,' said Melissa, 'in his case it was more than scare tactics. If it should bring about Aidan's death it would mean his sister-in-law and her daughter would be out of his clutches.'

'And Caroline wouldn't be able to shop him without dropping herself in it,' Joe said thoughtfully. 'If that is what he was planning, it's a pretty devilish scheme. More intricate than anything you've done in your novels,' he added with a grin.

'So what do we do now? Did you find Holistic Health Laboratories on the net, by the way?'

'A few near hits, but not the precise name. It may be a new outfit that hasn't found its way into cyberspace yet.'

'Suppose I ask Mike Mellor to have a root around?'

'That's not a bad idea. Tell you what' – Joe stood up and flexed the muscles in his back and shoulders – 'we could both do with some fresh air. How about a walk along the valley before we start thinking about dinner?'

'I was just about to call you,' said Mellor when Melissa telephoned him the following morning. 'I've done a bit of research on Doctor Harold Finn. He's head of a highly respected scientific institute, has a string of letters after his name and seems to be a graduate or fellow of more learned societies than you can shake a stick at. Prepares forensic reports for the police on a regular basis. No record of any hands-on activity, though. That's all carried out by staff in the laboratories.'

'That must mean he has access to all the facilities he'd need to get hold of this stuff, surely.'

'Oh, yes, but all tests, experiments and materials used

have to be logged and countersigned on account of Home Office involvement. Sorry, Mel, but I think you're barking up the wrong tree this time.'

'Oh well, thanks for trying.'

'No problem. You'll get my bill in due course, but it'll be a modest one for old times' sake.'

'That's nice of you, but I haven't told you yet why I called.'

'There's something else?'

'Yes.' She gave him a rapid account of the events of the previous day.

'Well, that does alter things,' he said when she had finished.

'What do you advise me to do?'

'This isn't a job for a private investigator,' he said without hesitation. 'You've got friends in the police; go to one of them and tell him the full story. My guess is that he'll send that pot of cream for analysis and if your suspicions are correct, try and track down the source.'

'I was afraid you'd say that,' she said sadly.

'Why? What's the problem?'

'If it is what I think it is, the police are sure to want to question Caroline, and she'll think I've betrayed her trust.'

'Seems to me she hasn't really told you anything incriminating,' he pointed out, 'and in any case, this pot of goo you found wasn't in her house. For all you know she'd never set eyes on it.'

'That's true. It would be interesting to know how it got there, though.' The question sent Melissa's thoughts flying off in a new direction and sparked a fresh charge of adrenalin as she thanked Mellor and hung up. Her next call was to the hospital; after considerable delay the ward sister informed her that no decision concerning Caroline's discharge would be taken until Doctor Constantine had seen her later that morning. That meant she had time to contact her old friend Detective Sergeant Matt Waters.

27

When Melissa called the hospital again at midday she was put on hold while the ward sister contacted Doctor Constantine. After a couple of minutes he came on the line and said, in the lilting voice that seemed to carry a hint of his native sunshine, 'I have arranged for Mrs Cresney to be seen by a psychiatrist tomorrow, so we shall be keeping her in at least one more night. I think,' he continued before Melissa had a chance to ask any questions, 'that her relatives should be informed. In view of her mother's delicate health, I wonder if you would be kind enough to have a word with her sister first, to minimise the shock and distress the news will undoubtedly cause.'

'Yes, of course I'll do that,' she said. 'What should I tell them? Caroline begged me not to say anything about her suicide attempt.'

'I'm afraid they will have to know eventually, but for the time being I suggest you simply say that Mrs Cresney has suffered a breakdown, brought about by the double tragedy, and that in my opinion – which I am confident the psychiatrist will endorse – she should remain in our care at least until there is someone at home to look after her for a while. If the sister – Miss Jennifer Blackley, I believe her name is – could arrange to come to the hospital, Doctor Fairclough and I can put her fully into the picture.'

'That makes good sense. How is Caroline at the moment?'

'She is making a good physical recovery, but mentally she seems quite apathetic and indifferent to what is going on around her. She made no objection to remaining here for at least one more day, but I am not convinced that she was taking in what I was saying and I have not said anything in her hearing about contacting her relatives. Is there any chance that you could call me later today, after you have spoken to Miss Blackley? I shall be here until at least five o'clock. We could then agree on what we tell Mrs Cresney.'

'Yes, I'll certainly do that.'

'Thank you, Mrs Martin.'

'Poor Caroline!' Melissa exclaimed as she hung up. 'She seems to be sinking deeper and deeper into the mire.' She repeated Doctor Constantine's advice in response to Joe's raised eyebrows.

He compressed his lips and gave an impatient shake of the head. 'I had a feeling right at the outset that it was a mistake to get too closely involved with her,' he said. 'Anyway, once the sister's been put in the picture, our responsibility should be over and we can get back to normal. Have you got her number, by the way? I thought you left Caroline's bag at the hospital.'

'I did, but I had a hunch something like this might happen so I sneakily kept her address book.' Melissa had taken it from her own handbag and was riffling through the pages as she spoke. 'Here we are.' She tapped out the number and waited.

Mercifully, Jennie Blackley answered. Her response to Melissa's carefully prepared message was, 'Poor Carrie. I can't say I'm altogether surprised, though. She's been under terrific strain ever since Aidan died, and her life was far from easy even before then.'

'That's been our impression,' Melissa said.

'I was planning to come next week anyway to talk about the proposed move. One of our neighbours has promised to keep an eye on Mother while I'm away and I'm sure she won't mind moving the arrangement forward a couple of days. Assuming there's no problem, I'll catch the first train tomorrow and I should be in time to have a talk to the psychiatrist.'

'That would be wonderful. I'll tell Doctor Constantine and he'll pass the message on to Caroline. More than anything in the world I think she needs company. Being in that big house alone can't have been much fun for her.'

'I'm sure you're right. It was a rotten thing for Quentin to do, walking out and leaving her like that. I expect Carrie told you the story of his serial marriages.' It was a statement rather than a question.

'Yes, she did, but I believe there's something she isn't telling me – something she feels guilty about. Have you any idea what it might be?'

'Not the slightest, I'm afraid.'

'Well, never mind. Maybe she'll tell you when you see her. By the way, if you need to contact me for any reason, you might care to make a note of the number.' She studiously avoided Joe's eye as she dictated it.

'Is this a social invitation or do you want to pick my brains in aid of some mystery plot Mel's hatching? She sounded quite mysterious on the phone.' There was a humorous glint in Matt Waters' blue-grey eyes as he accepted a gin and tonic from Joe, helped himself from a dish of nuts offered by Melissa and sat back with the relaxed air of a man among friends.

'If only!' Joe rolled his eyes in mock despair. 'Not only has she become embroiled in what she's convinced is a particularly fiendish murder plot, she's also managed to con me into joining in the sleuthing.'

'Not true – you volunteered,' Melissa interposed.

'Only so I could keep tabs on you,' he retorted, 'but in any case, it soon began to look like a wild-goose chase, although I have to admit that was before Caroline Cresney staged her little drama. I'm beginning to regret getting involved, but you know Mel. She's given up writing mysteries, but give her so much as a whiff of a real one and she's on it like a wasp to a honey-pot.'

'Do you mind choosing your similes a bit more carefully?' she said with a shudder.

'Sorry!' said Joe, looking anything but as he winked at their visitor. 'Anyway, cheers!' He raised his glass and the others did likewise. 'It's great to see you, Matt.'

'It's great to be here. I must say married life seems to suit you both.' His smile held a hint of wistfulness; he had lived a bachelor existence since the death of his wife some years ago and so far as they knew there was no woman in his life. 'How's your mother settling in, Mel?'

'Fine, thank you,' she replied. 'She's going to join us for dinner in a little while, but we wanted a private chat with you first. If Mum got wind of what it's about she'd insist on joining in, and that would quite likely mean some of her gossipy friends picking it up.'

'So this is all very hush-hush?'

'Only as far as the locals are concerned – and of course, if you consider it's something that needs investigating and

your lot start poking around, it's bound to get out. Here.'
Melissa handed Matt the résumé she had earlier shown to
ex-Detective Sergeant Mellor and to which she had added
an account of Caroline's suicide attempt and their subsequent conversation in the hospital. 'That's a potted account
of the situation from the beginning.'

'Thanks.' Matt read through the printed sheets without
comment. Then he laid them aside, picked up his glass and
sat sipping it, apparently deep in thought. After few
moments' silence he said, unconsciously echoing Mellor's
verdict, 'It's certainly a rum business. Have you got that pot
of cream handy?'

'Right here.' Melissa fetched it from a drawer and handed
it to him.

He smiled at the sight of the layer of cling-film.
'Protecting the fingerprints then?'

'Protecting herself, more like,' Joe grinned. 'She came
rushing in as though an entire swarm of bees was pursuing
her!'

'I'm afraid the idea of preserving prints never occurred to
me at the time,' she admitted. 'Anyway, in all probability the
most recent ones on it would be Sarah's, but as she's dead
there's no way of checking.'

'And you found this in a bag of rubbish in the Quentin
Cresneys' kitchen?' said Matt. Melissa nodded. 'Was there
an envelope or any other form of wrapping it might have
been in? Or a leaflet giving information about the product?'

She shook her head. 'I didn't see anything like that. Most
of the stuff in the bag was food waste. There were several
other bags that Gloria took out to the wheelie-bin, but I've
no idea what was in those.'

'Hmm.' Matt finished his drink, but shook his head when

Joe offered him a refill. Then he carefully peeled off the cling-film, unscrewed the lid of the pot and sniffed. 'You're right,' he said, 'there is a distinct smell of bananas. If it isn't genuine banana extract, have you any idea what it might be?'

'There's a chemical called isopentyl acetate that smells of bananas. It's also a constituent of what is known as the stinging pheromone of bees. When other bees get a scent of it they think their colony's under attack and come rushing to the defence.'

'By stinging what they assume to be the enemy?'

'I assume that's how it works.'

'So what do you know about this chemical?'

'Doctor Harold Finn told me it was commercially available and we checked it on the internet for further information,' said Melissa. 'It seems to be quite common – in fact it was used in a recent experiment to test people's sense of smell. Apparently women have more sensitive noses than men, which I thought was quite interesting.'

'I know one woman who has a nose for trouble,' said Joe darkly, earning a gleeful grin from his wife.

'This is probably a silly question,' said Matt, 'but is it likely to be used as a cosmetic ingredient?'

'I wouldn't think so,' Melissa said. 'It's liable to cause skin and eye irritation.'

'So what you're suggesting is that someone added a quantity of this chemical to some basic, odourless material – cold cream, for example – put it in this little pot, dressed it up as a free sample of a fancy skin treatment and sent it to Sarah Cresney with the deliberate intention of inducing bees to sting her?'

'Not only that, I think it was the same person who

somehow contrived to use the same substance to bring about the death of her brother-in-law.'

Matt picked up the notes he had laid aside and read through the final paragraph a second time. 'I see you refer to Caroline Cresney as having more than once hinted that she had something on her conscience,' he said. 'I imagine you suspect her of being an accessory to the crime . . . assuming, of course, that there was a crime.'

Melissa bit her lip as a mental image of Caroline's haunted expression and pale, drawn features seemed to float in front of her eyes. 'I'm afraid so,' she said sadly. 'The best I can hope for is that she was somehow inveigled into it without appreciating how serious the consequences would be.'

Matt rewrapped the pot in the cling-film and sat fingering it for a minute or two without speaking. Then he said, 'I think, on reflection, it mightn't be a bad idea to get this stuff analysed. Are you happy for me to take it, and your notes, Mel? I'd like to show them to our DI and get his reaction.'

'Sure,' she said and Joe nodded in agreement.

Matt folded the notes and put them in his pocket along with the pot of cream. 'If this stuff does contain the chemical you mentioned,' he said, 'it would certainly suggest, at the very least, that someone has been guilty of supplying a noxious substance — possibly through the post. It's a pity you didn't find the envelope it came in. A postmark might have given us a lead.'

'If it hasn't been destroyed already, it's probably in one of the other bags of rubbish that Gloria was putting out for collection.'

'Which will be when?'

'Next Monday.'

'That's a pity. Without some positive evidence to support our suspicions, there'd be no chance of organising a search – certainly not by Monday.'

'How long do you think it will take to get a result from the lab?' asked Joe.

'Could be up to a week, I'm afraid.'

Further discussion was ruled out by Sylvia's arrival, but later, after the guests had departed, Melissa said, 'It's a shame it's going to take so long to get the lab report. If there is any evidence in those rubbish bags, it'll have been lost by the time we find out.'

'I'd have thought there was enough in what we've given Matt to justify going through their contents, even without the lab report,' said Joe. 'He certainly took it seriously. Still,' he added with a shrug, 'I suppose, with the civil liberties and human rights lobbies breathing down their necks, the police have to do everything by the book nowadays.'

'Of course they do,' she agreed, 'but we don't.'

It took him a few seconds to grasp her meaning. Then he said, 'Mel, I don't think I want to know about this.'

'Then I shan't tell you.'

'I suppose there's no point in my doing the heavy husband and ordering you to stay home and do the house-work?'

She sidled up to him and put her face close to his. 'None whatsoever, my love.'

28

The following morning, after an early breakfast, Melissa set off on the half-mile walk to Cold Wells. The route took her away from the main village street and there was little chance of meeting anyone at that hour; just the same she went at an easy pace as if taking advantage of an exceptionally pleasant early autumn morning to go for a stroll.

The precaution proved unnecessary; there was no one about and as she approached the house she became aware of an unfamiliar stillness in the air. Apart from a few birds darting about, nothing stirred. It took her a moment to realise that the uncanny silence was caused by the absence of bees. Colin Palmer had kept his promise to remove the hives, so instead of using the drive she cut through the orchard, pushed the wheelie-bin containing the three bags of rubbish to Caroline's front door, let herself into the house and took the bags into the kitchen. She found a pile of old newspapers under the sink, spread one on the floor, emptied the first of the bags on to it and began rummaging through the contents.

It soon became apparent that Quentin had lived largely on convenience foods for the few days he had spent at home alone following Sarah's death. Melissa carefully examined each empty packet and plastic container before returning it to the bag, but found nothing of any significance. She repeated the process with the second bag, but again drew a blank.

The third bag was more promising. Among a large quantity of junk mail and inserts from newspapers and magazines were numerous envelopes. Careful inspection revealed that most of them were of ordinary letter size; a few larger ones appeared to have contained documents or catalogues and bore the names of well-known companies or mail order firms. She was beginning to give up hope of finding anything remotely suitable for posting a sample pot of cream when she gave a little exclamation of triumph. Right at the bottom of the heap was a small padded envelope bearing a typewritten label addressed to Mrs Sarah Cresney, Cold Wells Manor, Upper Benbury. It bore a Swindon postmark and from the date of posting she calculated that it would have been delivered very shortly before the day when Sarah was attacked by the bees. She turned the package over and found the sender had omitted to give an address. It might not be significant, of course; not everyone bothered with such details, but it would be an obvious precaution on the part of a person with something to hide.

She had been kneeling on the floor while carrying out her examination. Now she sat back on her heels and studied the envelope with rising excitement. She lifted it to her nose and sniffed, half hoping to detect a trace of the banana-like smell, but was disappointed. 'Never mind,' she said aloud as she laid the envelope aside and began returning the rest of the rubbish to the bag. 'If there's even the faintest smidgeon of the stuff on it, the lab will find it.'

She glanced at her watch. It was still too early for Roger to arrive with the post, but the public footpath that skirted

the Cresney property was popular with village people exer-
cising their dogs. She had already agreed with Joe that it
would be advisable, should she meet anyone she knew, to
be ready with a convincing pretext for her visit. Having
resealed the bags of rubbish she went up to Caroline's room
and quickly put a change of clothes into a shopping bag she
found hanging up in the kitchen. They might in any case be
needed if Caroline should be discharged from hospital
within the next day or two. She put the bags back in the
wheelie-bin, returned it to its original place outside
Quentin's back door and went home.

She found Joe at his desk in the study. 'Look what I
found!' she exclaimed, waving the envelope under his nose.
'What's the betting this contained that pot of doctored
cream I found in Quentin's kitchen?'

He took it and turned it over in his hands. 'It could have
done, I suppose, but it's not much of a clue when there's no
indication of where it came from.'

'But don't you see, that's exactly why it's suspicious?'

'Darling, not everyone bothers to write their name and
address on the back of their letters.'

'I know, I thought of that, but that sample of cream
purported to come from a commercial laboratory. You'd
expect them to have their address on their labels, don't you
think?'

'I suppose so.'

'I think it's worth investigating. I'm going to show it to
Matt.'

'Is that wise?' Joe looked dubious. 'You had no authority
to go ferreting around in the Cresneys' dustbins. The police
can be quite touchy about people taking the law into their
own hands, you know.'

'I'll chance being nicked for unlawful entry,' she said cheerfully. 'By the way, what have you got there?' She pointed to some printed sheets lying on his desk.

'Just doing a follow up to your research about isoamyl acetate. I've been learning about bananas.'

'Bananas? Why on earth–'

'As it's common knowledge that this stinging pheromone smells of bananas I thought it might be interesting to find out why. This article has the answer.' He handed her the printout. 'Read the bit on the top of page 2.'

She scanned the paragraph he indicated. 'So bananas contain isopentyl acetate, aka isoamyl acetate,' she said. 'Surely you aren't suggesting that pot of cream I found contains mashed-up fruit?'

'I think that's most unlikely. I'm no chemist, but I'd say it would make a pretty disgusting mess that no one would want to put on their face.'

'So how does this article help us?'

'Bananas contain a number of other chemicals as well and I happened to recognise two of them, namely serotonin and dopamine.'

'What are they?'

'They occur naturally in the human nervous system. A deficiency of dopamine is thought to be a cause of Parkinson's disease.'

'How do you know all this?'

'My uncle suffered from it for several years before he died. He was treated with a drug containing dopamine.'

Melissa put the article back on the desk and sat down. 'If I read you correctly,' she said slowly, 'you're suggesting that someone might be exploring the possibility of obtaining the substances naturally from bananas. Isoamyl acetate wouldn't necessarily be of any use for their particular purpose, but it might well occur as a sort of by-product during the experiments. Maybe that someone wrote a paper about it, and that paper was read by another person who thought of a different use for it altogether.'

'Something like that.'

'You're thinking of Doctor Harold Finn?'

'Well, he is a biochemist of some eminence,' Joe reminded her, 'and he happens to be very knowledgeable about the chemistry of bees.'

'He also had good reason to wish Aidan Cresney out of the way.' Melissa rested an elbow on the desk and cupped her chin in one hand. 'Caroline guessed he was having an affair and hired Mike Mellor to get the evidence,' she said after a moment spent weighing up the implications of Joe's discovery. 'When she confronted him with it he more or less gave her two fingers, having got things sewn up so that a divorce was pretty well out of the question. That must have made her feel pretty sick, to say the least. Maybe she got in touch with Finn, knowing he shared her feelings about the liaison, and suggested they put their heads together to find a way to get rid of the old bugger. I'm positive she knows more about his death than she's prepare to admit,' she went on. 'Remember the phone call I overheard?'

'You've no proof she was talking to Finn.'

'She was talking to someone who didn't need to be told how Aidan had died, and she's obviously weighed down with guilt about something. If only I could get her to talk about it.'

'She's not likely to do that if it means incriminating herself.'

'True,' she agreed, 'but it still doesn't explain why they tried the same trick on Sarah.'

'You're right. As far as we know, Caroline had no reason to want her out of the way. She took Aidan's death quite calmly, but she was really distressed when Sarah died.'

'Maybe that was Finn acting on his own. Maybe Sarah had somehow found out what he and Caroline had done and threatened to blow the whistle.'

'It's possible, I suppose.'

'And there's something else it doesn't explain,' Melissa went on. 'Finn says this chemical is readily available commercially, so why go to the trouble of extracting it from bananas?'

'Because he had no legitimate use for it in his official capacity?' Joe suggested.

'So he might have been stewing it up in his garden shed? Unlikely, don't you think?'

They fell silent again, each mentally sifting over the few shreds of information they had managed to glean so far. When the telephone rang, they both jumped. Melissa picked up the receiver and said, 'Hullo.'

'It's Jennie Blackley here. I'm at the station, waiting for a taxi to take me to the hospital. I'm awfully sorry to trouble you, but I'm wondering if I could possibly see you before I meet the doctors who are treating my sister. You see . . .' there was a pause as if she was searching for the right words, 'you said yesterday that you thought Carrie had something on her mind and you asked me if I knew what it might be?'

'I remember,' prompted Melissa as Jennie hesitated again.

'I said I had no idea, but that wasn't entirely true. I've been giving it a lot of thought since then and I'd appreciate an opportunity to discuss it with you. I get the impression that you're the only person she's had to confide in since Sarah died. If you could possibly spare a few minutes–'

'Yes, of course, no problem. When you get to the hospital, go to the cafeteria on the ground floor and I'll meet you there in about half an hour.'

'Oh, thank you, thank you so much.' A tide of almost tangible relief flowed along the wire.

'It seems an awful imposition, lumbering you with all our family problems when you must have so many other things to think about,' said Jennie. She sat opposite Melissa at a Formica-topped table in the hospital canteen, stirring a cup of coffee that she had made no attempt to drink.

'It's all right, I'm in no hurry,' Melissa assured her. If she was about to learn something that could help to explain Caroline's suicide attempt she was prepared to be patient.

'I promise I won't take up a lot of your time. I've left a message on the ward that I'm here and they'll call me on my mobile when Doctor Constantine is ready to see me.'

'It's all right,' Melissa repeated. 'I've got nothing special on this morning.'

'It's so good of you to . . . I mean, there's no one else I can talk to. Sarah's dead – not that I was ever particularly close to her, although she and Carrie seemed to get on okay – and as for Quentin, so far as I know he's been faithful to Sarah since they re-married, but deep down Carrie and I still believe he never stopped loving Poppy. Just the same, it was rotten of him to run out on Carrie like that.' She took a mouthful from her cup, pulled a face and put it down again. 'It's got cold,' she muttered.

'Let me get you another one.'

'There's no need–' Jennie began, but Melissa ignored the protest, went to the machine and brought a fresh cup back to the table.

'Drink that first and then we'll talk,' she said. Watching Jennie as she obediently sipped the coffee, Melissa was struck by the contrast between her and her younger sister. It was easy to see why she was the one who had stayed at home to care for their handicapped widowed mother; she was as homely in appearance as her sister was attractive. She wore no make-up, her clothes were undistinguished and her figure was on the dumpy side. Yet beneath her natural anxiety lay a hint of serenity, as if she accepted her lot without resentment. Perhaps Caroline's experience of marriage had been enough to reconcile her to her own situation.

When her cup was empty she put it back on the saucer and wiped her mouth with a tissue. Then she looked directly at Melissa and said, 'Did Carrie tell you that Aidan manipulated things so that Quentin left Poppy and went back to Sarah?'

'Yes, but she didn't explain how.'

'A year or two after he married Poppy, Quentin was taken ill and rushed into hospital. Poppy happened to be away at the time so it was a golden opportunity for Aidan to take charge. He knew the top people in pretty well every profession you can think of and he arranged for Quentin to be transferred to a private clinic. Poppy wasn't even consulted; in fact Aidan omitted to let her know of her husband's illness and when she came home – she'd been abroad on some international convention – she found herself completely sidelined. Aidan took every decision regarding Quentin's treatment and from then on he seemed to regard getting him back with Sarah as a kind of mission.'

'But why, if he and Poppy were happy?'

'I don't think their happiness was important to Aidan. All he was interested in was regaining control over his brother. Sarah was the wife he had chosen for him and he couldn't rest until he'd restored the status quo, so to speak.'

'Presumably Sarah wanted Quentin back?'

'I suppose so, but even if she hadn't, I doubt if Aidan would have taken much notice. I know it sounds fantastic, but that's the kind of man he was.'

'Yes, we always thought of him as something of a control freak,' said Melissa. 'He managed to ruffle quite a few feathers in the village, pushing his ideas through after he joined the parish council.'

'As far as the family was concerned, for control freak read tyrant. No one could stand up to him.'

'I see.' Melissa toyed absent-mindedly with her empty coffee cup. 'Look, Jennie,' she said awkwardly, 'I don't want to sound unhelpful, but I don't quite understand why you're telling me all this.'

'I was awake most of last night trying to figure out exactly what caused Carrie's breakdown,' said Jennie, and once again she looked directly into Melissa's eyes. 'She and I both suspected that Quentin had come to hate his brother for the way he'd controlled and manipulated him throughout his life. He'd managed to break away once and find real happiness with Poppy, only to be reeled in a couple of years later like a fish on the end of a line. I believe that was the last straw for him.'

Melissa stared at her, open-mouthed. 'Jennie, what are you saying?'

'You might think this sounds crazy, and I can't begin to imagine how he did it, but I think Quentin killed Aidan and somehow or other tricked Caroline into playing a part in the murder. Now she realises what she's done and she's weighed down with guilt. That must be what sent her over the edge.'

29

'Q uentin?' Melissa exclaimed in astonishment.

Jennie nodded. 'That surprises you?'

Melissa found herself momentarily lost for words. Her mind had flown back to Rosalie Finn's visit to Hawthorn Cottage after Aidan's funeral and the girl's confident assertion that his brother had been responsible for his death. Only after Sarah's death in similar circumstances to Aidan had she and Joe been prepared to believe that a crime might have been committed, but in spite of Rosalie's allegations Quentin had never seriously featured on their list of suspects. What Jennie had just revealed showed him in a different light. If everything she said were true, it was possible that the destruction of his marriage to Poppy had aroused something more than the mere jealousy that Rosalie had put forward as a motive. Had Quentin developed over the years a deep and corrosive hatred of his brother? Hatred was an emotion that had led down the ages to conspiracy, violence and death. The more Melissa learned about the dark forces at work within the Cresney family, the more inclined she was to believe them capable of almost anything.

'Yes, it does surprise me,' she said after a long pause. 'To be frank, I've always thought of Quentin as a bit of a wimp. Then when he started chucking his weight about after

Aidan's death, doing his "I'm the head of the family now" act, I found him pretty objectionable. It wasn't until Caroline told me something of the family history that I began to feel more sympathetic towards him. Just the same, I'd never have thought him capable of plotting murder.'

'But you do now?' Jennie's tone sounded almost urgent, as if it was important that Melissa should share her conviction.

'Nothing's impossible,' Melissa said slowly, 'but what about Sarah's death? You aren't suggesting he had anything to do with that, are you?'

'I suppose not, except that it wasn't until after that happened that Carrie started to get really screwed up and talk about guilt.' Despite the admission, Jennie sounded doubtful. 'Her reaction to Aidan's death was relief, liberation, call it what you like, although of course she had to be careful not to let anyone except me know exactly how she felt.'

'I'm afraid her very controlled response to widowhood did arouse some comment in the village,' Melissa said.

'Yes, I know. She was aware of that and felt she could handle it, but it was different after Sarah died. It was almost as if she held herself responsible for the double tragedy.'

'Couldn't it have been the sheer trauma of it all that sent her over the edge?' Even as she spoke, and recalling Caroline's virtual admission that she was holding something back, Melissa realised that in a sense she was playing the devil's advocate. She toyed briefly with the notion of taking Jennie into her confidence, but decided this was hardly the moment. It was more important to listen, to glean every scrap of new information this conversation might reveal.

'I don't think so,' Jennie replied. 'The last time I spoke to Carrie on the phone, she muttered something to the effect that Sarah should have kept her mouth shut.'

'You think Sarah found out how Aidan's death had come about and tackled Quentin about it?' said Melissa. 'Is that why she had to die too?' It was not the first time such a notion had occurred to her, although she had never pursued it. Now, it began to look like a hideous possibility. Was there no end to the horror that threatened to engulf the entire Cresney family?

'I don't know, I don't know.' Without warning Jennie's voice disintegrated, her face crumpled and her eyes filled. Melissa waited while she struggled to control herself. 'When I asked her what she meant by that,' she resumed after wiping her eyes and blowing her nose, 'she back-tracked and made me promise to forget it and not repeat it to anyone. I've kept that promise so far – even Mother doesn't know – but now I'm wondering whether . . . that's why I'm telling you. I'd really appreciate your advice. If Quentin really is a double murderer he shouldn't be allowed to get away with it, but how can I betray my own sister?' Her eyes, even more than her words, were pleading for help. She looked young, vulnerable and desperately unhappy. Melissa was reminded of her son Simon when, years ago, he had laid some cause for teenage angst at her feet, hoping she might solve his problems with a few words of maternal wisdom.

Melissa decided that the time for prevarication was over. 'Look, Jennie,' she said, 'neither Joe nor I seriously thought Quentin might be involved, but we have both come round to the idea that Caroline knows more about Aidan's death than she's admitted. That doesn't mean that she deliberately contributed to it, but like you I think she may have been tricked into it because she once blurted out, "How was I to know?" and then clammed up when I asked her what she meant.'

'I wish there was some way we could prove it without hurting her more than she's been hurt already.' Jennie wiped more tears from her woebegone face.

'The problem all along has been that there seemed no doubt it was apparently a bizarre and terrible accident. Then Sarah was also the victim of a similar incident and it seemed too much of a coincidence. I've been doing some research and it does seem that such attacks could be contrived, but it would need a particular expertise plus the right facilities to bring it off.'

'What sort of expertise?'

'Some knowledge of the chemistry of bees, for a start. As a matter of fact, I think I may have found such a person, but–'

Jennie's hand flew to her mouth and her eyes jerked wide open. She stared at Melissa as if transfixed, then started violently as her mobile phone rang and began scrabbling in her handbag. 'I hate these things . . . I can never find . . . whatever have I done with the silly . . . oh, here it is . . . hullo? Speaking . . . oh, thank you, I'll come at once.' She switched off the mobile phone with shaking hands, put it in her handbag and stood up. 'That was the ward sister. The doctor's with Carrie, so I have to go now. Please, can we talk again?'

'Of course. You have my number.'

'Thank you.' Jennie's voice was unsteady but she managed a weak smile before hurrying to the exit.

★   ★   ★

'Jennie looked really shocked when I mentioned the chemistry of bees,' said Melissa when she returned home and told Joe about their conversation. 'It obviously rang a bell, but unfortunately she was called away before I could ask her any more questions.'

'There are sure to be other opportunities,' said Joe. 'She said she wanted to talk to you again.'

'Breaking off just when you think they're about to say something interesting seems to run in the family,' Melissa complained.

'At least you've learned something this morning.'

'About how Aidan engineered the end of Quentin's marriage to Poppy, you mean? It doesn't really add much to our store of knowledge, does it?'

'That isn't what I meant, although it's interesting that both Jennie and Rosalie suspect Quentin.'

'What did you mean then?'

'Doesn't Jennie's reaction to bee chemistry suggest an acquaintance with someone who fits your description? Our old friend Doctor Harold Finn, for example? I'm surprised you didn't spot it.'

'It did cross my mind that she might have heard of him,' said Melissa, 'but she's hardly likely to know of his connection with Aidan's fancy woman. Mike Mellor didn't know anything about him until he did some investigation on our behalf, so Caroline wouldn't have done either.'

'Mel, you're slipping. What were we saying the other day about books on beekeeping?'

'Gosh, yes, of course. We'd figured that could explain how Caroline and Finn got together . . . but would she have mentioned it to Jennie? She obviously doesn't tell her everything.' She was struck by another thought. 'Jennie never mentioned the legacy to Rosalie.'

'We don't know for certain that it was left to Rosalie,' Joe pointed out. 'It might have been to her mother.'

'True, but it doesn't make much difference, does it? I wonder if Jennie knows?'

'Surely Caroline would have told her?'

'She might have done, but without letting on that it had become a cause for gossip in the village. I still think that was enough, on top of the guilt and the trauma, to push her over the edge. And none of it is going to go away.'

'Well, there's nothing we can do at the moment except wait for Jennie to phone.'

When Jennie did phone, towards the end of the afternoon, her message was brief. 'They want Carrie to stay in hospital over the weekend and I'm going to stay with her,' she said. 'She's explained everything to me and she's feeling loads better after getting it off her chest. I'm planning to take her home with me for a few days after she's discharged. We're going to put it all behind us now and start a new life once the house is ready.'

'Well, it's good to hear you speaking so positively,' said Melissa. 'Perhaps it was being on her own so much that blew things up out of all proportion.'

'Yes, I'm sure that's what it was. It's such a relief to know that it's all over.' It seemed to Melissa that the acceptance of her suggested explanation was a shade too enthusiastic. Her suspicions were aroused still further when Jennie added, 'Carrie sends her love and says she's sure you'll be glad you don't have to bother with our problems any more. You've been so good to her and we can't thank you enough.'

'I'm glad things are working out for you both. If there's anything else I can do–'

'Oh, I'm sure we'll manage just fine. Goodbye for now.'

'In other words, call off the bloodhounds,' said Melissa after relaying the message to Joe.

'You reckon Caroline's made her confession to her sister and they've decided to keep stumm?'

'That's what it looks like to me.'

'Are you going to go along with it?'

'Am I heck! I've already told Matt the story so far and he's sent the pot of cream for analysis. We'll just have to wait until he gets the result, but in the meantime–'

'Suppose it turns out to be completely innocuous?'

'I suppose that'd be the end of the matter, but after hearing Jennie all but pleading with me not to do any more research I'm pretty sure it won't be.'

'In which case, wouldn't it be better to leave it to the police?'

'There's no guarantee they'll follow it up. They're always complaining about shortage of manpower.'

'But surely, in a case of murder–'

'Even if there is isoamyl acetate in that cream, they may not consider it's strong enough evidence that a crime's been committed, but . . . all right, I suppose we might as well wait and see what Matt has to say.'

Seeing Joe's look of relief at her final words, she decided not to tell him for the time being about the idea forming in her mind.

On Monday, Melissa had an appointment with her accountant in Swindon. Joe had elected to stay at home and work, for which she was secretly grateful as, while he was busy in the garden on Sunday morning, she had done some further research on the internet. This had yielded some interesting information, which she decided to keep to herself for the time being. After her meeting she drove to an industrial estate on the outskirts of the town. A short while later she entered the modern premises of HAF Laboratories Limited, Industrial Chemists, where she asked to speak to the chairman, Doctor Harold Finn.

'I'm sorry, he isn't in today,' said the girl on the reception desk. 'Can anyone else help you, or would you like to leave a message?'

'I'm trying to contact these people.' Melissa handed over one of her business cards, on the back of which she had written the words 'Holistic Health Laboratories'. I asked for Doctor Finn because I happen to have met him, but maybe someone else here knows them?'

'I'll ask Doctor Pendleton. She has a lot of outside contacts.' The receptionist picked up the phone, waited a moment and then said, 'I have a lady here who's trying to trace an outfit called Holistic Health Laboratories. Do you know anything about them?' After a moment, she said, 'Thank you, I'll tell her,' put down the phone and said, 'would you like to go up to the first floor? Doctor Pendleton's office is the first door on the left.'

Doctor Penelope Pendleton was a slight, sharp-featured woman with bright intelligent eyes, whom Melissa judged to be in her mid-forties. She greeted Melissa with a pleasant smile and a brisk 'Good morning' and offered her a seat. She scrutinised the card, frowned and shook her head. 'I'm afraid I don't know these people,' she said. 'How did you come to hear of them?'

'They sent a free sample of one their skin creams to a

friend of mine. She said it was rather nice and we thought we'd try and get some more, but we can't find it in the shops. She lost the envelope it came in so we don't know their address, they aren't in the phone book and they don't appear to have a web site.'

'They're not likely to sell much of their product if no one knows where to get it,' Doctor Pendleton commented. 'What made you come to us, by the way? Our business is mainly with the food and brewing industries.'

Melissa was momentarily thrown; evidently her research had not been quite thorough enough. Fortunately, her inventive mind came to her rescue. 'I happen to have met your chairman recently,' she explained, 'and as I was in the neighbourhood I thought I'd call in on the off-chance.'

Doctor Pendleton frowned. 'It must be a very new outfit,' she said. 'Would you like to leave this with me? I'll ask around and if I find out anything I'll give you a call.'

'That's very kind of you. Thank you.'

As she returned to her car, it occurred to Melissa that perhaps she had been too impatient. Perhaps she should have made an appointment to see Harold Finn so that she could tell him face to face the story she had concocted and observe his reaction. Of course, even had he been there, he might have refused to see her. On the other hand, there was no guarantee that Doctor Pendleton would refer the query to him.

'Oh well,' she said to herself as she set off for home, 'all I can do now is wait and see.'

She did not have long to wait.

30

Roger was late with his deliveries on Wednesday. He arrived just as Melissa and Sylvia were unloading their purchases after a shopping trip to Cheltenham.

'Morning, ladies,' he said as he got out of his van. 'That looks heavy. Want a hand with it?' Without waiting for a reply he put the pile of letters he was carrying on top of a half-case of wine in the open boot of Melissa's car and picked it up. 'When's the party?'

'No party, just our dinner-time tipple,' replied Melissa. 'That's kind of you, Roger. Would you mind bringing it through to the kitchen?' This was the up side of life in a village, she thought to herself as he followed her and her mother along the narrow hallway and dumped the box on the table. It might number a few gossips among the inhabitants, but there was always someone willing to lend a hand with even the smallest task.

'No trouble,' said Roger. 'Sorry to be late this morning. I got talking to the ladies at Cold Well Manor. Mrs Cresney seems a whole lot better now she's got her sister with her.'

'Yes, I'm sure she is.'

'Must have been a shock, passing out like that. Wonder what caused it? Couldn't have been a stroke, could it? She seems a bit young for that.'

'I understand she had a fall,' said Melissa.

'That's right,' said Sylvia. 'It was so lucky that I happened to be on the phone to her at the time. I heard her cry out and then a bump, so I knew something was wrong.'

'I wonder what caused the fall?' Roger glanced first at Sylvia and then at Melissa. 'It must have been something serious. Mrs Parkin's sister-in-law works in the hospital and she said Mrs Cresney was in intensive care and they had to send for her family.' From the expectant look on his ruddy weather-beaten countenance, it was evident that he was looking to the two women for more details.

'We haven't heard the medical reports, but we understand that her sister was coming to spend a few days with her anyway,' said Melissa.

'Oh, I see. Well, I'm sure she'll be better for a bit of company.' He hovered in the doorway for a moment as if hoping she would add to her statement, but she merely nodded and began unpacking one of the bags she and Sylvia had already brought in. 'That the lot, then?' Despite his late arrival he seemed in no hurry to leave.

'There's only a couple of things left and they're not heavy. Many thanks for your help.'

'Any time.' After a further moment's hesitation he went back to his van and drove off.

'Who's Mrs Parkin?' asked Sylvia as soon as he had gone.

'Gloria, who else?' Melissa rolled her eyes in exasperation. 'She and her Stanley between them seem to have friends and relatives round every corner. It's like a mini mafia, except there's no malice in any of them, just an insatiable appetite for gossip.'

'At least Roger didn't know the real reason for Caroline being in hospital,' said Sylvia. 'I'm glad you didn't tell him.'

'If it had been left to me, I wouldn't have told him as

much as you did. If he tells Mrs Foster that we were the ones who alerted the medics, you'll have old Cynthia Long-nose Thorne and her cronies after you for details in no time.'

'Well, they won't get them. They're terrible gossips, you know,' said Sylvia with an air of virtue that made her daughter turn away to hide a smile. 'Had you heard Caroline was home, by the way?'

Melissa paused in the act of stowing dairy items in the refrigerator. 'No, I hadn't,' she said, frowning. 'I'm surprised Jennie didn't let me know.' There had been no word from either of the sisters since Jennie's phone call late on Saturday afternoon.

'Well, I expect they want to put it all behind them now. It's been a dreadful time for them. Has Quentin come back, by the way?'

'Not so far as I know.'

'I do think it was inconsiderate of him to go off like that.'

'Inconsiderate's not the word.' It crossed Melissa's mind to tell her mother the true reason for Quentin's absence, but she decided to leave it for the time being. It was possible that once things were more settled, she might learn it from Caroline herself.

'I wonder if that was why the poor girl took those tablets?' Sylvia said. 'She must have felt so lonely. Oh, look!' While she was speaking, she had been sorting the pile of letters Roger had left. 'Someone's sent you a prezzie!' She handed Melissa a small padded envelope. 'It's something quite small; I wonder what it is.'

Melissa's stomach went into a spasm as she took the envelope, which she saw immediately was identical to the one she had found in Quentin Cresney's kitchen and had handed over to Matt for possible forensic examination. She gave it an exploratory squeeze and felt the shape of something round. Seeing her mother's eyes fixed on it, she put it casually to one side with her other letters and said, 'It feels like a cassette. It's probably from some wannabe writer desperate for a bit of encouragement. I'll listen to it some other time. Would you like to join us for lunch, Mum?'

'Thank you, dear, that would be lovely. I'll just go and put my shopping away and read my letters. Oh dear, those look rather sorry for themselves.' She pointed to a vase of wilting dahlias on the kitchen windowsill. 'I've got some beauties in my garden; I'll cut a few for you and bring them round.'

'Thanks, Mum, see you later.'

The minute the communicating door to Brambles closed behind her, Melissa snatched up the envelope and opened it. She felt her throat tighten and her pulse give a leap as a small round pot slid out on to the kitchen table. It bore a label reading, 'Free sample of Fruit and Herb Skin Cream with the compliments of Holistic Health Laboratories'. As she anticipated, there was no clue to its origin. She was still staring at it when Joe entered the kitchen.

'That was quick work,' he exclaimed as he saw the pot. 'What's the verdict?'

'Verdict?' she said bemusedly.

'From the police lab. Isn't there a report with it?'

For answer, she handed him the envelope. He peered inside and then explored the interior with one finger. 'It's empty,' he said, his voice sharp with concern.

'Exactly. I'll bet the one addressed to Sarah was empty as well.'

'This is getting altogether too close to home.' Joe scrutinised the envelope more closely. 'It's postmarked Swindon like the other one. I wonder why it's addressed to Melissa Craig and not Mrs Martin.'

'There's no mystery there. When I met Harold Finn I gave him my card.'

'But why should he send you one of his nasty pots of cream?'

'Because he's afraid I'm on his track and he's trying to get me stung to death,' said Melissa. 'Joe, there's something I haven't told you.'

His expression became grim as she told him of her visit to HAF Laboratories on Monday. 'Well, of all the stupid, hare-brained things to do!' he exclaimed furiously when she had finished. 'Whatever you hoped to achieve, I'll bet it wasn't this. Why on earth didn't you leave it to the police? A few more days wouldn't have made any difference.'

'Please don't be angry with me, Joe. It was a spur of the moment thing; I thought, even if the police do find that chemical in the cream, there's no direct evidence of criminal intent, but I thought if I told the story I'd concocted to Harold Finn face to face he might give himself away.' Even as she spoke, she realised how lame it sounded.

'Too right, I'm angry. Now he knows you're on his track he's put you on his hit list. This' – Joe pointed to the pot of cream – 'is his first shot. If it doesn't work he'll no doubt be thinking up some other devilish way of disposing of you. I must say,' he went on, 'it doesn't seem to be a particularly smart thing for him to do. The very fact that you've tried to track down this phoney laboratory should have told him you're wise to what happened.'

'It is surprising, now you come to mention it,' Melissa agreed. 'I'd have thought any intelligent person would have realised . . . oh well, the damage is done now. We'd better hand this over to Matt right away and let him take care of it. I'll see if I can get him on the phone first and tell him the whole story.'

'Before you do that, wouldn't it be a good idea to have a word with Doctor Pendleton and ask her if she mentioned this to anyone else?'

'I suppose I could, but why?'

'Just to make sure Matt has the complete picture.'

'All right. The number's upstairs, I'll call from there.'

'I'll come with you.'

The receptionist at HAF Laboratories answered immediately. When Melissa asked to speak to Doctor Pendleton she said, 'I've got a feeling she's . . . just a moment.' She broke off and Melissa heard her say to someone nearby, 'Janice, do you know if Poppy's gone to lunch?'

Melissa barely heard the receptionist's offer to take a message. She put down the phone and sank into a chair. Her head was reeling and her stomach churning. 'How in the world could I have been such a fool?' she muttered.

'Mel, what is it? You're as pale as a ghost.'

'Poppy,' she said shakily. 'Doctor Penelope Pendleton is known to the staff at HAF Laboratories as Poppy.'

It took a moment for him to understand. Then he said, 'My God! Quentin's wife! So she's behind all the mayhem!'

'So it would seem.' She grabbed at the phone again. 'Matt must know about this right away.'

She had barely keyed in the number when they heard an agonised scream from outside. 'That's Mum! She must have hurt herself!' She threw down the phone and together they rushed downstairs and out into the garden. They found Sylvia frantically waving her arms in an attempt to drive off a small cloud of angrily buzzing bees that seemed to be attacking her hands. Joe tore off his jacket and began using it as a flail to drive them off while Melissa dragged her mother indoors and into the kitchen, leaving him to close the patio door and deal with a few bees that had followed them into the house.

'I don't understand,' said Sylvia, her face contorted with pain. 'I wasn't disturbing them, I was just cutting a few dahlias when a bee landed on my hand and stung me, and then it seemed like a whole army of them appeared. Look what they've done!' She held out her hands, showing several angry-looking red spots.

'Don't rub them!' said Melissa sharply. 'Try running them under the cold tap to ease the pain, and then sit down and let me see to them. Iris told me how to deal with bee stings last time she was here. It may hurt a bit,' she went on as Sylvia meekly did as she was told, 'but we have to avoid the venom getting into your system.' The tension was almost unbearable as one by one she extracted the stings with a fingernail. Her own hands were none too steady, but at last she succeeded in prising them all out intact. 'There you are,' she said, almost crying with relief.

Joe came in, closing the door behind him. 'I think I've dealt with them all,' he said. 'Are you all right, Sylvia?'

'Yes, thanks to Lissie knowing what to do.'

'Thank goodness there were only a few bees about. If Colin Palmer hadn't taken Aidan's hives away there'd have been thousands.'

'It seemed like thousands,' said Sylvia shakily.

'Let's go back next door,' said Melissa. 'I've got some sting relief stuff in the first aid cupboard, and I think we could all use a drink. Joe, would you do the honours?'

'Coming up. G and T everyone?' He led the way back to

Hawthorn Cottage and began setting up the glasses while Melissa hurried upstairs to fetch antihistamine ointment. 'I hope you put that pot of cream somewhere safe, Mel,' he said as she returned to the kitchen and began anointing the afflicted hands. 'We don't want any bees to get a sniff of its contents.'

'I haven't put it anywhere; I left it on the table.'

'Well it's not there now.'

'Do you mean that one?' Sylvia pointed at the pot, which was now on the draining board. 'I pinched a little smear when I washed my hands after throwing your old dahlias away.' She made a little *moue* of disgust. 'Their stalks had gone all slimy; I didn't think you'd mind. It's got rather a nice smell, hasn't it? Like bananas. Where did you get it, by the way?'

'You used some of that stuff, thinking it was hand cream?' Melissa stared at her mother in horror. 'Oh, my God, what have I done?' she whispered. 'I could have killed you!'

Sylvia looked bewildered. 'What on earth do you mean?' she said.

'I thought I was being so clever, and all I did was put you in danger.'

Joe put a glass into her hand. 'Here, love, have a swig of this,' he said. 'It wasn't your fault, and thanks to your quick action there's no harm done.'

'Will someone please tell me what all this is about?' said Sylvia.

'In a minute, after I've had a word with Matt.' Melissa reached for the phone and keyed in DS Waters' mobile number.

He replied almost immediately. 'Mel, you must be psychic, I was just about to call you,' he said. 'I got the report from the lab a few minutes ago. It's positive all right; as you suspected, that sample is simply cold cream laced with a significant amount of isoamyl acetate. So far we've been unable to track down Holistic Health Laboratories, so that's obviously a false name. I don't suppose you've managed to find out anything more?'

'Oh, yes I have, and it's brought about some rather frightening results.'

Matt whistled when she told him of the latest development. 'The woman must be out of her mind to think she could get away with it.'

'So what happens next? I shan't feel comfortable while she's at large, dreaming up alternative ways of bumping me off.'

'I'll have to have a word with my DI about our next move, but in the meantime I'd better collect that second jar of cream, and the envelope it came in. We might get some useful prints off them, although she probably wore latex gloves.'

'When do you want to pick them up?'

'Now, if it's convenient.'

31

'I can't understand why you didn't tell me all this before, and I don't believe you've told me everything even now.' Sylvia's tone was petulant. 'Why should these people Sergeant Waters was talking about want to kill Aidan Cresney? What had he ever done to them? And why did they send you that little pot of cream that caused all the fuss?'

'Because they knew I was on to them and I suppose they had some wild idea that it might have the same effect on me as on Aidan and Sarah,' Melissa replied.

Matt Waters had been and gone. Despite tactful hints that it would be a good idea for her to take the opportunity to go somewhere quiet to relax and recover from the shock of her experience, Sylvia had remained hovering in the background when he arrived to collect the new evidence. Melissa herself was in none too good a mood since she was certain that, had her mother not been present, Matt would have been more forthcoming about his discussions with his senior officer. She had omitted, in her account of her investigations, any reference to the Cresney family's turbulent history. Sylvia, it seemed, was determined to learn more.

'You haven't explained what made you suspicious in the first place,' she pointed out.

'No, and for the moment I'm not going to.'

'Why not?'

'Because there are things I prefer to keep to myself for the time being. It's as simple as that.' Her tone was sharper than she had intended and a hurt look crossed Sylvia's face.

'I don't understand why you have to be so secretive,' she persisted.

Melissa felt her patience wearing thin. 'Just leave it for now, Mum. You'll know all about it eventually.'

'Anyone would think you don't trust me.' The hint of reproach in her mother's voice only increased Melissa's irritation.

'It's the people you associate with that I don't trust,' she retorted, 'and while we're on the subject, I want you to promise not to say anything to them about what happened this morning.'

'I'm sure I don't know what you're talking about.'

'Oh, yes you do. Cynthia Thorne and the school for scandal she's pleased to call a bridge club. If they get the slightest hint that you know something interesting, they'll have it out of you in no time.'

'Well, I'm sorry you have such a poor opinion of my discretion,' said Sylvia huffily.

'Oh, don't be so silly, Mum. That's not what I meant.'

'She means it's not you, it's the others.' Joe's remark, spoken in a jocular tone, failed to mollify his mother-in-law, who continued to look offended.

'Perhaps you'd like me to leave you to continue your discussions in private,' she said. She stood up with the obvious intention of returning to her own quarters.

'But we haven't had lunch yet,' Melissa reminded her. 'Why don't you sit down and have another drink? It's only cheese and salad and things, it won't take long to rustle up.'

'I'll make you one of my special omelettes if you like,' said Joe.

'Thank you, I'll have lunch in my own place.'

'Then you'd better let me come with you to make sure there aren't any bees lurking in dark corners,' he said, 'and perhaps you should give your hands another good wash, to make sure you've got rid of all that stuff.'

'Oh, yes, perhaps I'd better.' Sylvia looked down at the angry spots on her hands. The sight of them evidently reminded her of her recent harrowing experience. Her air of self-righteous resentment fell away and she suddenly appeared frail and old.

Melissa felt a pang of compunction. 'Come on, Mum,' she said more gently. 'You know I didn't mean to upset you, but you have to respect my loyalty to Caroline.'

'Caroline? Is she the one who's been telling you things?'

'Not only Caroline.'

For a moment Sylvia appeared to be on the point of asking further questions, but changed her mind, went to the sink and began washing her hands. Melissa noticed as she gave her a towel to dry them that they had begun to shake again.

'Now, do stay and have lunch with us and then go and have a lie down,' she said. 'Have you got your pills with you? Perhaps you should take one to guard against delayed shock.'

'Very well, dear,' said Sylvia meekly.

The meal was a subdued affair; Sylvia ate with little appetite and after Joe had, as promised, pronounced her home clear of live bees and disposed of the dead ones, she seemed only too ready to lie down for a nap. Melissa went with her, helped her off with her cardigan and shoes and put a light blanket over her as she lay down on her bed with a little sigh of mingled weariness and relief.

'Have a nice sleep,' she said. 'I'll pop round and make you some tea presently.'

'Thank you, dear, that will be lovely.'

When Melissa returned Joe had just finished loading the dishwasher. 'I've made a pot of coffee,' he said, indicating a tray with two mugs and the cafetière set out on the table.

'Brilliant!' She sank into a chair and closed her eyes. 'A good shot of caffeine will be just the job after this morning's fun and games.'

'I thought we'd have it in the sitting room. The chairs are more comfortable and we both need to relax.'

'Good idea.'

They drank their coffee in silence for several minutes before Melissa said, 'Do you think we should warn Caroline to expect a visit from the police in the near future?'

'I've been thinking the same thing,' said Joe. 'The danger is that it may drive her to another attempt at suicide.'

'That danger will be there in any case once the police enquiry gets under way, but at least Jennie's there to keep an eye on her.'

'That's true.' He considered for a moment and then said, 'Why don't you have a quiet word with Jennie first and let her know what's happened? Then she can break it gently to Caroline if she thinks it advisable. Now she's on a more even keel she should be in better shape to take it.'

'Theoretically, yes, but I'm still convinced the pair of them are hiding something. If they're forewarned it will give them time to concoct some fairy story.'

'They may have done so already.'

'That's a point,' she said. 'Perhaps we should just let things take their course.'

They sat back in their chairs and relaxed, Joe with the latest issue of *The Bookseller* and Melissa with *The Times* crossword, unaware that the final act in the tragedy was about to begin.

The telephone at Hawthorn Cottage rang a little after half past ten that evening, just as the TV news was ending.

'Who the heck's calling at this time of night?' Joe grumbled. 'Whoever it is, get rid of them quickly. There's a good film starting in a few minutes.'

'I'll take it in the kitchen.' She went out of the room.

When she returned, Joe took one look at her and said, 'Something's wrong, I can tell by your face. It's not Sylvia, is it?'

'No, it's not Sylvia, it's Poppy.'

'That was Poppy on the phone?'

'No, Jennie. They're all in a fearful flap. Poppy's had a breakdown and been taken to hospital, Quentin's come flying back to Caroline begging to know what's going on and Caroline's in a state of near hysteria. Jennie says she's babbling about asking my forgiveness before she gives herself up to the police.'

'Ask your forgiveness? What in the world for?'

'For all the trouble she's given me and for having deceived me and made me what she calls an accessory to her crime.'

'Her crime?' Joe's eyebrows nearly climbed into his hair. 'Do you reckon this means she and Poppy have been in this diabolical scheme together?'

'It looks like it, but there's only one way to find out.' Melissa went out into the hall and returned with an outdoor jacket and her car keys. 'I promised I'd go right away and hear Caroline's confession before she goes completely bonkers. Quentin's gone to pieces and poor Jennie's beside herself trying to cope with the pair of them.'

'Can't it wait till tomorrow?'

'No, love, it can't. You sit down and watch your movie.'

'Don't be daft, I'm not letting you go to that nuthouse on your own. Hang on while I get a jacket.'

They went in Joe's car. Neither spoke during the short drive; when he pulled up outside the front door of Cold Wells Manor it flew open and Jennie came rushing out. As Melissa got out of the car she grabbed her by the arm and burst into tears. 'Oh, I'm so thankful you're here!' she sobbed. 'It's all so dreadful, Carrie keeps saying she's a murderess and deserves to be locked up for ever and Quentin's prowling up and down like a wild animal in a cage saying it's all Aidan's fault. I just don't know what to do; I couldn't think of anyone else but you to turn to.'

'Let's go somewhere quiet first while you tell me exactly what's happened,' Melissa suggested.

'I'm afraid to leave Carrie on her own for long in case she does something silly.'

'Isn't Quentin with her?'

'Yes, but he's in pretty bad shape himself.' Jennie's voice rasped with contempt.

'Why don't I stay with her while you and Mel have a chat?' Joe suggested. 'She's been to our house, it's not as if I'm a stranger.'

'Would you, love?' said Melissa. 'This is my husband, Joe,' she explained, turning to Jennie.

'Oh, how do you do?' Despite her distress, Jennie politely offered him her hand. 'Please come this way.'

She led them to the sitting room. When they entered, Melissa had the sensation of walking on to the set of a Victorian play as the final act was about to begin. No one had thought to close the shutters and the reflection in the tall windows of the room and its occupants added to the dramatic effect. 'Seen through a glass darkly,' she thought as she took in the scene.

Quentin was on his feet with his back to the door; he swung round and froze on seeing them. He too appeared to have been weeping; his mouth was compressed and his jowls sagged. He stared at the newcomers for a moment without speaking, then shrugged and turned away. Caroline was sitting bolt upright in an armchair with a glazed expression, giving no sign of having noticed their entrance. Jennie touched her gently on the shoulder and whispered in her ear; she started as if she had been awakened from sleep, murmured something in reply and then sat back in her chair and closed her eyes. Melissa thought she saw a more peaceful look settle on her face.

Jennie beckoned to Joe, pointed to a chair beside Caroline, drew Melissa back into the hall and closed the door behind them. 'I've told her you'll be here very soon and she said "Thank God".' More tears spilled from her reddened eyes as she added, 'It felt like bringing comfort to the dying.'

'Oh, come now, I'm sure it isn't as bad as that.' Melissa put more conviction into her voice than she felt. 'Where shall we go for our talk?'

'In here.' Jennie opened the door of the room Aidan had used as a study. It contained two chairs, but she made no move to sit down or invite Melissa to do so. 'It started about an hour ago,' she began. 'We'd had a quiet evening watching television and we were talking about our plans. Carrie's not ready to be left alone in the house and I have to get home to relieve Mrs Banks, so we agreed she should come back with me. We were thinking about getting ready for bed when we heard a car pull up outside and the next minute Quentin was banging on the door demanding to be let in. He was beside himself, practically gibbering. We managed to calm him down and he said Poppy had had a breakdown and was telling everyone she'd brought about Aidan's death and Sarah's too – he didn't say how but he gabbled something about "some witch's brew" – and at this point Caroline gave a scream and said she was as guilty as Poppy because she'd helped her and she was going to tell the police what they'd done. Then she said she wanted to talk to you and I said I'd speak to you tomorrow and she grabbed me by the shoulders and said, "No, now!" She was like a wild thing. I'm terribly sorry to have to bother you with all our troubles, but–' The final words were washed away in a further flood of weeping.

'Hush, it's all right, we'll get it sorted,' Melissa soothed, knowing all too well that the worst was to come but filled with pity for the unfortunate victim of what she was beginning to think of as the curse of the Cresneys.

'It's Carrie I'm worried about,' Jennie wailed. 'I don't give a hoot for Quentin and I hardly know Poppy, except what Carrie's told me.'

'What has she told you?'

'She's very clever; she's a biochemist and she was one of Quentin's parishioners when he was a vicar.'

'I wondered why you reacted so strongly when I mentioned chemistry. I had no idea Poppy was a scientist, and I didn't know either that she and Carrie were friends.'

'They chummed up when they all went to Quentin's church, and Carrie went on seeing her after Quentin left Sarah to live with her. Aidan forbade it, of course, but she managed to get away with it. And she did her best to comfort Poppy after Aidan manipulated Quentin into leaving her and coming back to Sarah.'

'I think I'm beginning to see the picture,' said Melissa. Despite the appalling tragedy of the situation, she couldn't help feeling a twinge of satisfaction at having her hypothesis at least partially confirmed. 'Poppy wasn't prepared to leave it at that, was she? I guess she realised Quentin would never have the guts to break free a second time so she devised a plot – a particularly vicious one – to kill Aidan. But of course, you know all this, don't you? Caroline had already confessed to you what she'd done and that's why you did your best to make sure I wouldn't ask any further questions.'

Jennie nodded. Tears were streaming down her face but she made no attempt to wipe them away. 'Sarah noticed that Carrie had been washing the protective overall Aidan was wearing when he died, instead of leaving it with the other laundry for her cleaning lady to do. She didn't say anything at the time, but she must have thought it over, become suspicious and tackled her about it later. Carrie begged her to keep quiet, but somehow Poppy got to hear about it and decided she was a threat to the pair of them, so she had to die too.'

'Because she "couldn't keep her mouth shut", as you suggested the other day. Do you think your sister had a hand in that death as well?'

'She swears that she didn't. I pray that she hadn't.'

'You do realise, don't you, that the police are going to be involved?'

Jennie nodded miserably and mopped her face with a handful of sodden tissues. 'Yes,' she said. The word was barely audible.

Melissa was on the point of telling her about the abortive attempt Poppy had made on her own life, but decided she had had enough to cope with for one day. It was, she reflected, hardly surprising that Poppy had had a breakdown. She must have been dangerously close to madness to conceive such an ill-thought-out plan.

'Perhaps I'd better go and talk to Carrie now,' she said, 'or rather, listen to what she's got to say.'

32

'I didn't know it would kill him. I never meant to kill him.' In contrast to her sister, Caroline showed little outward sign of distress. Her voice was without expression and her features composed, as if all feeling had been sucked out of her. Only her eyes, as she looked directly at Melissa, betrayed her inner torment.

'I never meant to kill him,' she said again, like a child repeating a lesson. 'She never said it might kill him.'

Melissa sat down in the chair that Joe had vacated and took her hand. Jennie knelt on the floor at her feet and said, 'We believe you, Carrie. Don't we, Quentin?' she added sharply, glancing over her shoulder to the window-seat where he sat with his head bowed, nervously clasping and unclasping his hands. He looked up briefly in response to her question and muttered something inarticulate. She had suggested before the conversation started that it might be better to allow Melissa to hear in private what Caroline had to say, but he had insisted on remaining and Caroline raised no objection; in fact, she hardly seemed aware of his presence. Joe had retired to the kitchen saying if anyone wanted coffee he was willing to make it, but the offer had gone unheeded.

'When you say "she" I take it you mean Poppy?' said Melissa.

Caroline's head rose and fell two or three times, as if manipulated by an invisible puppeteer. 'We both hated him,' she said in the same dull monotone. 'We both wanted to teach him a lesson. We kept thinking of ways to–' she broke off for a moment as if searching for the right words – 'knock him off his high horse. He was such a know-it-all and so arrogant, always riding rough-shod over everyone. One day we – Poppy and I – were talking about the bees and how he was always boasting that no one who knew what they were doing ever got stung. I said I wished he would get stung and then maybe he wouldn't be so bloody cocksure any more.'

'None of us liked the beastly things,' Quentin remarked. 'I think he only started keeping them because he knew we were all against it.'

The interruption appeared to break Caroline's concentration and for a moment her gaze flickered in his direction. An odd expression, something that seemed to Melissa like a blend of pity and contempt, flitted across her hitherto blank features. He drew a quick breath as if about to speak again, but Melissa put a warning finger to her lips.

'Let's hear her out before we start asking questions,' she said quietly. He appeared about to object, thought better of it and sat back in his seat.

It was a full half-minute before Caroline spoke again. 'We didn't say any more about it then, but next time I saw her Poppy said she'd had an idea. She said there was this stuff they used in the laboratory, something to do with flavouring beer, that made bees angry. She gave me some and told me to put it on his bee veil and the bees would smell it and start stinging him. "That'd teach the bastard a lesson," she said. I said the bees couldn't get inside the veil and she said, "Easy-peasy, make a little hole for them, somewhere he won't notice." So I did. I didn't know so many of them would get in; Colin Palmer told me later that the number of stings he'd suffered was nearly as bad as being bitten by a rattlesnake. But I never meant to kill him, and I couldn't believe at first that Poppy did either.' There was a long silence; Quentin began fidgeting and once again Melissa made a warning gesture.

'I didn't want to be around when it happened,' Caroline resumed at last, 'so I pretended to have a headache that morning and stayed in bed. And the next thing, Sarah came running to tell me they'd found his body. His body,' she repeated. She knotted her brow and looked puzzled, as if reliving her initial disbelief at the news.

'That must have been a dreadful shock,' said Melissa.

'Dreadful?' For the first time there was a spark of animation in Caroline's voice. 'Do you want to know what I really felt?' Her gaze went from one to the other. She drew a deep breath and sat a little more upright. 'I felt relief! It was a shock, yes; it never occurred to me that he would die, but in spite of the shock I found myself thinking, I'm free of him at last! I phoned Poppy and told her he was dead and she didn't seem at all surprised, she just said, "Wash the overall in case anyone asks to see it." It was only later, when I thought about it, that it dawned on me we'd as good as murdered him. But I still didn't feel guilty, not until Sarah–' For the first time her artificial composure showed signs of cracking; she bowed her head and put her clasped hands to her mouth. 'Poor Sarah!' she whispered. 'Why did she have to go telling Poppy what she knew?'

'Did she threaten to tell the police?' asked Melissa.

'She promised to keep quiet if Poppy made no attempt to

steal Quentin away from her a second time. Poppy meant to get him back, you see, once Aidan was out of the way, but Sarah was just as determined to hang on to him.'

There was a muffled groan from Quentin. 'Poppy was as ruthless as Aidan in her way,' he said in a voice thick with emotion. 'More ruthless in fact – at least my brother never killed anyone. She made a terrible scene when I told her I'd decided to stay with Sarah, said she'd been ripped off over the divorce and she wanted some of her money back. She had a point there; I agreed she'd been badly treated by Aidan and I offered to pay back some of the money. It seemed the right thing to do.' He raised his head and squared his shoulders, and for the first time Melissa caught a glimpse of the idealistic young man he had once been. 'That must have been why she decided to dispose of Sarah in the same way as she'd killed Aidan,' he went on. 'Of course, she couldn't enlist Caroline as an ally, but she knew Sarah was allergic to bee venom because I once mentioned she'd had a bad reaction when she was stung as a child.'

'We all knew that,' said Caroline. 'I remember pointing it out to Aidan when he was talking about buying his first hive. And do you know what he said?' Her gaze swung round the little group as if calling them to attention. 'He said, "Then she'd better keep out of their way, hadn't she?" He'd made up his mind to start keeping bees and nothing, but nothing, was going to stop him.'

There was a short silence while they all digested this further example of Aidan's overweening selfishness. Then Quentin muttered, half to himself, 'I'd like to know how she fixed it so Sarah got stung.'

'She sent her what looked like a free sample of skin cream

that she'd laced with the same substance she used to kill Aidan,' said Melissa.

'How on earth d'you know that?' he asked.

'Because she tried to dispose of me in the same way. She might have ended up killing my mother instead if I hadn't managed to get the stings out of her hands in time.'

He gaped at her in bewilderment. 'Why on earth should Poppy attack you?'

'She saw me as a threat and made one last desperate throw of the dice. I'm not surprised she's gone barking. No rational person could have hoped to get away with it.'

'I don't understand.'

'I'll explain some other time. I think Caroline's had enough for now. She looks utterly exhausted.'

'I think we all are.' He leaned back and closed his eyes. 'Poor Poppy, it was frightening,' he muttered. 'I've never seen anything like it – she went completely bananas.'

His choice of expression was so ludicrously apt that for a moment Melissa had a wild impulse to laugh. Her voice shook a little as she said, 'She must have been under a lot of stress for a very long time.'

'Haven't we all?' He covered his face with his hands and choked back a sob. 'Where's it all going to end?' he said brokenly.

33

'I always said there was something not quite right about the way Mr Cresney died, didn't I?' Cynthia Thorne addressed the handful of customers in the village shop with an air of triumph.

It was Saturday morning. Melissa and Joe had remained at Cold Wells until the small hours of Thursday, by which time Caroline had become calm, composed and declaring herself ready to face whatever consequences of her actions lay ahead. Apart from a brief telephone call from Jennie on Friday evening to say that Quentin had left and that the police had agreed to her taking Caroline home for a few days, they had no further news of the case. Melissa, who was in no mood to discuss it with anyone, least of all Cynthia Thorne, deliberately kept her back turned and paid un-usually close attention to the contents of the frozen food cabinet.

There was a slightly embarrassed silence before Cynthia continued, 'It just wasn't natural, the way his widow took it so calmly.'

'They do say the poor lady's nerves are in a bad way after what she's been through,' said Mrs Foster. 'You have to feel sorry for her, no matter what she's done.'

'*I* for one don't feel sorry for her,' said Cynthia with a sniff. 'Murder is murder, that's what I say.'

'Do we know for certain it was murder?' someone asked.

'Well, conspiracy to murder then. Roger saw a man he recognised as a plain-clothes policeman driving away from her house, so it's obvious she knows more than she's let on about how her husband and her sister-in-law died.'

Melissa, who had been listening with mounting irritation, swung round and looked the speaker straight in the eye. 'I would remind you, Mrs Thorne,' she said, keeping her voice level with some difficulty, 'that no charges have been brought against Caroline Cresney. I'd think twice about spreading unsubstantiated rumours if I were you.'

'I'm sure you know better than most that it takes time for the police to prepare their case before making an arrest,' Cynthia said in a patronising tone, 'and I see no reason to disbelieve the report in the *Gazette*.'

'I read the *Gazette* as well, and all it said was that the police were following several lines of enquiry as the result of in-formation they had received concerning the deaths of Aidan and Sarah. I don't recall seeing any mention of either conspiracy or murder.'

'I would have thought it was obvious, even if they didn't say it in so many words.'

'It might be obvious to you, but people who "know better than most" as you put it may see the case differently.'

'Well, if that includes you, Mrs Martin' – Cynthia's voice, normally on the shrill side, rose even higher – 'perhaps you'd care to enlighten us as to why the police have been to see Mrs Cresney, and also why she should have taken an overdose if it wasn't because of a guilty conscience.'

A little gasp arose from the other customers, who had so far remained silent.

'You mean, she tried to do away with herself?' said Mrs

Foster in an awestruck whisper. 'However did you hear that?'

'I'd like to know the answer to that one as well,' Melissa snapped. 'No, don't bother to tell me, I think I can guess.'

'So you don't deny it?' said Cynthia triumphantly.

'I neither confirm nor deny it, because it's none of my business or yours either,' Melissa retorted. She felt her anger on the point of boiling over. 'When I was at university,' she said through her teeth, 'I remember once having a discussion on the proposition that for prying into human affairs, none are equal to those whom it does not concern. You might care to give that some thought yourself.'

Cynthia's face turned a dull red. 'Well, really!' she exclaimed indignantly.

'Yes, really,' said Melissa. She took her change, picked up her shopping and stalked out of the shop, observing with some satisfaction that the remaining customers were reacting with barely concealed amusement to Cynthia's discomfiture.

She was still seething when she reached home. 'That bloody Thorne woman!' she exploded as she entered the kitchen and dumped her shopping bag on the table. 'If I ever contemplate committing a real life murder, she'll be top of my list of potential victims. You should have heard her holding forth about conspiracy to commit murder . . . and she's somehow found out that Caroline took an overdose. Mrs Wilson, I suppose, via Gloria and one of her umpteen contacts. Joe, it's not funny!' she protested as he greeted her account of the episode with a hearty laugh, but in spite of herself she found her indignation melting away.

'Was there anyone else in the shop?' he asked.

'Some ladies from Lower Benbury. One of them questioned whether it really was murder and Mrs Foster was inclined to be charitable towards Caroline on account of all she's been through, but Cynthia would have none of it. Then I quoted Victor Hugo at her; that took the wind out of her sails.'

'You really gave the old bat an earful, didn't you?' said Joe gleefully. 'Joking apart, though, do you reckon the police will bring charges?'

'Who knows? On the face of it it's unlikely because the real culprit is Poppy and she's been sectioned, but of course it's early days yet. Matt won't tell me anything, which is only to be expected, and I've no idea what further information Caroline's given them. It's a pity she admitted to damaging Aidan's veil so the bees could get in, but a good defence counsel would make mincemeat of any attempt to prove it was a deliberate attempt to kill him, or even cause GBH. Unless Poppy recovers sufficiently to make a coherent statement and enter a plea, they'll be hard put to it to make a case that would stand a chance of getting to court. Gosh!' she added as another thought struck her, 'from what I've seen of him, I'd never have thought Quentin would have been the object of a tug of love between two women – although according to Caroline he was quite attractive, and much kinder, years ago.'

'Before Aidan licked him into shape, you mean,' said Joe. 'He doesn't strike me now as the type to make husbands jealous, but you never can tell.'

She finished putting her shopping away, glanced at the clock and said, 'I think I'll pop round and have a word with Mum before lunch. I ought to warn her that I've upset her pal Cynthia and she's liable to have her ear bent about my rudeness.'

She found Sylvia in her garden, dead-heading roses. 'It's sad to think summer's nearly over, isn't it,' she said wistfully, glancing round her little patch. 'I have to admit I'm not looking forward to the winter. Everyone tells me it's a lot colder here than in town.'

'That's true, but you'll soon get acclimatised,' Melissa assured her. 'All your windows are double-glazed and the house has central heating and–'

'Yes, I know, dear, you did everything you possibly could to make me comfortable. I don't want you to think I'm complaining, it's just–'

'Never mind that now, Mum,' Melissa broke in impatiently, 'there's something important I have to tell you.'

'About Caroline? Have there been any more developments?'

'Not exactly.'

Sylvia listened in silence to the story of her daughter's brush with Cynthia Thorne; when it ended she burst out laughing and clapped her hands in delight.

'Good for you, Lissie!' she exclaimed. 'I wish I'd had the nerve to tell her off a bit more strongly when she phoned me yesterday.'

'Did she say the same things to you as she was spouting this morning?'

'More or less. I told her we shouldn't be too quick to judge Caroline until we knew the whole story, but she just brushed it to one side.'

'I imagine the harpies at the bridge club will have a field day at her expense next time they meet.'

'Probably, but I'm glad to say I shan't be there.'

'Oh, why not?'

'My friend Lottie Haynes – you remember her I'm sure – has invited me to stay with her for a few days. I hope you don't mind.'

'Why should I mind? It'll make a nice change for you.'

The few days that Sylvia planned to spend with Lottie Haynes, who lived close to her old home in a small town near Reading, turned into a couple of weeks. Shortly after her return she took an opportunity when she and Melissa were alone to say, 'Lissie, there's something I want to talk over with you.'

'Yes, Mum?'

'First of all, I'm not going to the bridge club any more, or the flower club either.'

'Why not? You enjoy your flower arranging so much, and you said the other day that your bridge was coming on quite well.'

'Yes, I know, but to tell you the truth, I found myself giving them all a piece of my mind, especially Cynthia. Yesterday at the bridge club they were all so horrid about poor Caroline that I told them they were being thoroughly unchristian and they should be ashamed of themselves, and then I walked out.'

'Well done, Mum, I'm proud of you!'

'Thank you, dear, I thought you'd be pleased.'

'Is that it, then?' Melissa asked, as Sylvia, instead of appearing relieved, looked down at her hands and began fiddling with her wedding ring.

'No, there's something else,' she said in a voice husky with embarrassment. 'I don't quite know how to tell you this because you and Joe have gone to so much trouble and expense to help me settle here, but–' She hesitated again and avoided Melissa's eye. 'The fact is, while I was staying with Lottie we went to visit an old friend of ours who's selling her bungalow and going into a home.' Her colour deepened as she hurried on. 'It's a dear little bungalow, very close to the shops and the church, and several of our other friends live nearby; it was so lovely to see them all again. I haven't liked to say anything to you and Joe, you've been so good to me and I don't want to seem unappreciative, but lately, with all this unpleasantness in the village and the winter coming on and everything–'

"You're thinking of leaving Brambles and buying this bungalow?' said Melissa as her mother lapsed into an uncomfortable silence.

'Well, yes,' Sylvia admitted. 'It's hard to explain, but somehow it felt just right for me. As soon as I saw it I knew . . . there was something about it . . . . I'd been there before to visit Mrs Tripp, but this time it felt special, sort of homely and welcoming–'

'I think I understand,' said Melissa. 'It must have been like the feeling I had when I first saw Hawthorn Cottage, as if it had been waiting for me to find it.' She gave her mother an impulsive hug. 'We'll miss you, of course, but if that's what you really want, go for it.'